FOUR LITTLE BOYS

by

Elizabeth R. Lovell

FIRST EDITION

Copyright 1993, by Elizabeth R. Lovell
Library of Congress Catalog Card No: 93-93975
ISBN: 1-56002-351-1

UNIVERSITY EDITIONS, Inc.
59 Oak Lane, Spring Valley
Huntington, West Virginia 25704

Cover by Connie Ludwig Troutman

The attempt to kidnap the Kaiser is a true story.

All other characters and incidents in the book are fictitious. Any resemblance to persons living or dead is purely coincidental.

I used some of my own family names for the fictitious characters i.e. REID, HUTCHERSON, MCKAY, GREER and BIRDSONG.

"Forest Home" was the name of my great grandfather's home in Denmark, Tennessee. "Inglenook" was the name of our home in Franklin, Tennessee. The home named "White Haven" exists only in my dreams.

Dedication

Dedicated to
Gene and Reid and the two
I didn't have.

A special thanks to Mary Louise Lea Tidwell, daughter of Colonel Luke Lea, for sharing the story about the attempt to kidnap the Kaiser.

I am thankful for having a family, especially my sister, Betty Jane, who showed me the meaning of love and family pride.

To my teachers, Dr. Louise Morrison and Joanna Long.

To my friends who believed in me, Janie and Ora Pearl.

And a big hug for Lanieve and Florine who kept cheering me on!

The Nightingale Pledge

I SOLEMNLY PLEDGE MYSELF BEFORE GOD AND IN THE PRESENCE OF THIS ASSEMBLY:

TO pass my life in purity and to practice my profession faithfully.

I WILL abstain from whatever is deleterious and mischievous, and will not take or knowingly administer any harmful drug.

I WILL do all in my power to maintain and elevate the standard of my profession, and will hold in confidence all personal matters committed to my keeping, and all family affairs coming to my knowledge in the practice of my profession.

WITH loyalty will I endeavor to aid the physician in his work, and devote myself to the welfare of those committed to my care.

The reporter was gathering her materials to leave when she glanced curiously at a little patched up paperweight on some papers in the center of Dean Lee's desk. It looked as though it had been broken into a hundred pieces and then painstakingly glued back together. It was the figure of four little boys.

"There must be quite a story back of that broken figurine," she observed. The dean smiled, picked up the paperweight and held it almost caressingly as she answered, "Yes, there is . . ."

The reporter hesitated hopefully, but the dean remained silent. Realizing the interview was terminated, she bade the dean goodbye and left.

Dr. Leslie Jane Lee

It was November, 1942. World War II was raging and Americans were fighting on both sides of the world. General Eisenhower was beginning his westward push towards victory in Morocco and Algeria.

On the home front, anxious families were grasping at every news item they could get. Glaring newspaper headlines and almost on-the-site radio reports gave accounts of fighting, bombings, air raid attacks and the atrocities being inflicted by the enemy. Ernie Pyle's homespun column and Bill Mauldin's cartoons brought both humor and pathos to the deadly struggle and some comfort to the homefolks. To their readers it was almost like hearing from a member of the family who had visited their sons.

Women were coming to the forefront in this war more than ever before and The Globe Newspaper decided to do a series of articles about the women. Since nurses had been a major part of the armed forces dating back to The Crusades, one of their top reporters was assigned to interview Dr. Leslie Jane Lee, Dean of Vale University School of Nursing, about nurses and their role in the war effort.

In preparation for the interview, the reporter had searched the files for some background information on Dean Lee and the school. Her research revealed that Vale University School of Nursing was one of the leading collegiate schools of nursing in the country. It was the first to start a Cadet Corps program to prepare nurses for the armed forces and Dean Lee was a nationally recognized leader in her profession.

The reporter also learned the dean's educational vitae was most impressive—a Bachelor of Science degree in Nursing at Vale University, Masters Degree in Nursing, at the University of London, England and a Doctorate at Columbia University, New York; she had served in most every position in the state nursing organization and was a past president of The American Nurses' Association; she had worked in all levels of her profession and was now dean of the school where she had once been a student; she was a published author and her text books were used in many of the major schools of nursing.

As the reporter was ushered into the office, her first impression was wall to wall books. Then her feet sank into the luxurious blue carpet and she noted the tailored, yet feminine looking drapes, the antique pine desk with work neatly stacked in the three tiered basket. Several comfortable chairs were grouped around a large oval coffee table in front of a bay window. Nan caught her breath in admiration as she saw this strikingly beautiful woman standing at the window, looking at the bird feeder outside. A little squirrel was trying to crawl up with the birds.

She knew the dean was 44 years old. She had expected to meet a capable, brilliant, middle-aged woman—not this.

As the dean stood there in slim, fashion model elegance, she could easily have passed for thirty years of age. She was about five-feet-five-inches tall and was dressed in a navy blue wool crepe suit with a white blouse. She was patriotically wearing the new wartime rayon hose. She looked immaculate from her carefully manicured nails to her highly polished shoes.

The most striking thing about the dean was her jet black hair which she wore in a bun at the nape of her neck. A small streak of grey through the center contrasted sharply with the blackness. She used very little make up except for lip rouge. Rounded thick brows and long eye lashes framed her large green eyes.

Dean Lee was most gracious as she greeted the reporter. She was glad to grant this interview as she felt the publicity would be beneficial to the school and the nursing profession in general. Nan settled down in one of the chairs opposite the dean. The reporter, not one to waste time with small talk, plunged right into the interview. Her questions were concise and to the point. Dean Lee's answers were thought-provoking and inspiring. Her eyes sparkled when she talked

7

about nursing. She was so beautiful and her voice so mellifluous that in spite of her seemingly tough facade, Nan was intrigued. She would have loved knowing more of the dean's personal life. What had inspired her to become a nurse? Why hadn't she ever married? But then, Nan reminded herself, she had an assignment to do. At her request they toured the hospital and the nursing school and she had the opportunity of interviewing some of the cadets.

During the tour, the reporter was impressed with the obvious respect the dean seemed to command from everyone from the chief of staff to the maids and orderlies. Dean Lee was familiar with every facet of the hospital operation from the autoclave to the whirlpool and explained them all in detail. Nan took voluminous notes and the camera crew took pictures.

Back in the dean's office, Nan summarized her findings and explained that the article would be published in the Sunday Magazine section. "I'll look forward to seeing it," said the dean.

As the door closed on the reporter, Dean Lee continued to hold the paperweight. As she sat there looking at the treasured little momento, she could almost see it flying through the air and crashing against the wall. How well she remembered the day she had hurled it at Marshall.

Thoughts and events long suppressed rolled through her mind. She visualized the dance back home in Tennessee just before she had entered Vale University in September 1916.

Leslie Jane Lee

The country club was gaily decorated for this, the closing dance of the season. The younger set had turned out in its entirety as most of them were preparing to return to their respective schools.

The European war was in its second year but it all seemed very remote from Jackson, Tennessee. Some Americans still believed this conflict did not concern them. President Wilson had already proposed that both sides begin peace negotiations and so far he had managed to keep America neutral.

Leslie Jane was an excellent dancer and was having a good time. Her gown was a light green crepe de Chine with a full skirt that flared gracefully as she danced. Her straight black hair was braided and coiled around her head. A few strands of hair escaped around her ears and the back of her neck giving the appearance of a little girl trying to look grown up. She wore a sprig of cape jasmine in her hair. Her naturally fair skin was tanned due to a summer spent almost entirely out of doors.

Leslie and her partner were doing the intricate steps of the tango. Since it was a relatively new dance, there were only a few couples on the floor and they were attracting quite a bit of attention. Among the most interested observers were Mack Lee, Leslie's older brother, and Marshall Chadwick his life long friend and now roommate at Law School.

"Leslie's really grown up this past year, hasn't she? How old is she now?"

"She's almost eighteen," Mack answered absently.

Marshall waited until the dance was over and then strode across the room and claimed Leslie for the waltz.

"Well, if it isn't the young lawyer." Leslie was both surprised and pleased with this partner. Marshall had always treated her as a child.

"You may refer to me as 'Your Honor.'"

"We do have a high opinion of ourselves,

don't we? And where do you hold court?"

"Right here, in just a few minutes." It was surprising how well they danced together. He held her closely and firmly. He'd known her all of her life, but tonight it was as though he was seeing her for the first time. And was was flattered to be noticed by an "older" boy.

"What is this?" Even though their eyes had been locked together and Marshall seemed to be concentrating only on her, he had skillfully managed to dance her right through the door and they were now outside on the terrace.

"I just wanted to have you to myself. We'd never have a chance to talk in there." He put his arm around her and guided her towards the garden. Marshall had always been affectionate towards her as a little girl, but tonight it seemed different. Leslie felt a tingle of excitement as she walked beside him. His six-feet-four-inch frame towered above her. She started appraising him too from a different viewpoint. He had light brown hair and blue eyes that smiled a lot, a rather large nose which balanced well with his jutting jaw. Then, as if to belie the strength of his square chin, a big dimple nestled in the center of it. Everytime Leslie looked at that dimple, the silly little jingle ran through her mind: "a dimple in the chin, a devil within."

"What are we going to talk about, your honor?" Leslie sensed his changed attitude towards her and was feminine enough to feel some satisfaction, especially after having been overlooked for so long.

"You."

"Well, that's not very exciting. Let's talk about you."

"Later. Mack tells me you're leaving college to enter a school of nursing." His arm tightened around her as they walked through the garden.

"Yes, that's right." Leslie braced herself for the lecture she felt coming on.

"Leslie, are you sure this is what you want? I hate to see you start out on such a wild goose chase."

"What's so wild about wanting to become a nurse?" She pushed away from him. "You and

10

Mack and all of you make me sick! I know what I want to do."

She flounced back towards the club house, realizing that she was acting childish which was probably the way he still thought of her.

"No, wait, little Lessie Lou." Marshall reverted back to his childhood nickname for her as he caught up with her. "I'm sorry, honey. I blurted it out all wrong. I didn't mean to offend you. I just don't want to see you get hurt, that's all. I've always thought that nursing is such hard work and I just can't imagine your being cut out for it." He was so gentle and persuasive that Leslie relented. She walked towards a rustic bench and sat down. She knew it was foolish of her to throw a tantrum everytime someone tried to reason with her, but she'd been through so many scenes at home since she'd announced her intention of changing her major to become a nurse. Her parents had objected violently at first but had finally relented.

"It's all right, Marsh. I'm sorry I lost my temper. I know you were only trying to help. Really, I'm not expecting it to be a bed of roses. Nursing is so important though and offers such a promising career opportunity for a girl. I do want to give it a try and if I'm wrong, I'll be the first to admit it." She was so sincere, he smiled.

"Please forget I even mentioned it, honey. I can see it's very important to you and I know you'll give it your best. Now let's talk about more exciting things." He moved closer to her and took her in his arms. "Do you realize you're very beautiful?"

Leslie gave a little shiver of delightful anticipation. She thought sure he was going to kiss her. Marshall suddenly seemed confused as he dropped his arms. "Oh, I'm sorry. You're cold. Maybe I'd better take you back inside." They walked towards the club house in silence. Leslie felt foolish and disappointed. Marshall was silently cursing himself. He felt like he'd bungled the whole thing. His intention of giving her some brotherly advice had backfired. And he really did want to kiss her but this sudden transition from a child to a young lady was too

11

fast for him. He'd have to wait.

As they returned to the dance floor, Leslie was instantly claimed and Marshall went off in search of Mack.

Later in the evening when their dates brought Leslie and her cousin, Margaret Reid home, they were surprised to find Mack sitting in the parlor reading.

"Why, Brother, what are you doing up so late?"

"Waiting for you," he said calmly shutting his book.

"Well, that let's me out," said Margaret. "I think I will have a glass of milk before going to bed though." She made her way towards the kitchen where, in all likelihood, Janie would have a dainty tray of sandwiches and cookies waiting for the children. Margaret lived on the adjoining farm, "Forest Home." She and Leslie were the same age and more like sisters than cousins. For the first time in their lives, they would soon be separated as Leslie had been unable to persuade her cousin to join her in the nursing school.

Margaret had decided to leave Union University, however, and finish her degree in a larger college in the east.

"Bring me something when you come back," Leslie requested.

As the door closed on Margaret, Leslie turned towards Mack suspiciously. She had promised herself she would not lose her temper again. Her voice sounded calm as she said: "If you've waited up all this time to tell me what a mistake I'm making, you're wasting your time."

"Just keep your shirt on, Sis. I don't give a damn what profession you choose. All I want to do is give you a little brotherly advice."

"Really?"

"I just want to discuss a few, cold, hard facts of life with you." He was smiling but his eyes were serious. Mack, like his parents, dreaded the thought of Leslie going away to school. He rather wished she would be coming to his college where he could look out for her, see that she met the right fellows, etc., but since this was not possible, he had taken this "talk" upon himself. He hardly knew how to broach the subject, and as he saw the mischievous gleam in Leslie's eyes, his self-imposed task became even more difficult.

"Leslie—" he began just as Margaret re-entered the room with a tray of sandwiches and cookies and a glass of milk for Leslie. The two girls exchanged knowing glances before Margaret departed for bed.

"This should be interesting, Brother, but remember Mother has already told us the 'facts.'" She knew she was being facetious, but she'd had about all the advice she could take. She munched on a sandwich as she looked at Mack with pretended seriousness.

"Little girl, I doubt if your mama even knows some of the things I could tell you."

"Oh," delightedly. "What?"

"Well, er—" Mack floundered around seeking a beginning. Leslie wasn't helping any with that silly look on her face either. "Leslie, I guess you've been around enough to know a few things. Has anyone ever kissed you, for instance?" he blurted out. His face got as red as hers. Leslie practically choked on her sandwich. She was too surprised to answer immediately.

"Well, I haven't spent these past two years at college studying in my room all the time! Of all the silly things! Why?"

"Leslie, just spare me your righteous indignation." He was groping for words. "What I'm trying to say is—aw hell!" He jumped up and walked around the room. "All I'm trying to do is warn you that things are going to be different for you away from home. Here, you've dated boys you've known all your life and whose families Mother and Father know and approve of. You are known as Thomas Lee's daughter and Archibald McKay's granddaughter, but when you get to Vale, you'll be more or less on your own without this protection. No one there ever heard of the Lees or the McKays and could care less.

"Most likely you'll meet a lot of nice people and will think how wrong I was for having any
13

fears for you and yet again there might be others who aren't so nice and might try and take advantage of you. It boils down to this: You've always been selective in choosing your friends, so up there be doubly careful. Well, that's it! You can do what you want to with it," he concluded rather ineloquently.

"You're right, of course." Leslie surprised him by answering in this way. "I'm glad you care about me, Brother, but I'm sure I can take care of myself. Thanks." She really appreciated Mack's concern and realized the truth of his remarks at the same time. However, since she had been coddled and protected all of her life, she was actually looking forward to being on her own.

"Well, good night, Miss Sophistication. I hope you don't fall too hard when someone knocks you off your high horse." Mack started for the door, "Say," he paused as though the thought had just occurred to him. "Why don't you stick around here and marry old Marsh. He's keen about you now that you've grown up and aren't all arms and legs like you used to be. He told me so himself."

"Really? Marrying is the least of my worries now. Good night." Leslie sauntered off upstairs to have a last confab with Margaret before they settled down to sleep.

The Lees were an old aristocratic southern family of English descent. The first Thomas Lee had settled in North Carolina, but between 1820 and 1830, the Lees along with the McBrydes, Whartons, McKays, Reids, Chadwicks, and many others left North Carolina and settled in Denmark, Tennessee.

Denmark was a thriving little town during the 1850s and was the center of social and religious life, for its citizens were of the best quality, most of whom were wealthy. Denmark began its decline in the 1870s when the railroad bypassed Denmark and came to Jackson. However, the plantations remained and the Lees, and many of their friends continued to farm the land.

The Lees had been prominent in American history since its beginning. Leslie's grandfather, Thomas Arthur had fought as a Confederate Colonel in the Civil War and was one of the original "Denmark Danes" who marched from Denmark to Jackson to become a part of the 6th Tennessee Regiment.

For such a glorious beginning with all the young men so eager to fight for "the cause," the bitter end was painful and degrading. The years following the war were the hardest. Having been brought up as a southern gentleman and not being skilled in any trade, Thomas Arthur adjusted poorly. He could hardly take care of himself, much less his growing family. It was largely due to his beautiful wife, Laura Hutcherson Lee whom he had married on a furlough during a more hopeful period of the war, that they were able to retain possession of the Lee's ancestral home, "White Haven." Laura had also been reared in the luxurious custom of the old south, but she had been better able to face reality and cope with poverty than had Tom.

Realizing that they couldn't wait for the crops to come in to have some money, Laura got together a flock of chickens, laying hens, fryers and some milch cows. She made a contract with the manager of The Southern Hotel in Jackson (even though it was filled with Yankees) to sell milk, eggs and fryers and home made cakes and pies. When the children, Thomas Jr., Elizabeth, and Clara were old enough, they helped with the chores and also worked in the cotton fields. Thomas Jr. trapped rabbits, and Tom peddled wood. Working together as they did, they not only managed to survive, but Laura was able to put aside some money.

The long years of struggle proved too much for Laura, however, and when Thomas Jr. was barely 16 years old, she died, thus transferring the responsibility to his young, inexperienced shoulders. They continued supplying milk, eggs, and fryers to the hotel. The cakes and pies were discontinued as the girls were not old enough to take on that task. Young Tom helped his father with the farm work. The only time he could be away from school or work was to hunt or fish—not so much as a sport, but rather to put some food on the table.

One thing in old Tom's favor was he insisted that the children complete their education. Since the town of Denmark had both a Male and Female Academy, they were able to attend. The Lee children weren't any different from their neighbors as most Southern families were poverty-stricken.

Another thing old Thomas decreed was that White Haven should go intact to Thomas Jr. His will would provide for the girls to inherit other farm lands, but the home and original acreage must be passed to the eldest son. This old custom of primogeniture stemmed from their English ancestry. It was strange, in a way, that the first Thomas should have continued this tradition as he had been a second son and for that reason had come to America to found his own fortune after his elder brother had inherited their father's title and lands over in England. Anyway, the custom had prevailed.

As the years passed and tensions eased, the Lees were able to reap the rewards of their labors. When White Haven was paid completely out of debt and restored, in some measure, to its former splendor, Thomas Jr. had more leisure time and he became interested in Janie McKay, a friend of his sister, Clara.

He and his father lived alone now, as Clara had married one of the Tyson boys and Elizabeth had married William McBryde.

Janie McKay was only 17 when she and Thomas were married. She and her family lived on an adjoining farm called "Forest Home." They had known each other all their lives, although Janie was nearer the age of his younger sister, Clara. Their marriage caused quite a bit of surprise, but yet approval as it linked two of the oldest families in the county.

The marriage was indeed a happy one and to an observer who did not know of the previous years of poverty, it was almost like a reversal of time—a handsome man and his beautiful lady

16

living in a plantation house. Dogwood and Locust trees lined the drive leading up to the house. As the dogwood blossoms faded in late April and early May, the Locust started blooming. White snowball bushes, white crepe myrtle, white "flags" and white rambler roses along the fence row all combined to make a vision of white and people came from miles around in the spring to see it.

Even their first born child was a boy to carry on the tradition of the Thomases. He was christened Thomas McKay and later became known as "Mack." Thus, he became the first Thomas to be called by another name. Janie felt like it was too confusing to have so many Thomases living in the same house. It was gratifying that old Thomas lived to see and enjoy his grandchildren.

Their second child, a girl, was born four years later and given the name, Leslie Jane.

Their first real sadness came two years later when their second son was born with a heart condition known as a "blue baby." He lived only three months despite all the efforts of Dr. Miller and the loving care of the family.

They were still grief-stricken over this baby the next year when Janie gave birth to premature twin boys who also died in infancy. Dr. Miller felt that Janie shouldn't have any more children as she was so frail following these last two pregnancies.

Janie waited five years before their last child was born. A little girl who was a healthy, happy child and helped compensate somewhat for the loss of the little boys. She was christened Elizabeth Ann but would always be called Betsy. Thus she was nine years younger than Leslie.

Janie and Tom were so proud of their family and indulged the children in every way. Thomas wanted them spared any of the worries and hardships he had known as he was growing up.

Life had been kind to them in a material way and, except for the loss of the infant sons, they had been lucky with their remaining family. Mack was a son to be proud of and Janie fairly beamed with pride everytime she looked at him.

He was now a handsome 22-year-old man preparing to enter his second year of law school this fall. He had inherited Janie's fair skin and golden wavy hair and blue eyes, whereas Leslie had straight black hair and green eyes, with thick lashes and brows. She was not as beautiful as her mother but her appearance was striking. She had a short, slightly tilted nose and a rather large mouth but when she smiled her dimples seemed to counteract any defects her features might have. Under Janie's watchful eye, her boyish impulses were curbed, but her sparkling personality was always evident. Now at age 18, she was a poised, self-assured young girl.

Betsy, at the tender age of nine, showed every evidence of becoming Janie's counterpart. She was small and dainty with curly blonde hair and blue eyes. The Lees tried hard not to spoil her but she was so fragile and beautiful that Leslie and Mack joined in with the whole family in worshiping this lovely child.

The Lees had never dictated to their children regarding their plans. They guided and directed when needed but never more than that. They had more or less left it up to the children to select their college courses and choose their major. Mack had made his own decision to become a lawyer.

No definite plans had been made for Leslie upon graduation. They just took it for granted that she would return home. A trip abroad was impossible at this time because of the European War. Janie didn't want to abandon the idea altogether however, as she considered this an important part of a young lady's education. No thought was given to a vocation. College was merely an interlude whereby Leslie could develop a more cultural background and grow a little older before settling down to marry one of the eligible young men in the county. They hoped it would be Marshall.

It was, therefore, a genuine shock to both parents when, after completing her sophomore year in college, Leslie bluntly announced her desire to enter a school of nursing. Although the Lees were supposedly reasonable parents, they really didn't want their daughters to work—maybe teaching for a while would be all right, but they were astonished to think she would consider being a nurse. Neither Janie's tears nor Tom's stormy protests could change her mind. Aunt Clara and Aunt Elizabeth were scandalized. Aunt Margaret (Janie's sister) who had always been Leslie's favorite, was the only one who showed any understanding and offered encouragement. It was largely due to her intervention that the bewildered parents finally agreed to let Leslie give her wild idea a try. Neither of them believed she would actually complete her course and as Tom theorized: "She's either stirred up over the assassination of Miss Edith Cavell or she's read a book where the heroine was a nurse. We'll have to let her try. I just hope she won't be hurt."

Tom didn't know his own child very well. Leslie never did anything halfheartedly. She had made up her mind to become a nurse and she intended to give it the best she had.

As the time grew nearer, Leslie eagerly prepared for her departure. She couldn't help but feel some qualms due to the vehement objections she had encountered from all her family, but she was so sure of her own stamina and ability that she was soon able to suppress most of her misgivings. She was a carefree, idealistic girl and was leaving home for the first time.

Janie would often look back on that last day at the train station as she bid her young daughter goodbye. Both she and Tom wanted to put their arms around her and shield her from everything, but they knew that was impossible. They tried to accept the fact that it was right for little birds to leave the nest, but it was so hard for them to relinquish theirs. Leslie looked so small and helpless as she eagerly clasped her hands and said:

"Mother, you'll never be sorry you let me go. I'll make you and Father so proud of me."

She was destined to fulfill her promise. She would make a name for herself.

Vale University

Leslie arrived safely at her destination. Although she had toured New York and other large cities with her parents, she was now somewhat overwhelmed. Maybe she'd been wrong to insist on being independent and coming alone. Being responsible for checking her own baggage amidst the hustle and bustle of the railroad station was another new experience. She was finally able to hail a cab and direct him to the university. She had only a few bags. Her trunk would arrive later.

As she arrived at the university, Leslie was impressed with the beauty of the campus and the old buildings. Truly an Ivy League College, she thought. If she was determined to be a nurse, her parents had insisted that she select the best school available.

As the cab driver stopped in front of the dormitory, she couldn't help but notice that the Nursing School and the hospital were located at the lower side of the campus almost apart from the rest of the university. She stepped out of the cab and looked around. The leaves were just beginning to turn, the marigolds were still in bloom and the chrysanthemums were budding. She felt a warm feeling as she looked up at the five story building which would be her home for the next three years.

On entering the dormitory, Leslie was immediately appropriated by some of the sophomores who fairly beamed with their newly acquired importance. They intended to see to it that the present freshmen would experience the exact same agonies they had last year. The entire morning was spent in the registration line, room assignments, and class schedules. It was a tired Leslie who was finally ushered over to the hospital for lunch. This was her first glimpse inside a large hospital and its enormity amazed her. The students were led to the section of the building set aside for the cafeteria and dining room. Leslie, being preoccupied with all her surroundings, marched towards the dining room door with her usual resoluteness, but was hastily drawn back by her guide who informed her that the nurses entered according to their rank. The graduates entered first, followed by the seniors and so on until lastly the lowly freshmen! After getting that little matter settled, Leslie found the dining area cheerful and the food was good. After lunch, Leslie was shown to her room and she gratefully laid down for some much needed rest.

That afternoon the new students were to be guests of honor at a tea in the large lounge area of the dormitory. By this time, Leslie had made friends with several of the girls. One of them, Helen Adams, was a tall dark haired girl from Texas with the largest brown eyes Leslie had ever seen. Alice Caraway, from Ohio, was a small girl with light brown hair and blue eyes. Another girl, Sharon Webb, from South Carolina, was a striking blonde whose beauty almost set her apart although she seemed utterly unaware of it.

The four girls went down together. They were greeted by a tall angular sophomore who was the "image" of the popular movie star Theda Bara, they were informed by another of the upper classmen. Leslie failed to see the resemblance, but she and her companions smilingly agreed. Beverly Bayne's double was also pointed out. Again the freshmen politely nodded agreement. At this point their informant left them.

"My, I can hardly wait to meet Mary Pickford and Ruth Roland," was Helen's dry comment. The girls were in peals of laughter over this remark when a tall, distinguished looking grey haired lady walked over to them.

"It's refreshing to hear such gaity," she said. "May I ask what the joke is?" She spoke with a low, vibrant voice. Her entire appearance gave the impression of a dynamic personality which demanded immediate respect.

"Oh, not really a joke. Just emotional reaction to some of our varied experiences of our first day here, I guess," spoke up Sharon with ease. The other girls were relieved that she

21

could carry it off so well and they gazed on in admiration while Sharon conversed with the lady. Sharon's wit and repartee were a match for her.

Miss Miller suddenly turned towards Leslie. "And I hear you are from Tennessee, my dear."

"Yes," answered Leslie. "This is my first time away from home."

She then talked to each girl, calling her by name, showing a remarkable knowledge of their backgrounds.

The girls did not realize it then, but never again would they converse with this lady with such freedom and ease and display their girlish enthusiasm. Miss Miller happened to be the dean, and most students never feel comfortable with, much less close to the dean.

The girls were presented to most of the faculty members and the other students and about 5 p.m. they went upstairs to dress for dinner.

That night they were invited to the roof for a "slumber party." The upper classmen were going all out to make the new students feel welcome. The roof garden was decorated with Japanese lanterns and card tables were scattered around for those who wanted to play cards and the center was cleared for dancing.

"Theda Bara" whose real name was Catherine Case came over to Leslie and started talking. "How many in your class?"

"Fifty of us," Leslie said proudly.

"Well, only twenty-five of you will make it to graduation. They always kick out half the freshman class."

"What?" Leslie was shocked.

"Oh, yes," said the cheerful sophomore. "There were forty-eight of us last year and only thirty left now and still another year to go. So you see the casualty rate is high."

"But why do they 'kick' you out?" Leslie unconcsiously mimicked Miss Case's crude expression.

"Oh, er, different reasons—poor grades, unsatisfactory work, but mostly for your attitude. There now, I shouldn't have frightened you. Forget all about what I said and have a

22

good time." She patted Leslie's shoulder and sauntered off in quest of another victim.

Leslie immediately sought her friends to tell them the alarming news. Sharon had already been told, but Alice and Helen had not. Thus the news spread like wild fire through the Freshman Class.

Every young student tossed fretfully in bed that night wondering who would be lucky enough to remain in school. Leslie just couldn't go to sleep as she laid in bed thinking of the fuss she'd made to come here to school and to think now there was a possibility that she might be rejected! She determined then and there that she would study harder than she ever had.

The following day was full, what with entrance exams, physical exams, unpacking and the like. The girls had very little time to think of their worries. The third day formal classes started.

Bull Sessions

It took Leslie a while to get adjusted to dormitory life. While attending Union University, Leslie had lived at home and although she had participated in all college activities, she had missed out on the nightly "bull sessions," so it was quite a revelation to her to sit in on one.

The eighteen-year-old girls were still young and naive and so eager to learn all about the mysteries of the bedroom. Anyone of them who had actually "gone all the way" certainly wasn't likely to admit it, but they shared whatever information they had been able to gather from whatever source.

Leslie sometimes felt guilty and embarrassed, but the fascination of it kept her listening anyway. She had always shared so much with her mother but there still seemed to be an "unseen portal" beyond which they had never ventured.

She remembered how her mother had called her in when she was twelve years old and showed her some neat, white pads made for her along with a belt and safety pins. Then her mother told her since she would soon be "growing up" she would need them. Menstruation was explained and Leslie was instructed that she must come and tell her mother when it happened to her.

Leslie had immediately sought Margaret and together they went to Leslie's cousin, Laura McBryde, who was a few years older than they were and had already started menstruating. Laura told them how painful the "cramps" were and that the monthly period was called "The Curse" because women were still being punished because Eve ate the apple.

Leslie had to wait two years before experiencing this mysterious event. Then she was instructed to put her soiled pads in the slop jar, filled with cold water and to be sure it was covered and hidden away from Mack. After the soaking, Mother or Mary would scrub the pads in hot soapy water and rub them on the wash

24

board. Then they were boiled and rinsed through "bluing water" to make them white again, pressed and put back in her dresser to wait until next month.

Thank goodness, the hospital now had disposable ones to furnish the students.

The bull sessions were mostly speculation and gossip until Pauline Baron revealed that she had mysteriously acquired a book about sex while she was at summer camp last year. All the girls gathered eagerly around.

Pauline was a methodical person and she went into great detail as she delivered her peroration:

"The penis was the male organ of copulation and was located in the groin—"

"For goodness sakes, Pauline! We know that. Actually, I wouldn't think of looking for it anywhere else!" interrupted Lucy Jones sarcastically. "Just get to the point and tell us what the book said about making love."

Pauline was undaunted and continued in her detailed, anatomical account. Leslie did learn that the clitoris was a vital part of the female anatomy. She did know of its existence from her study of anatomy, but not its significance.

Thelma Rogers confided that her sister had "Honeymoon Cystitis" after she got married. And so the girls would laugh and giggle until time for lights out.

In fact, they discussed their dates and they usually knew which boys were most likely to get "fresh" when they went out on a date. The medical students were older and more dangerous, they were told.

Leslie could look back now and understand many things that were so puzzling to her as a little girl. She remembered how once she had picked up a broom and tried to knock the rooster off the hen, shouting:

"Leave her alone, you big bully!" only to have Mack jeer at her,

"Stop that, Leslie!"

"Why?"

"Aw, Lessie, you're so dumb! Why don't you go back to the house and play dolls." He stalked off leaving her without any explanation. She knew she had done something wrong, but what? She sat down on a hay bale feeling very dejected.

Marshall had been standing by looking at his feet, trying to hide his embarrassment. He waited until Mack was out of sight, then he came over and gently touched her on the shoulder.

"Little Lessie Lou, the rooster wasn't fighting with the hen."

"What were they doing?"

"Well, that's the way they—er—well, make little baby chickens I guess."

"Oh—"

After that, she was careful not to make anymore blunders around the boys. She informed Margaret of her new found knowledge.

"Well, the hen certainly doesn't act very happy about it, does she?" was her comment.

Farm children had more opportunity to observe the animals than other children and as Leslie and Margaret grew older and compared notes with their playmates, they learned a lot about procreation, but the mysteries of the human animal still eluded them.

Another incident that could have ended tragically happened at Aunt Clara's. Leslie went over twice a week for art lessons and to paint in Aunt Clara's attic studio. Jerome, who was three years younger than Leslie was always underfoot. Aunt Clara could usually find something for him to do, but on his particular day, he was obviously excited and stimulated over something.

When Aunt Clara had given Leslie her assignment, and left the room, Jerome slipped in. He was grinning broadly as he clutched a packet close to his chest. Jerome was grossly overweight and therefore, the brunt of all sorts of cruel jokes at school. He tried to cover up his inferiority complex by continually making himself obnoxious.

"Lessie, I'll bet you wish you could see what I have."

"Probably not." Leslie was trying to concentrate on her painting and wished he would go away.

"I've got some hot pictures—" He proudly produced a pornographic magazine.

"Jerome! You should be ashamed of yourself. Now get out of here and leave me alone or I'll call Aunt Clara. I'll bet she'd just love to see your pictures." She started for the door.

"Aw naw! Don't do that," he protested. "I'm leaving. Tell you what I'll do though. I'll leave them here just in case you change your mind." Jerome went strutting out the door, leaving the pictures on the table. Leslie really felt sorry for him and thought how unfortunate it was that he couldn't relate to boys his own age.

She ignored the pictures and continued to paint on "The Harp of the Winds." She was trying to concentrate on the detail work of the trees when she kept hearing creaking sounds. It was kind of spooky up here on the top floor, but she continued to paint until all of a sudden she heard a splintering crash and a yell from Jerome. She rushed over to the window to find him hanging precariously to the ladder where two rungs had broken under his enormous weight. The ladder had tilted back and a small tree limb was preventing it from crashing to the ground. Luckily, there was a double window. Leslie raised both sashes, wrapped her right arm around the window casing and reached out her left hand and grabbed the ladder, but she still held it away from the wall.

"Jerome, just what do you think you're doing?" She knew exactly what he was doing.

"Lesslie, help me before I fall and break my damn neck!"

"First, tell me what you're doing up here peeking through the window." She was going to make him admit it.

"I was trying to catch you looking at the pictures. Now help me!"

"Did you see anything?"

"Hell, no!" He squirmed and she almost lost the ladder! Realizing she'd carried her self-righteousness too far, Leslie pulled the ladder to the house, praying that she hadn't waited too

27

long. Jerome was exhausted and scared. She reached down and grabbed him by the belt and he was finally able to grasp the window sill. His weight made the pulling very hard for her, but with both of them tugging, he was able to scramble through the window. On the final tug, they both fell to the floor. Leslie's right arm was skinned and bruised and her finger nails on her left hand were broken where she'd pulled on Jerome's belt. They were both mussed up.

Jerome scrambled to his feet, grabbed his pictures and went scampering off to remove the ladder before his mother found it. He didn't bother Leslie any more after that.

Explaining her injuries to her mother was difficult, but there was an unwritten law that the children wouldn't tell on each other. Janie treated her abrasions and didn't press her for more details than Leslie was willing to give.

Margaret's reaction was somewhat of a surprise: "Leslie you're so pious, it's pitiful! I wished you'd looked."

"Maggie! You know Jerome would have held that over me for the rest of my life."

"How else are we going to find out anything?"

"Not that way. Mother will tell me someday."

Gradually, she and Margaret began to realize there was more to being married than just sleeping together. Whenever the wife of a tenant farmer or one of the neighbors had a baby, her mother was often called to assist the doctor or "granny woman."

Somewhere along the way, they were told that a "seed" was planted in the mother and the baby grew inside her body until time to be born, but their informant would suddenly become tongue-tied when asked how the "seed" got there and how did the baby get out?

Leslie was sustained by the fact that she knew for a certainty her parents were happy and loved each other, so she could only anticipate what being loved would be like and with her present career ambitions, she was in no hurry to find out.

28

Mack's Visit

Leslie let out a squeal of delight as she read her letter from Mack.

"Whatever's wrong with you?" asked Sharon, looking up from her own letter.

"Oh, guess what! Brother and Marshall are going to stop by here this weekend on their way back from the football game."

Sharon looked at her with amused tolerance. She felt years older than Leslie while in reality she was only seven months older. Sharon had completed her junior year in college before deciding to major in nursing.

"Thank goodness, I'll get to meet that wonderful brother of yours. I'll take care of him and you can have Marshall all to yourself."

"I must tell Alice and Helen." Leslie went off in search of her friends. Sharon continued reading her letters.

The freshmen had been in school three months now. As yet, they had not seen inside the hospital except when they went over for their meals. As yet, Catherine Case's dire prophesy had not been fulfilled. The students were beginning to breathe easier and apply themselves more diligently to their work.

Leslie was determined to make the grade. She studied harder than she ever had in high school or college. Late every night she was either studying in the Medical library or in her room gleaning all the information possible. Every single procedure they were taught, she executed with such painstaking care that she surprised even herself. The real truth was that Leslie was terrified for fear she might be one of the unfortunate students who would be rejected. She recoiled at the thought of having to return home and face her parents. She knew they would be disappointed that she had failed in any undertaking, even if it was one of which they disapproved.

Therefore, Leslie continued her studious habits to such an extent her friends became alarmed that she was overdoing it and might get sick. Mack's admonitions shortly before her departure seemed unnecessary now because Leslie had not allowed herself any time for dates.

Sharon and Helen had lost no time in getting acquainted with some of the medical students and they had repeatedly asked her to double date but Leslie always pleaded some excuse. It was not that she wouldn't enjoy getting out, but she felt like there would be plenty of time for dates later. For the present, she must make good grades and convince herself and others that she was capable of being a good nurse.

It, therefore, gave Leslie a real thrill to receive Mack's letter. She decided she'd really take time off and enjoy every minute of their visit. The other girls joined in her enthusiasm and agreed they would all go to the station to meet the boys.

On their arrival the next day, Mack and Marshall were surprised and pleased to find four lovely girls waiting for them. Leslie threw her arms around Mack with such childish glee as to almost embarrass the young lawyer.

"Now, just a minute!" Marshall pulled her away from Mack. "Save some of that loving for me."

"But of course," Leslie laughingly gave Marshall a big hug also, then turned towards her friends: "I want you to meet my best friends in the whole school."

The girls were presented and they decided to have lunch in town after which they took a cab back to the university. The boys were shown around and introduced to innumerable girls. Mack declared he didn't know there were that many females in the world.

Leslie checked the activity sheet and learned there was an all school dance at the gym that night so they decided to go. Since Alice and Helen had other plans, the boys escorted Sharon and Leslie to the dance.

Marshall was relieved to finally get Leslie to himself. He'd been almost irritated during the afternoon at the way she'd clung to Mack.

30

Leslie loved dancing with Marshall, and Sharon, true to her promise, kept Mack busy.

"Lessie Lou, how about writing to me. I hate to get all my news about you through Mack."

"Why, of course, Marsh." Leslie was pleased. "I love writing letters and especially receiving them."

"Agreed, then?"

"Agreed."

"And now, tell me how you like being a nurse? I'll bet you've found out it's not all you were hoping for."

"I just love it and it's even better than I'd hoped for," twinkled Leslie. She didn't tell him that their first year would be mostly theoretical and that she still had no idea what nursing was really like.

"Well, honey, I think you're swell anyway."

At this point, a young boy cut in. Leslie recognized him as one of the university students she'd seen in the library. She'd rather continue dancing with Marshall but she didn't want to be rude so she danced off with the student.

"Nursie, I'm sick and need some attention." He was trying to be witty but only succeeded in irritating Leslie even more.

"Then I'm afraid you're in rather inexperienced hands," she said coldly, breaking away from him.

"Let's have some punch." She walked towards the ante room hoping that Marshall would come to her rescue but she didn't see him. Another student entered the room.

"Say, Bill, I just heard a good joke—oh, I beg your pardon—" the boy stammered as he saw Leslie for the first time.

"Aw, go and tell your joke," said Bill. "She's a nurse. She won't care."

Leslie's face turned crimson. She was embarrassed, but mostly angry. If she could have picked up the punch bowl, she'd have thrown it at Bill. Instead, she gave him a contemptuous look and holding her head high, walked out of the room. Luckily, Marshall found her almost immediately. It was a relief to get back in his arms and dance. She laid her head on his massive chest and he held her closely. Marshall sensed her feelings and asked if anything was wrong. She decided it was best not to tell him. It would only make matters worse, so she just said she was tired. She remembered then and understood Mack's concern about her being in a strange school among all classes of people.

The girls had to be in the dormitory before midnight and that hour was fast approaching. They found Mack and Sharon and started back.

The boys were leaving on an early train so Leslie had to say her goodbyes that night. Marshall was a little disappointed not to have been with Leslie more, but he felt like he'd made some progress.

After they had gone to their rooms, Leslie, clad in her gown and kimono came to Sharon's room and recounted her unpleasant experience.

Sharon showed no surprise or concern. "My dear, don't you know there's a lot of ignorant fools in this world? Forget it. You know, I really do like your brother. I wish they weren't so far away."

But Leslie wasn't willing to forget and it infuriated her for Sharon to be so calm. "But don't you see, Sharon, that was an insult to the whole nursing profession? I really wanted to pick up that punch bowl and throw it at him."

"Leslie, you did exactly right," soothed Sharon. "Always ignore offensive people. We both know he's wrong. Mr. Dickens certainly didn't do us any favor when he created Sairy Gamp,² but that image of a nurse still exists. The better informed people of today know that its distorted and that nursing is a great profession and a challenge for the finest type of women. We can contribute to the cause by living up to the highest standards set for us by Florence Nightingale."

Leslie was somewhat mollified by this earnest speech and felt better as she went off to bed. Two surprises were waiting for her the next day: flowers as a parting gesture from Marshall and a note of apology from Bill. She proudly displayed the flowers to her friends who were pleased for her. They knew now why Leslie never dated anyone at school—she was in love with Marshall. Leslie laughed off their good natured teasing. She showed Bill's note to Sharon privately. Sharon was amused.

"He'll probably call you tonight."

"I wouldn't dream of going out with him," fumed Leslie.

"Don't be silly. Go on with him. You might meet someone you really like." Sharon always had a practical way of looking at matters. If she didn't like her boyfriend, she merely used him as a means of meeting new ones.

Sharon's prediction proved true. Bill did call Leslie who was polite, but stood by her intention to have nothing to do with the boy.

Several days later, Leslie was accosted in the library by the other young man who had been a part of the unpleasant experience. He was most apologetic and seemed so sincere that Leslie relented. They left the library and went to the campus drugstore for a soda. He was a very pleasant youth and Leslie found herself enjoying his company. His name was Dennis Raymond and he was a sophomore in the School of Engineering.

"Miss Lee would you go to the picture show with me tonight?" he asked as they strolled up the walk to the dormitory.

"Thank you, but I have a term paper to work on." She had no intention of jumping at the first chance she had.

"Tomorrow night, then?"

"I'm sorry, but I have a class meeting to attend. You see, I'm president."

"I'll give you a call later," said Dennis as he bid her goodbye at the door.

Leslie came upstairs to find Alice and Helen in her room. They had been looking out the window when Leslie and her new friend were walking up the walk and immediately besieged her with questions.

"Do you have a date tonight?"

"No."

"Did he ask you for one?"

"Yes."

33

"Well, then I still say you must be in love with Marshall to be so content to stay home and study all the time," concluded Helen.

"Oh, no. Marshall is *years* older than me."

"Only four years older and that's about right," argued Alice.

"Have it your own way, but do run along so I can work on this nursing paper! You two should be doing the same thing."

When Leslie settled down to work after the girls left, she forgot all about boys, dates, etc.

The next week the class in Nursing Procedures was in progress when the blow fell! Ten students were called from class to report to the office of the dean. Five were rejected for various reasons and the other five were placed on probation and warned if their grades did not improve, they, too would be dismissed.

Neither Leslie nor any of her friends were called but the rest of the day was ruined for them anyway. Leslie was so upset she called Mack who tried to reassure her and laughingly predicted that she would be right there when Gabriel blew his horn.

After this trying day, she resolved more than ever she would stay home and study. When Dennis Raymond called, she politely but firmly refused.

Night after night, she could be seen studying late in the Medical Library. Every waking moment she spent either studying or practicing some nursing procedure. Her work was perfection itself.

The girls tried to get her to relax and slow down, but Leslie was thoroughly scared now and she continued to work and study late in spite of their admonitions.

After weeks of classes and practical experience, the students were now ready for final exams before the Christmas holidays. Leslie's grades were the highest in the class and her parents were well pleased with her progress.

The students had been told that upon their return from the holidays, they would finally be sent to the hospital wards for actual experience. This was a thrilling thought. Up until now, they

34

had been practicing on each other and the model doll they had named "Mrs. Case."

When exams were over, the students prepared to leave for a much needed vacation. Leslie packed her things enthusiastically. After these past three months of such intensive study and mental stress, she was really looking forward to this respite. She wanted to leave it all behind and enjoy being at home and attending the round of parties they always had during the Christmas season.

Christmas Holidays

"Oh, my darling! I'm so glad to see you." Janie clasped her young daughter to her. "Let me look at you. Why, baby, you've lost weight. We can't have that! Aren't they feeding you well?"

"Now, Mother, please stop imagining things." Leslie wished she wasn't so observant. She transferred quickly to her father's waiting arms and then to the impatient little Betsy. Leslie had missed this beautiful little creature more than she had thought possible.

"But, honey, you look so tired," persisted Janie as they walked towards the car.

"Father, please make Mother be quiet," teased Leslie. "She's trying to make me feel bad when I've planned such a happy holiday."

"Mother's just concerned about you. But don't worry, Mary will feed you so much, you'll have that weight back on in no time." The happy family drove leisurely home. Leslie felt unusually content and carefree. She was home now and could forget all about pressures, deadlines and studying.

"Guess what, Big Sis! Aunt Clara and Aunt Elizabeth are having a tea for you on Wednesday and I'm going to help serve." Betsy couldn't keep the secret any longer.

"How nice," said Leslie, remembering how strenuously they had objected to her entering the school of nursing. Oh, well, if they were willing to bury the hatchet, why shouldn't she also?

"There'll be lots of parties," said Janie.

They drove on to Denmark and as they made their way up the tree-lined drive to White Haven, Leslie realized how much she had missed her beautiful home and family. She didn't take time to unpack but started making her rounds over the house and farm, greeting the servants and farm hands as eagerly as she had her family.

Leslie was especially glad to see Mary. She'd missed her almost as much as her mother and father. Mary was an institution at White Haven and she ruled the household with an iron hand.

36

She was more like a friend than a servant as she and Janie had grown up together at Forest Home. When Janie and Tom married, Mary elected to come with them and soon afterwards, she had married Jake Jones, a sharecropper at White Haven.

Most Southern children had a "black mammy" and some had need of a "wet nurse." Mary filled both of these roles for the Lee children as she was having her brood of children at the same time Janie was having hers. Janie never seemed to have enough milk but Mary's ample bosoms always had plenty so she nursed both Mack and Leslie part time along with her own babies. When Betsy came along, Leslie was old enough to realize that Mary was more to them than just a nursemaid and she learned that all of them owed their healthy young lives to Mary's generosity in feeding them.

It was only natural for them to feel a special closeness to Mary, whom they affectionately called "Mae Mae." Mary pretended to be firm and stern with them, but she was usually a soft touch when they begged her for cookies or other favors.

Leslie had been home three days now and felt like all she'd done was eat and sleep.

"What do you have planned for tonight, dear?" asked Janie as she brought Leslie's mail to her.

"Oh, Marshall's coming over," answered Leslie as she eagerly opened her letter from Sharon. "Guess what, Mother! Sharon's boyfriend proposed. Of course, she said 'no.'"

"I'd think she was still too young to marry," Janie sat down to hear more of Sharon's letter. A real bond of understanding existed between Leslie and her mother. Janie never pried, she just waited for Leslie to reveal whatever she wished and Leslie always talked freely with her.

"I'm glad you're going out with Marshall. Sugar, I wish you'd be a little nicer to him. You know how much your brother loves him and Tom and I do too. We'd be so happy for you to see more of him."

37

"Why, Mother, I never thought of 'courting' Marshall. He'd always seemed older to me and you know yourself how he and brother used to use every means possible to be rid of me."

"I know, dear, but you're grown up now and the young man is very much aware of you."

"All right, sweet. I'll be especially nice tonight—all for you." teased Leslie, and then on a more serious note, "I love you, Mother, and I do thank you and Father for allowing me to go to Nursing School. I really do like it."

When Marshall arrived that night, he settled down in the parlor and talked to Janie and Tom like always. He enjoyed being with the Lees and they thought of him as part of the family. After a while, he turned towards Leslie, "Would you like to drive to Jackson and see a picture show?"

"That sounds like fun," said Leslie sweetly, remembering her promise to her mother.

The show was a good one and Leslie and Marshall laughed a lot and she found herself having an unusually good time. Just as Marshall had experienced difficulty in her transition from a child to an adult, Leslie also had to adjust from his being a big brother type tease to now, a possible suitor.

After the show, Marshall suggested stopping at the Corner Drug Store, a popular hanging out place for the younger set. As they entered they were hailed by several friends and stopped by two or three tables to exchange greetings before finally finding a quiet booth in the back.

Marshall was very solicitous, helping Leslie with her coat and getting her seated. As they sipped their drink and talked, Marshall surreptitiously slipped his hand in his pocket and pulled out a small package.

"I brought your Christmas present along."

"Why, Marshall, how sweet!" She eagerly reached for the package. "May I open it now?"

"I want you to."

"Glory be," gasped Leslie as she unwrapped the package and gazed upon the most beautiful bracelet she'd ever seen. Leslie had often heard her mother speak of the Chadwick collection of heirloom jewelry. This antique bracelet was

38

undoubtedly a part of it. "It's so beautiful. I don't believe you should give me such a nice present," she finally said.

"I want you to have it. The bracelet belonged to my grandmother. My mother wore it until she died."

"But you should reserve a present like this for your *best* girl." She realized immediately she'd said the wrong thing.

"I know. I want *you* to be my 'best' girl, Leslie Jane." He covered her small and with his large one and then helped her slip the bracelet on. "You know I've always loved you even as a little girl. Now that you've grown up, it seems the most natural thing in the world to keep on loving you."

"I don't know what to say, Marshall." Her honesty and sincerity would not permit her to answer him while she was so confused about her feelings. She was accustomed to the usual "line" of her boyfriends, but she knew Marshall was sincere.

"You don't have to say anything. I just wanted you to know how I felt about you. I realize it will be a long time before I have the right to speak to your father. I still have another year of law school and then it will take a while to get established. By that time you will have finished school also."

"Yes, but that will only be the beginning for me," exclaimed Leslie earnestly. "I want to work and do something really important."

"Isn't being a wife and mother 'really important?'"

"Well, er, yes. Of course, someday I want to marry," she added defensively. "In fact I'm going to have four little boys, but it's a long way off and you'd probably get tired of waiting by then."

"It's not that simple, little Lessie Lou. You'll find out someday. I really didn't intend to get into this with you so soon, but I see you so seldom, and I was worried for fear you might fall in love with one of those doctors. Also, the war situation is getting serious. We may get into it yet."

39

"Please don't talk about the war! It frightens me. And don't worry about the doctors either," she added. She wondered what Marshall would think if he knew she had not had one single date since she had been at Vale University. No need to tell him. He probably wouldn't believe it anyway. "You don't really think we'll get in the war, do you?"

"I hope not. Besides you just told me not to talk about it." He was teasing again. "Let's get started home."

They were quiet on the drive back. Somehow Leslie couldn't feel any triumph over this "conquest." She really did want to pursue her professional career, but also somewhere in the dim, dark future, she wanted to marry and have children. Maybe Marshall was the one. She just didn't know.

The lights were burning brightly as Marshall pulled into the driveway at White Haven. "Looks like Mother Jane is waiting up for you." He stopped the car in front of the house.

"Honey, forgive me for speaking out so tonight. I don't want to rush you, but I do love you and someday I'm going to ask you to marry me." He took Leslie in his arms and kissed her tenderly. Her first real kiss. What girl wouldn't have been thrilled? He escorted her to the door and kissed her again. This time with more intensity and passion.

As Leslie entered the hall, she found Janie in the parlor sitting on the floor by the Christmas tree wrapping last minute presents.

"Come in dear. Why didn't Marshall come in? I have some chocolate made."

"Oh, he had to go on." Leslie was a little shaken. She'd never been kissed like that before. She poured herself a cup of chocolate before sitting down to help her mother. "See my present." She extended her arm with the bracelet on it.

"What a lovely gift. I remember seeing Edie wearing it." Janie was as surprised as Leslie had been.

"You asked me to be sweet to him, Mother. I guess I overdid it. He told me he loved me and

40

that someday he was going to ask me to marry him."

"And what did you say?" gasped Janie. She was pleased but hadn't expected things to happen so fast.

"I didn't say anything. I've always loved Marshall, but not that way and, Mother, there's so many things I want to do. It will be years before I can settle down and have my four little boys."

"Well, dear, you're right to wait until you are sure of your feelings. However," she teased, "I think Marshall would make a wonderful father for my four little grandsons." Janie regarded her daughter fondly. Strangely enough, she had experienced some of the exact same fears Marshall expressed. She certainly didn't want Leslie to fall in love with some Yankee doctor. She tried so hard not to be a snob, but Janie just felt like people should marry their own kind.

The rest of her vacation was very busy. As far back as Leslie could remember, it had been the custom for each family on the Lee and McKay side to have their big "Christmas dinner" and everyone invited to these enormous spreads. Marshall and his father always attended because "Daddy Chad" was "kin" to the McBrydes. The main dinner on Christmas Day was held at White Haven because it was the home place. The entire family flocked in. There was Aunt Clara, Uncle Jerry and their sons, Lee, David, Thomas, and Jerome. Lee was married and brought his wife and two small children. David and Thomas were in college and Jerome still in high school. Then there was Aunt Elizabeth and Uncle William (the McBrydes) and family—Clara, Alice, Laura, William Jr.(Bill), Greer, and Archibald. The two older girls were married and had their husbands, babies and little children. Laura, Greer and William Jr. were in college and Archibald was in high school.

Janie's side of the family wasn't so prolific. Aunt Margaret was her only sister and Margaret was an only child. Aunt Margaret and Jim Reid had married soon after Janie and Tom.

There were greetings, ooing and aawing over the new babies and little children. "My, how you've grown" and "You look like your daddy."

Leslie remembered how she used to hate these inspections when she was little and she, therefore, made it a point to just greet the children, play with them and spare them her comments about their growth and which side of the family they resembled. Consequently, she was a favorite among the young set. The cycle was repeating itself. These little children would be dragged to the annual family reunions just as she had been.

Leslie rather enjoyed these clan gatherings now, but she remembered how they used to play, fight and argue and how Mack, Marshall and the other boys would gang up against the girls. They could reminisce and laugh about it now. She had even forgiven Jerome and they could laugh over their private little secret. It was gratifying to see how Jerome had slimmed down and seemed more mature.

She enjoyed her time with Marshall, but she saw other friends and almost by mutual consent, no further mention was made of his proposal, although it was uppermost in both of their minds. Margaret was the only person besides her mother that Leslie had confided in. Margaret and Tommy Tyson had suddenly become a twosome, similar to Marshall and Leslie, after having known each other all their lives.

By the end of the second week, Leslie was getting almost homesick for school and all the hard work she knew she would face upon her return. It was, then, with both joy and sorrow that she prepared to return to Vale.

Back To School

"Leslie!" squealed Alice as she rushed to greet her friend. "Did you have a nice Christmas? It is good to be back though, isn't it?"

"Yes, it is and I really did miss all of you," agreed Leslie as she gave Alice an affectionate hug. Helen and Sharon appeared and greetings were again exchanged. The girls helped Leslie unpack and then started showing their Christmas presents. Leslie hesitated for a moment but then decided to show them Marshall's bracelet.

"Heavens to Betsy!" exclaimed Helen as she admired the exquisite beauty of the bracelet.

"Looks like love to me," observed Sharon.

"Now, please, don't start that, girls! Are we really going on the wards tomorrow?"

"Yes, at seven o'clock, so we'd better go to bed early and get plenty of rest. I do hope they don't send me to the men's ward. I'd rather practice on women first," said timid little Alice.

The next day the young students reported to Miss Hicks who assigned them to various wards. Leslie couldn't help but feel nervous even though she had practiced faithfully. This was the real thing. This morning, she would actually have to bathe a real patient.

She was assigned to ward 2316, the men's medical ward, and reported for duty as the morning report was being given by the night nurse. The head nurse was young enough to be understanding and sympathetic to the students. Leslie read her patient's chart before she was escorted out and introduced. He was a nineteen-year-old boy who had rheumatoid arthritis. Leslie felt such compassion for him that she forgot all about her fears as she gave him his bath followed by a good back rub. She then made the bed, mitered the corners perfectly and had the unit in order. He was a nice patient and she enjoyed making him feel better. Everything proceeded smoothly and by the time the instructor came to check her work, Leslie was feeling quite pleased with herself.

After the instructor left, Leslie, feeling very secure now, picked up the basin of dirty bath water to be emptied in the utility room. At the same time she picked up the half-used bar of soap to exchange it for a new one. Leslie made her way down the hall and had almost reached the safety of the utility room when the bar of soap slipped out of her hand and slid down the hall right in the path of an oncoming medical student. Her cry of warning was unheard as he was walking rather briskly, holding his head very high in the air.

Leslie stood frozen to the spot as he slipped and started sliding down the hall right towards her. And then, horror of horrors, as if matters weren't bad enough already, as he rolled into Leslie, the impact was so strong, she slipped and fell right on top of him spilling the water!

"What in the world is happening?" called the head nurse as she rushed out to see what all the commotion was about.

"I've just about been drowned, that's all!" stormed the indignant medical student as he scrambled to his feet.

"Oh, I'm so dreadfully sorry," wailed Leslie. She was so embarrassed. She just wished she could disappear or something. Miraculously, Leslie had escaped getting wet. All the water seemed to have landed on the unfortunate medical student.

"I guess you think that excuses everything. If I'd broken my leg, it would have been all the same. And because of you and your clumsiness, I'm going to be late for rounds!" He was glaring at her with such fury, she though she was going to melt. "Miss Moore, I have to go home and change clothes. Will you please explain my absence to Dr. Williams?" Then without another glance at the lowly student nurse, he marched out as grandly as his dripping clothes would allow.

"Oh, Miss Moore, I'm so ashamed. I know that boy could just kill me." Leslie looked at the head nurse with such consternation that Miss Moore smiled in spite of herself. She dismissed the crowd that had gathered, most of whom were

44

sympathetic towards Leslie, after hearing the medical student's tirade.

"Don't worry about it, child. Just be thankful it wasn't the Chief of Staff." She looked at her watch. "It's time for you to be off duty. Write up your charts and then you may go."

Leslie managed to write her nurse's notes and then left immediately. The tears started before she could reach her room. It had started out to be such a wonderful day to have ended like this. If only he could have been a little nicer instead of looking at her as though she were a worm or something less. She was lying on her bed weeping bitterly when Alice, Sharon and Helen appeared to discuss their morning's experiences.

"Whatever's the matter, honey? Did you have a nasty patient?" asked Helen.

"Please don't cry, dear," begged Alice who couldn't stand to see anyone unhappy.

"All right, stop crying and tell us what happened." Sharon was matter-of-fact.

"Oh, I made the awfulest blunder! I'll never be able to go on that ward again. I'm going to ask to be reassigned. I might see him."

"See who?" persisted Sharon.

"That awful medical student." Between sobs, Leslie managed to tell them about the accident. Instead of sympathizing, they all broke into gales of laughter.

"Oh, I wish I could have see it," laughed Helen.

Gradually, Leslie began to feel better as the girls continued to laugh. They each told of their first experience caring for a patient and by the time Alice confessed that she told her patient to breathe so she could count his respiration, she actually smiled.

"What did the medical student look like, Leslie? Don't you have any idea who he was?" Sharon had been dating some of the medical and knew quite a few.

"He was tall, had black hair, a black mustache and the meanest black eyes I ever saw."

"We'll just have to find out who he is," persisted Sharon.

"Please, Sharon, I want to try and forget it. I'll just die if I ever see him again."

Leslie was to see him sooner than she expected. That night Sharon begged her to go out on a blind date with her and Bob Harper. Leslie finally allowed herself to be persuaded. After all, she had resolved while home during Christmas that she would stop studying so hard and go out occasionally. After her trying day, she needed some relaxation.

As the girls entered the reception room to meet the boys, Leslie thought she would faint as she recognized the tall, dark medical student with the snapping black eyes. He recognized her at the same time and his reaction was the same as hers—as though he wanted to bolt. It was too late to retreat—too late to tell Sharon.

"Bob, may I present my friend, Leslie Jane Lee." Sharon was completely unaware of the by-play. Leslie automatically acknowledged the introduction. Then Bob Harper introduced his friend.

"Miss Webb, Miss Lee, this is Stephen Southall."

Oh why did I ever let Sharon persuade me to come out tonight, Leslie wondered as she allowed Stephen to escort her out.

"What'll it be, girls?" asked Bob as they left the dormitory. He was such a likeable person.

"Would you like to go to Monty's and dance, Leslie?" asked Sharon.

"Oh, yes, anything—" She knew Bob must think her terribly stupid as she hadn't uttered a word since the introductions. They were in Stephen's new Pierce Arrow automobile and Leslie was thankful he'd have to drive. As they drove along, she had a chance to really look him over. She had to admit that, in spite of his daredevil arrogance, he was one of the most handsome men she'd ever seen. They scarcely spoke a word, but Sharon and Bob kept up such an animated conversation, that Leslie and Stephen's silence went unnoticed.

When they arrived at the tavern, much to

46

Leslie's relief, several students whom they knew were there. When Dennis Raymond walked over, Leslie fairly beamed with pleasure. Others joined their table and the conversation was lively. Stephen looked very bored and held himself aloof. The girls were kept busy dancing and Leslie was beginning to have a wonderful time. She was an excellent dancer and the boys were delighted with her.

Finally, as though he considered it all in the line of duty, Stephen asked her to dance. They glided smoothly across the floor and Leslie was thinking what a good dancer he was. Just as she was having good thoughts about him, he said:

"Well, I certainly hope my life won't be endangered while I'm out here with you."

"Maybe if you get your head out of the air and watch where you're going, you'll be safe." This kind of remark was not at all like Leslie. She'd never been sarcastic in her life, but Stephen was so obnoxious, she felt justified.

"You seem to forget that I was the injured party! The least you could do would be to say you were sorry, especially considering the bawling out I got from Dr. Williams. He wouldn't even let me explain why I was late." They were glaring at each other, but didn't miss a step as they danced.

"I told you this morning I was sorry, but you wouldn't listen."

"Would you have been in a listening mood, much less a forgiving one if you were on the floor in a puddle of dirty bath water and a dumb student nurse on top of you?"

"Well, this 'dumb student nurse' is ready to go home." Leslie walked away from him before the music stopped. Bob and Sharon were already getting up from the table as they approached.

"We'd better go. The girls have to be in by 10:30," Bob said.

On the ride home, Stephen and Leslie were very quiet. At the door, they did manage to bid each other a civil good night.

As the girls started to their rooms, Leslie's sense of humor returned and she turned to Sharon and said: "Sharon, do you realize *WHO* you got me a date with?"

"Why yes. Stephen Horatio Wainwright Southall III of Boston, no less. I hope you're properly impressed."

"Oh, I am. He's also His Dripping Majesty I—the self same medical student I spilled water all over this morning—no less."

Sharon was flabbergasted. "Oh NO, Leslie NO," she squealed. "I can't believe it! Of all the medical students in school, Bob has to bring *that* one." The girls were laughing so much that all along the hall, heads started popping out to see what all the commotion was about. "I wondered why you were so quiet."

The entire Freshman class had heard of Leslie's escapade that morning and now they gathered in her room to hear the details of her blind date with the victim.

Sharon was simply beside herself. "Oh, this is so funny. I had never met him before, but I think everyone has heard of the 'great' Stephen. Some of the medical students don't like him because he's so stuck up. He's an only child of very wealthy Boston parents."

"Dear old Boston," chimed in Helen looking very sleepy and cute, "the land of the baked bean and the cod, where the Lowells speak only to the Southalls and the Southalls speak only to God."

The girls went into peals of laughter over this, and Sharon said, "Leslie, you really are a mess. When I *finally* persuade you to go out on a date, it's a disaster. Have you always gotten into scrapes like this?"

"It would seem so," laughed Leslie who seemed to be enjoying herself. "Actually I started at a very young age. Once I was in a school pagent and was supposed to do a Greek dance with two other little girls. We were dressed in loose flowing tunics and were supposed to float out on the lawn in our bare feet. Our number was called 'The Dance of the Three Graces.' My whole family was there and Mother was so proud. Well, I came gliding out and as I started into the dance, my foot landed on a thorn! Being the true trooper that I was,

48

however, I felt the show must go on and I kept dancing. Every time I put my poor foot down, the thorn would go deeper and my expression more agonized. I literally hobbled through the dance. My mother, my teacher and I were all in tears over my disgrace, not to mention having to be rushed to the doctor to extricate that awful thorn." The laughter was getting louder and Leslie suddenly remembered the time! "Now, you've heard the story of my life, please go home. It's past time for lights to be out." The girls were about to leave, when a loud knock sounded at the door. Before anyone could answer, Dean Miller walked in.

"What's going on here? Doesn't anyone know the rules?" Lights were supposed to be out at 10:30 and no visiting in the rooms after that time. The students were too frightened to answer. They knew the rules, of course, but this had been such a spontaneous occasion that no one had remembered.

"Miss Lee, are you in the habit of holding open house at this hour?" She seemed to turn her full fury on Leslie.

"No, mam. I, er—that is we were—"

"Never mind your excuses. Since you seem to be the one doing the entertaining, you can receive the punishment. Your privileges will be taken away for two weeks. The rest of you get to your rooms immediately." With this, she marched out, leaving a frightened group of students behind.

"As if we weren't all equally guilty." Alice came over and put her arms around Leslie.

"Never mind. Please leave before something else happens." Leslie couldn't help but feel hurt over Dean Miller's unfairness.

After she retired, Leslie was restless as she lay in bed reviewing the events of the day. FInally, she drifted off to sleep. He *was* good looking.

Florence Nightingale

Several days had passed since that eventful first day on the wards and Leslie was beginning to feel more like a real nurse. The students went on duty every morning at seven and came off at nine. She was no longer afraid of her patients and was really enjoying her work. The young arthritic boy was her favorite patient and he had shown marked improvement under her care. She was patient and persistent with him and he finally cooperated with her (in spite of the pain it caused) in doing the passive exercises prescribed by the doctor and thus contractures were prevented.

Her two weeks without privileges was really getting on her nerves, but it would be over soon. During this time, she was not allowed to leave the dormitory except to go on duty, to class or to the library. She could not communicate with or visit the other students.

Stephen would really be gratified if he knew she was being punished for her sins. Leslie smiled as she thought about him and was actually feeling kindly towards the big dark villain when a sarcastic voice interrupted her thoughts.

"Well, if it isn't Florence Nightingale in person."

Leslie turned around. There he stood smirking at her.

"Sorry I can't compare you with some equally famous doctor." She snapped her chart shut and prepared to leave.

"Aw say now, must you always treat me as though I were poison?" The tone of his voice changed and he looked almost contrite. "I know we got off to a bad start, but can't we bury the hatchet now?"

Leslie's good nature returned immediately and she gave him a sparkling smile. "Of course, and let me say again that I am truly sorry and even more sorry for my conduct later."

"This is much better." He gave her a boyish smile. Why his eyes didn't look mean at all. Leslie's heart started acting very queerly as the handsome fellow walked along with her out of the hospital. As they neared the dormitory, she suddenly remembered that her two weeks without privileges wasn't over yet.

She mustn't be seen with Stephen. Nor did she want to tell him about her punishment. She still didn't trust him.

"You'd better go back now, Steve," she said.

"What! Just as I've begun to break the ice? I should say not."

"Now, Stephen, really. I have a class and have to do some preparation for it. Please go," begged Leslie, glancing frantically around to see if that dreadful Miss Miller was anywhere about. "You may come over some other time when I don't have a class."

"All right, Florence. I'll go, but I'm going to see you again real soon," he stated emphatically as he started back towards the hospital.

Leslie breathed a sigh of relief as she hurried on to her room and started studying. Oh how she resented having to stay in and being treated like a child, but there wasn't much she could do about it.

That night Stephen called her but she made an excuse.

"Now see here, Florence Nightingale, don't be coy with me," he said breaking in on her excuse. "Either say 'yes' or 'no.'"

There he goes being overbearing again, thought Leslie. "Well, if that's the way you want it, the answer is 'no.'" She was campused for another week but she had no intention of telling him.

"Then will you give me a date sometime in the future?" His tone changed and he tried being persuasive.

"Yes."

"When?"

"Call me next week. Exams will be over then."

Since there was only one phone to a hall and it was located about midway, Sharon had heard the telephone conversation. When Leslie returned to her room, Sharon slipped in.

"Oh, Sharon, you mustn't be seen in here!"

cried Leslie. "We'd both be punished and I can't stand this isolation much longer."

"I just had to know who was calling," whispered Sharon, who couldn't stand not being in on everything.

"Stephen Southall," answered Leslie. "Now please go at once."

"Why, Leslie, that's wonderful. The Med school dance is next week. Maybe he'll ask you."

"Sharon, please leave. I don't care about the dance. All I want is to be free again." She fairly pushed her out the door.

The next week seemed to drag by and Leslie was becoming so cross and irritable, she knew she couldn't stand it much longer.

Stephen Southall met her several times on the halls and repeatedly asked her for dates, but she put him off each time. This sort of treatment stimulated his interest even more. He wasn't accustomed to being refused and here was a little upstart student nurse who actually tried to avoid him.

Finally, the long week did pass, and Leslie gave Stephen a date for Sunday afternoon. They decided to go ice skating. Stephen looked very handsome in his skating outfit and he gave a whistle of appreciation as Leslie appeared in her new skating suit of red trimmed with white fur. He waited while she signed out.

"Florence, I can't believe we're going out together and on speaking terms too." He held her arm lightly and she felt a strange tingle of excitement.

"My real name is Leslie, you know."

"No." He shook his head. "Leslie is a sweet, clinging vine type of name and that doesn't suit you at all. I imagine you have as much of the devil in you as the original Florence. You'll always be Florence to me," he said emphatically.

"And who do you think you are to criticize Florence Nightingale? She was the greatest nurse of all time."

"True enough. I only said she wasn't a clinging vine. But remember, we're not supposed to fuss today," he protested. "Must you always take issue at everything I say?"

52

Leslie laughed and tried to forget how irritating he could be at times. When they reached the skating area, she was entranced watching the good skaters perform. Steve was an excellent skater. Leslie was only fair since she'd lived in the South all her life and had not had much opportunity to learn. They skated several hours and Stephen gave Leslie some helpful instructions. It was a most enjoyable afternoon.

As they drove home in the gathering twilight, Stephen talked to Leslie of his life. As a young child, he had private tutors and later attended private schools. When he was only thirteen, he was sent away to a boarding Preparatory School. His father's shipping business necessitated his being out of town on frequent overseas trips. His mother had a very busy social life as well as traveling frequently with his father, and it was, therefore, necessary for Stephen to be placed in a boarding school. He told Leslie that he'd made more friends and found more happiness since being in medical school than he'd ever known before. Leslie was quick to realize now that his bold arrogant manner was only a shield to cover his loneliness.

Her whole attitude towards him changed. It made her realize just how lucky she was to have Mack, Betsy, and the most loving parents in the world. From his description, she knew that Stephen's home in Boston and even their summer home was more pretentious than White Haven but she wouldn't trade places with him for anything.

Stephen parked his car and escorted her up the walk to the dormitory. "It's been fun not fussing with you, Florence."

"It most certainly has, Stephen," agreed Leslie, "and please let's try and forget our first date. My mother would be so ashamed of me if she knew how I talked to you that night."

"Well, I wasn't exactly what you'd call a knight in shining armor either, but that's all in the past. We'll start over again from this afternoon. I'm even going to try and forget what a hard time I had getting a date with you. Which reminds me—when am I going to see you again?"

They made a date for the following Wednesday and Leslie went to her room to study. She also wrote Marshall a long letter, but she couldn't get Stephen off her mind. She had an uneasy feeling that she had just embarked on a collision course.

Capping

The months sped by and Leslie liked her work better all the time. She knew she'd made the right choice of a profession and her parents were convinced too. Now that their probationary time was over the students had earned the right to have a cap. During a very impressive candlelight ceremony, they marched single-file into the auditorium, singing "Follow the Gleam." Each student carried a lighted candle in a Florence Nightingale candle holder. The dean placed their cap on. Vale nursing caps were very unique, and distinctive, made in the shape of a V to symbolize the school. The ceremony was concluded with the students repeating the Nightingale Pledge. Reaching this milestone was a real achievement. Leslie felt a sense of pride and loyalty as she joined the ranks of so many nurses before her.

Each day brought new patients and new experiences. The students were assuming more responsibility and they were on duty longer. Leslie felt more sure of her position now, but she continued to study hard and her grades were the highest in the class. The students were granted "late leave" according to their grades—that is: A students had two late leaves a week (12 midnight), B students had one late leave a week and C students only two a month, otherwise 10:30 was the curfew.

Leslie seldom used more than one of her leaves. Stephen called her frequently, but she allowed him to come over only once during the week and maybe on Saturday or Sunday. Since she was getting out more and meeting other students, she was very popular. Occasionally she dated Dennis Raymond and others but Stephen remained the main one in her life.

Stephen liked for her to be popular at the dances as he felt this was proof of his good taste, but he was very jealous when she dated other boys. Leslie only laughed and went right on with them. Having other friends, she felt would be a "safety valve" for her as she had no intention of forming any entangling alliances for a long time yet.

Leslie was happy and content most of the time. She wrote Marshall regularly and received letters from him at least once a week.

The war news was upsetting and there was always the haunting fear that the United States might get involved. If that should happen, she knew both Mack and Marshall would have to go.

World War I

The Americans (at least half of whom) could trace their ancestry back to British roots, sympathized strongly with the Allies. Also, the hearts of Americans went out to their traditional friend, France. France had helped us win our independence and we felt we owed her an unpayable debt.

Germany sank even lower in American esteem when she began the brutal assault on "poor little Belgium" whose neutrality had been solemnly guaranteed.

The execution of Miss Edith Cavell, an English nurse who had aided scores of allied soldiers to escape, was another of the reasons most Americans were pro-Ally. Several other factors such as the continual sinking of our merchant ships by German U-Boats and finally, the Lusitania where one hundred and fourteen Americans lost their lives, seemed to be moving us inexorably towards war.

It wasn't until April 1917, that the United States declared war on Germany. Leslie was so upset she called home to try and get some information but Janie had not heard from Mack. Since this was their last year in law school, she hoped they would be allowed to graduate before being drafted.

The next day, Leslie received a special delivery letter from Marshall which gave her a twinge of conscience. She had been worrying about her brother but Marshall's first thoughts were of her. He told her that he and Mack had already volunteered. "After all," he wrote, "we have to be true sons of 'The Volunteer State.'" They would be allowed to graduate, he said, but would have to postpone taking their Bar Exams.

Leslie immediately made an appointment with Miss Miller to request leave during the time the boys would be home before going to camp. The dean could be very considerate and understanding at times, and she granted Leslie the time off.

That night Stephen called and asked her to

meet him in the lab. He had to work late and thought she might like to come over and see some of the specimens he was working on. Leslie was delighted. She was an ardent student of Chemistry and Anatomy and any opportunity to work with the microscope fascinated her. Also it would help get her mind off her troubles.

Stephen was waiting for her at the door. He looked very handsome in his white lab coat and Leslie was keenly aware of it.

"I appreciate your coming over to keep my company while I work."

"It's nice of you to let me come and look at your bugs."

He ushered her into the large laboratory where several other students were bending over their microscopes. Stephen succeeded in isolating an acid-fast bacillus from a tuberculosis patient's sputum. He also showed her a spirochoete on a dark field. She became so absorbed that, for a time, she forgot about the war and her worries. Finally, Stephen looked at his watch.

"It's getting near your signing in time," he said and started putting his equipment away.

They walked towards the dormitory. Stephen hadn't mentioned the war all evening although it was uppermost in both of their minds.

"Well, Florence, it's come at last." He finally broke the silence.

"I know. I still don't want to believe it."

"And here I am just a junior medical student! It makes me sick."

"I know how you feel. I'm just a first year student nurse. I wish I were in a position to join the army."

"I'm glad you're not," he said emphatically. "I wouldn't want you to be in the army."

"Do you realize there's a real need for nurses in the army?" She bristled.

"Yes, but you're still a student—just like me." Stephen grinned, deciding to avoid a fuss. "You can't go anyway and that's that. However," he added thoughtfully, "I might go on and volunteer even though I haven't finished yet."

"Oh no, Stephen! You mustn't do that," protested Leslie recovering from her feeling of

58

antagonism. "You must finish Medical School. Please promise me you won't do anything foolish."

"Dear Florence, your concern is gratifying, but I'll probably wind up doing what every other draft-age man will do—that is just as he's told."

How was it possible for him to be so sweet and considerate one minute and so irritating the next, Leslie wondered. "My brother and Marshall didn't wait to be told. They both volunteered." Leslie proudly lifted her chin.

"Florence, I must say you're most inconsistent. When I mention volunteering, you appear to be concerned and beg me to finish school and then when I mention waiting for the draft, you rub it in by telling me what heroes your brother and that Marshall chap are for volunteering. And, by the way, who is that Marshall anyway? This isn't the first time you've mentioned him."

"'That Marshall' is my brother's dearest friend and a friend of the family. His father is a prominent lawyer back home and my mother loves him almost as much as she does us."

"And your mother's daughter is quite fond of him too, isn't she?"

"Quite," agreed Leslie.

"Now see here, Florence. Is there an understanding between you and this chap?"

"No, that is—not exactly," evaded Leslie.

"And exactly what do you mean by that?"

"It means I'm not ready to make up my mind about anyone just yet. Everything's so uncertain and besides I'm just finishing my first year in nursing. I still have two more years and when I graduate, I want to work and do something really important. I want to help make nursing one of the top ranking professions for women. Nursing should rank along with Medicine, Engineering, and other schools as an integral part of the University." During this declaration, Leslie was speaking earnestly and emphatically.

Stephen looked at her quizically, "And you demurred when I first called you 'Florence.' There's no other name for you, honey." He regarded her with unusual tenderness. "And then after you've made the world a better place for nurses or should I say, the world better because of nurses, what then?"

"Maybe then I can settle down and have my four little boys."

By this time they had reached the dormitory. As they stood in the doorway, Stephen took both of Leslie's hands in his and looked her steadily in the eye. "Good night, Florence. We've left a lot of things hanging and I still want some answers, but just remember this: the real thing comes only once in a lifetime. Don't be so blind you'll let it pass you by." He kissed her lightly on the cheek.

"Good night, Stephen. I'll remember." Leslie's throat suddenly felt very tight. She had never seen Stephen like this before.

As she was undressing for bed, Sharon came in. She'd had a date with Bob Harper.

"We saw Stephen lingering over his goodnight," she said.

"You know, Sharon, I really am beginning to like him a lot. He's so different from what we first thought."

"Oh, honey, I'm so glad," said Sharon, giving Leslie a hug. "Have you heard from Mack yet?"

"Marshall wrote that they'd both volunteered." Big tears welled up in her eyes.

"Well, you knew that's what they would do and what you'd want them to do." Sharon tried to console Leslie, her own eyes bubbling over with tears.

"Why, Sharon? Why do there have to be wars?"

"I don't know dear. Because there'll always be greedy, selfish, power hungry leaders, I suppose," she answered simply.

"You know, Leslie, the war coming at this time is really hard on the medical students. They can't enlist as doctors. Bob said tonight he felt like he should go on and volunteer anyway, but I begged him to wait."

"Why, Stephen said the same thing!"

"And when I mentioned that I wished I was

a graduate nurse so I could join, you should have seen what a fit he threw."

"And so did Stephen," cried Leslie, amazed that their conversations should have been so similar.

Sharon gathered up her things and said good night. Leslie decided to answer Marshall's letter. She didn't feel like she could sleep anyway. In her heart, she felt that Stephen was falling in love with her and this was the last thing she wanted now. She still couldn't separate her feelings for him against her feelings for Marshall. The trust and security she felt with Marshall lacked the excitement and adventure she had with Stephen.

Farewell

"Ummm, that's delicious, Mae Mae," exclaimed Leslie, tasting the icing of the cake she was beating up.

"Now don't eat too much and spoil your dinner, honey," cautioned Janie stirring away on another bowl of goodies.

The kitchen and the whole household for that matter was a scene of activity. The servants were busy either cooking or cleaning in preparation for the party Janie was having that night. Leslie had been home almost a week enjoying a round of parties with Marshall and Mack. Everyone wanted to give the boys a good send off. Tonight, Janie had invited some of their closest friends and family in for a farewell dinner and dance. Leslie's cousins, Tommy Tyson, and Greer McBryde would also be leaving in a matter of weeks. Lee and David Tyson were married men but it was almost certain that they would have to go also.

Mack's girl friend Virginia Neal had been a house guest all week as had Leslie's cousin Margaret Reid. Margaret just lived on the adjoining farm, but since she was an only child, she felt as close to Mack as Leslie did. Besides, it was easier for her to see Tommy Tyson at White Haven because it seemed to be the hub of all the activities. Marshall spent every waking moment there also. His father said he guessed he'd have to move in too if he expected to see anything of his son.

Janie loved having her children's friends around. Her heart was so full of love that she could gladly open it to anyone who loved her loved ones. Janie was determined that the boys' last memories of home should be happy ones. Leslie, however, could read her mother like a book. No one else noticed the dark circles underneath Janie's eyes, but Leslie knew this meant she wasn't sleeping well. She also noticed that Janie was tense and her laughter strained. Leslie's heart ached for her mother because she knew that back of all the brave front, her heart was breaking. Her only son was going off to war along with his cousins and best friend. No one would have guessed her anguish as she worked in the kitchen. She was wearing a little blue pinafore and looked very young and girlish in spite of her forty-two years.

"What are you doing this afternoon, darling?" she asked as she fondly regarded her daughter.

"Marshall, Betsy and I are going horse back riding," answered Leslie.

"How sweet of you to take Betsy. I know she'll enjoy it."

"Oh, I'm not being sweet to Betsy," she smiled. "I'm just trying to help Brother. Even if he wanted to pop the question to Virginia, he hasn't had much opportunity the way Betsy's been hanging around him."

"Virginia's a lovely girl and if Mack wants to 'pop the question' it's fine with me," declared Janie.

"Well, tonight's his last chance," laughed Leslie, tasting another cookie.

"And it's Mr. Marshall's las' chance too," interrupted Mary. "Miz Jane, don' you spec we oughta keep that chile Betsy at home wif us today?"

"Glory be! Hush, Mae Mae," exclaimed Leslie, noticing that the two colored girls in the kitchen were silently giggling as they stirred their mixes.

"You're absolutely right, Mary," agreed Janie putting her bowl of icing down and starting towards the door. "I'll see to it that Betsy doesn't interfere with either of my children's romances."

"But, Mother, I promised Betsy she could go," argued Leslie, following Janie down the hall.

"And I promised Mary that she should not go."

Leslie let the matter drop, secretly deciding that she'd get Margaret to go with them. However, when Marshall arrived that afternoon, Margaret had a date with Tommy.

Leslie dreaded being alone with Marshall.

She definitely did not know her own mind and did not want a decision forced on her at this time. Although she loved Marshall dearly and felt such a sense of security with him she knew something was lacking that she hadn't realized until she met Stephen.

"Where shall we ride, Les?" he asked as he helped her mount her horse.

"Let's just ride around over the farm," she answered.

They rode over the fertile fields of White Haven where the farm hands were busy plowing the fields for spring planting. The soil had a good fresh smell as it was turned back to receive the new plants and seeds. The fruit trees were blooming and spring flowers dotted the yards and fields. It was a beautiful day. As they rode around and saw familiar sights and reminisced, Leslie's tumultuous spirit felt more at rest than it had for days.

"Lessie, see the old oak tree where we built our tree house? Part of it is still up there." Marshall pointed to the giant tree.

"Yes, and do you remember how you and Brother would climb up and pull the ladder after you so Margaret and I couldn't come up," reminded Leslie.

"Remember the old grapevine swing where I broke my collar bone trying to play Tarzan?"

"—And Daddy Chad was ready to spank me for daring you to do it!"

"Let's ride down to the creek and water the horses," he suggested.

Leslie sat down on a fallen tree and watched him as he led the horses to get a drink.

"Marsh, wasn't it right about here, where Margaret and I came upon you, Brother, Jerome and Tommy swimming and we tied knots in your clothes?" She laughed as she thought about it.

"Yes, and the only reason you didn't run off with our clothes, we told you that if you did we would come after you—clothes or no clothes."

"They say it's a sure sign of old age when you start looking back," remarked Leslie. "We've been reminiscing all afternoon."

"We do have a lot of happy memories," he

said wistfully. "I hope there will be more happy times to look forward to."

Suddenly Leslie felt very sad and discouraged. They'd all been so brave this week and so careful not to say anything sad, and now here, right at the end, she had let this slip upon her. The anguished look on Marshall's face and her own heavy heart caused her over-taxed nerves to snap. She leaned her head against the tree trunk and began to cry.

"Darling, please don't!" cried Marshall, rushing over to her. He gently pulled her towards him and rested her head on his broad chest. He stroked her hair and kissed her forehead and softly spoke soothing words to her.

Leslie couldn't stop. She'd held back the tears so long for her mother's sake that it was now a relief to cry. War was such a horrible thing. People's lives and plans had to be changed to conform to a war none of them wanted—not even the enemy.

It was so comforting to relax in his strong arms until suddenly, Leslie realized that Marshall thought she was crying over him. Well, she was, but also for Mack, herself and the whole world. He was so sweet. She just mustn't hurt his feelings. Her numb brain finally grasped his words.

"Leslie, please marry me before I leave. I love you so."

"But Marshall, honey, I can't marry you now. I told you why before."

"But Leslie, the war has changed all that. We have such a short time," he protested. "We must marry now."

"But can't you see, Marshall, the war makes it even more important for me to finish school. They may need me," argued Leslie.

"Look at me, Les," commanded Marshall. He held her face between his hands. "Do you love me?"

Leslie faced Marshall and her clear green eyes met his blue ones.

"I love you dearly, Marshall, but whether it's the kind of love you want and deserve, I do not know."

65

"But, hon, you'd have to know that."

"It's never been my wish to deceive you, Marshall. I must have more time."

"You've written me about this Stephen. What about him?"

"He's a fine person, but I'm not in love with him either."

"Will he be going to the army?"

"I don't know. No decision has been made about Junior medical students yet."

"And while I'm gone, he'll steal my girl," said Marshall bitterly.

"Oh, Marshall, don't talk like that," cried Leslie. "We mustn't let the war do this to us. It can't last forever. If there hadn't been a war, we'd have waited several years to have a showdown."

"I'm sorry, Les. I just can't bear the thought of losing you."

"We'd better start back, Marsh. It's getting late and Mother will want me to help her with some last minute preparations for the party."

"In just a minute, Leslie. Will you promise me one thing?"

"Why, yes, Marsh. What is it?"

"Please promise me you won't marry anyone until I get back. Is that asking too much?"

"No, that's not asking too much. I'll promise."

"Now, I have something for you." He reached in his pocket and produced a beautiful antique ring—a diamond surrounded by emeralds. "This was my grandmother's engagement ring. It was truly a gift of love and I'm passing it on to you."

"That's the sweetest thing I ever heard." Leslie was sentimental. He slipped the ring on her third finger, left hand.

"A perfect fit."

"Thank you, Marshall. It's so beautiful. I'll take good care of it for you."

Marshall took her in his arms and kissed her tenderly. He tried to show restraint, but as his desire grew, he became more intense. Leslie gently broke away from him. She knew she would be safe with Marshall, but this had to stop.

Marshall recovered his equanimity. "I'm sorry, honey. It's just that I love you so much."

"I know."

They mounted their horses and rode back home where Leslie slipped upstairs. She wanted to bathe her face before her mother could see that she'd been crying.

Leslie was in the bathroom which she shared with Betsy when a knock sounded at the door.

"Who is it?" Sudden panic seized her. She just couldn't face her mother now.

"It's me, Sis," answered Mack. "May I come in?"

"Oh, sure, come on in," called Leslie dabbing her eyes with the towel.

"I wanted to talk to you before tonight," he began, then his sharp eyes noticed Leslie's tear swollen eyes. "What have you been crying about?"

"Nothing that you can do anything about," she answered. "What do you want to talk about?"

"Oh, I don't know—just things." Mack knew if he didn't press Leslie, she'd eventually tell him what was troubling her. "Tonight's our last night." He took a deep breath. "It may be a long time before I get back." He walked over and sat down on the window seat. He was looking out over the spacious grounds of White Haven as though he wanted to etch every detail of it on his mind. "You know, Sis, I'm not really afraid to go to war. I expect to come back, of course, but I do have such a hollow, empty feeling."

Leslie began to choke up again. "Please, Brother, let's try not to get upset. We've got to get through the party tonight for Mother's sake."

"I know. We're lucky to have such fine parents, aren't we?"

"Yes, of course. Brother, you do understand that Mother and Father are just being brave, don't you? They certainly don't feel as calm as they've been acting all the week."

"You don't have to explain my parents to me, Leslie. I've known them longer than you have. Besides, that's not why I came in here."

67

"You said you wanted to talk?"

"Hmmmm-m I see you're wearing Marshall's ring."

"How did you know it was his?"

"He showed it to me. Are you going to marry him?"

"I don't know."

"Then why did you accept his ring?"

"He wanted me to have it, even though I told him I wasn't ready to make any kind of commitment. I did promise him that I wouldn't marry anyone else until he returned. By that time, I should know."

"He's a great guy."

"Yes, he is, but I can't marry him just for that reason."

"Well, actually I have to agree with you. I don't think people should get married before going off to war."

"We're *not* agreeing either!" Leslie protested. "I think two people who *know* they're in love should get married—war or no war. Do you love Virginia?"

"Yes, and she wants to get married."

"Then why don't you?"

"I just told you why," he said impatiently. "Besides, you refused Marshall."

"Yes, but not because of the war. Your situation is different. You know you love each other."

"Sis, I just couldn't marry a girl and then go off and leave her. There's no telling how long I'll be gone or what kind of condition I'll be in when I return." He looked so miserable.

She walked over and put her hands on his shoulders. "Everything's in such a turmoil. Marshall wants to get married and I don't. Virginia wants to get married and you don't! Why couldn't things have worked out for at least one of us?"

"I don't know, Sis. Just hang in there and take care of the home front until we get back." Mack got up and kissed her lightly on the forehead. "I'd better leave and let you get ready for tonight."

Leslie awakened early the next morning. They had danced until a very late hour, but she was bathed and dressed before the others woke up. Everyone seemed to have had a good time at the party and she was glad.

Leslie hurried downstairs to help her mother and Mary with breakfast. Janie had decided to serve their last meal out on the long back porch. She already had the table out and set with her finest linen and china, and she was rushing around giving orders to the servants.

Janie looked very pretty, but Leslie noticed the circles under her eyes were deeper and darker in spite of her efforts to hide them with make-up.

"Mother, I want to show you the ring Marshall gave me." She held out her hand.

"Oh, it's so beautiful!" Janie held her hand and scrutinized the ring carefully. "Is it an engagement ring, dear?"

"Well, no—" Leslie tried to explain the situation.

"I see." Janie was always so understanding.

The family and guests came drifting down and there was no more opportunity for conversation. They were all very quiet during breakfast. It was as though they felt there was no longer any need for pretense. Leslie's father and Daddy Chad would drive the "children" to the station. Janie said she preferred to say her goodbyes at home.

Leslie dreaded this last moment most of all. Her mother had spent the past week as though she were playing the leading role in a life drama. The curtain would soon ring down and the climax, where Janie would bid her boys goodbye and really send them off to war, was about to begin. Would she be able to act out her final scene?

Mary's boys had already loaded their baggage in the car. Leslie gave her mother a hasty kiss and then ran to the car to climb in beside her father. He was sitting there very quiet, and Leslie slipped her small hand in his and they silently waited for the others.

Margaret came next and then Virginia.

69

Marshall, who had been playing with Betsy, tossed her over to Mack for a final tussle.

"Do I get a goodbye kiss, Mother Jane?" he asked.

"Of course! You're my child too." Janie held out her arms to him. Then Mack put Betsy down and came towards his mother. Janie smiled bravely as she put her arms around him. Mary was crying openly in her apron and the other servants were standing around observing this scene with bowed heads.

"You'll be sure to write, won't you, Son?"

"Just as soon as I arrive, Mother." He was afraid to say much for fear they would both start crying. "Please try not to worry. This is something that we have to do. We'll try and get it over as soon as possible." With that, he gave her a final kiss and ran towards the waiting car.

She was smiling bravely as they drove off. As long as they could see her, she waved her little white handkerchief. Now that they were out of sight, she could let the tears flow.

The boys were in camp only a short time and then shipped overseas where they were to receive 6 weeks of special artillery training on the French 75—the supreme weapon of war, and rigorous training on both trench and open warfare. They were granted only a 24 hour pass which did not allow enough time to come home. Marshall and Mack called Leslie and she did get to say goodbye.

The arrival of the Americans brought new victories for the Allies and Leslie would read about every battle—Scieheprey, Cantigny and Chateau Thierry, and the the grim reality set in—Americans were beginning to be wounded, to be gassed, to die.

The weeks that followed were a nightmare and Leslie wondered how she'd ever live through it. She would awaken at night, cold and trembling after having dreamed that something had happened to her brother. An uneasy, gnawing feeling gripped her and she just knew that eventually the Kaiser would come and get them all!

70

The heavy case load in the hospital and rigid classroom schedules helped. As long as she could stay busy, she could forget, for a while at least.

Americans voluntarily rationed their food with wheatless and meatless days. Back home, her mother was busy knitting socks, doing volunteer work with the Red Cross and helping with the War Bond drive. Tom increased his corn, wheat, and cotton crops to aid the war effort. Each in his own way helped.

Surgery

Leslie and her friends were working in surgery now and it was a blessing in disguise. An electrifying atmosphere always prevailed during an operation and the thrill and excitement of the operating room seemed to grip everyone. This did more than anything to help Leslie suppress her fears. Even the most minor operation was a miracle to her, and she never tired of helping and would even volunteer for extra duty. She never ceased to marvel at the skill of the surgeons. Usually the doctors were so absorbed in performing the operation, they had little time to notice anything so lowly as a student nurse—except when she made a mistake! Then she was the center of attention to everyone from the surgeon on down to the intern. Leslie never took any of their curt remarks personally, however. She knew the doctor had to be under a terrific strain and could understand his irritation if he was handed the wrong instrument or if he was delayed when they were slow getting the sutures ready.

Sharon didn't share this feeling though and when the doctor yelled "suture" at her, during an operation, it was all she could do to keep from throwing it at him.

One day after Leslie had scrubbed for her first major operation, she came back to the supply room to relate her experience to Sharon in glowing terms. Sharon was folding sponges and helping wrap supplies for the autoclave.

"Sharon, guess what! I just scrubbed for Dr. Lawson! We did a cholecystectomy. It was so exciting and he didn't have to ask me for a single instrument. I knew what he would need and had it ready before he could ask."

"So *we* did it, you say? I imagine his version would be the big *I*, not 'we.'"

"Oh, Sharon, don't be so mean," Leslie protested. "Dr. Lawson is a great surgeon. Anyone could do what I did, but it takes skill and years of study and practice to do what he did."

"Please forgive me, Les!" Sharon put her arms around Leslie. "You're such a sweet child. I wish I had your enthusiasm and zest for living." At that moment, Miss Hance, the operating room supervisor came in.

"Miss Lee, Dr. Lawson would like to see you. He's in his office."

Leslie, still wearing her surgical cap and gown, rushed down the hall trying to imagine what he wanted. She was sure she'd done everything right. As she entered the doctor's office, he was dictating a letter to his secretary. He motioned her to a chair until he finished. When the secretary left, he turned to Leslie and said: "Young lady, you did remarkably well assisting me this morning. I just wanted to compliment you."

"Oh, thank you, Dr. Lawson!" Leslie was relieved and exuberant. She felt like she'd just been conferred knighthood. "I think you did real well too," she added seriously.

Dr. Lawson was a little taken aback by this remark but when he looked into her clear green eyes, he knew she was sincere. "Miss Hance told me this was your first cholecystectomy. How were you able to anticipate my needs and have the right instrument ready?"

"Well, I've had the opportunity to observe you for a long time and also I've made it a practice to always read up on an operation I'm to help with."

"Hmmm—" the doctor was at a loss for words. This was a new breed of student who evidently wasn't intimidated by doctors. "I hope you will assist me again." He dismissed her then.

Christmas 1917

The weeks dragged into months, and gradually Leslie was able to adjust to the reality of a cruel war. During this time, she turned more and more to Stephen for comfort. he could reassure her when the news sounded bad and Leslie, in turn, was a great help to him when he was restless and unsure of his own position. When he would feel an urge to volunteer, she would make him understand the importance of finishing medical school.

Stephen was almost convinced until one day he was in a downtown store and a young woman looked at him scornfully and said, "Why aren't *you* in the army?"

This cut Stephen to the quick. In spite of his seeming arrogance, he was actually a very sensitive soul. He rushed out of the store before the clerk could give his his change, and went immediately to the draft board and volunteered. They took his name and gave him an appointment for a physical.

That night, he told Leslie what he had done. "Honey, you can't let some ill-bred woman ruin your whole career."

They argued on and on and on. When Leslie was worrying about Stephen, she could forget her fears and when he was consoling her, he could reduce his own restlessness. Without either of them quite realizing it, they each filled a great need for the other.

When the draft board learned that Stephen was a medical student, he was given a deferment.

That Christmas, Leslie nor any of her friends were allowed to go home. The hospital was understaffed since so many nurses and doctors were in the army. The students were well into their second year now and were able to assume more responsibility.

This was Leslie's first Christmas away from home and she was very homesick. The hospital census was low because as many patients as possible had been discharged to spend Christmas at home. The students knew the remaining patients were homesick also and did everything in their power to cheer them. Some of the medical students were persuaded to go out and cut down cedar trees and then everyone joined in decorating each ward and the lobby. The private patients' rooms were checked also to be sure they had Christmas cheer.

Also the students had been practicing for weeks on another little surprise they had planned. Miss Moore, their Biology instructor, had been coaching them. The excitement was at a high pitch on Christmas morning. The student nurses were up at 6 a.m. before time to report for duty, donned their uniforms with the white slip over aprons and their caps. Each one carried a lighted candle in a Florence Nightingale candle holder as it was not yet daylight at that hour. Their big moment had arrived! They marched through the hospital corridors singing Christmas carols! It was a very impressive sight and sound as some of them had really beautiful voices. The patients enjoyed it so much and later one patient told Leslie that when he awakened and heard the sweet music and saw the nurses in the dim light with their lighted candles, he thought he must have died and was waking up in Heaven!

The girls had the afternoon off and Bob Harper's parents invited them to their hunting lodge for Christmas dinner. Sharon, Bob, Helen and Stephen drove up earlier to decorate the tree and get the cabin ready for their party. Leslie and Alice stayed to attend a prayer service at the Presbyterian Church. After the service, Tom Lodge and Barney Cook, two medical students who dated Alice and Helen drove them up to the lodge.

A light snow was falling and the log cabin nestled among giant pine and cedar trees emulated a scene on a Christmas Card. As they arrived, the party was in full swing. Some of the couples were just returning from a sleigh ride. Stephen was looking out the window and rushed out as soon as he spotted their car.

"Hurry, Stephen!" called Bob from the doorway. "Just think, it's been all of three hours since you saw her."

"I was getting worried," Stephen said sheepishly, putting his arms around Leslie.

"We had to drive slowly because of the snow," she explained. "We're here now though and a big merry Christmas to you!" She laughed as he gave her another hug and ushered her inside.

A big log fire was burning in the fireplace and the long, rustic living room was cheerful and cozy. The smell of hot cider and spice permeated the air. Momentarily they could almost forget that a horrible war was being waged across the ocean. Sharon and Bob were setting the table and Mrs. Harper was placing food on the hunt board for their buffet dinner.

"It's so sweet of you to share your Christmas with us, Mrs. Harper," beamed Leslie. "This helps us forget to be homesick."

"We're delighted to have you, my dear."

Leslie observed that Mr. and Mrs. Harper seemed to be very fond of Sharon. She was glad to see this as she suspected that Sharon and Bob were falling in love. For the first time, she wondered what Stephen's parents were like and if they would approve of her. She quickly brushed this thought away as the group gathered around the table and joined hands. Mr. Harper offered a prayer of thanks for their blessings and a special one for the soldiers so far from home.

After dinner they gleefully flocked to the Christmas tree where all shapes and sizes of presents were piled underneath. Bob acted as Santa Claus and distributed the gifts. There were nice, serious gifts and also funny ones for everyone.

The girls squealed with delight as they opened their presents. Stephen's gag gift was a bar of soap! Leslie covered her face with her hands amid all the laughter. She guessed she would never live that escapade down but now they could both laugh about it. Stephen even said, "If it hadn't been for that bar of soap, I might never have met Florence." Helen gave Sharon a cartoon she had drawn of an operating room scene and to the side, she had scribbled some prize quotes of sarcastic remarks the surgeons had made to the students helping them. Leslie's funny present was also beautiful—a ceramic figurine of four little boys grouped together.

"How sweet!" she exclaimed. "They'll look just right on my desk."

Stephen's gift to her was the Nightingale Pledge done in petit point cross stitch and framed in a lovely antique maple frame. The card simply read, "To Florence II, with love, Stephen." This pleased Leslie more than anything he could have given her.

After dinner, they played records on the victrola and danced. As they danced, Leslie and Stephen seemed to cling closer together with a new awareness of each other. "I'd like to talk to you, Florence. Could we go over and sit by the fire?" Leslie sensed what this conversation would be about, but she knew of no way to avert it. The other couples were dancing and Mr. and Mrs. Harper were in the kitchen packing up leftover food and supplies to take back home.

They found a big cushion by the fire and snuggled down in it. He had his arm around her and she rested her head on his shoulder. Oh, if they could just sit here peacefully and watch the fire, Leslie thought, but she knew that was not to be.

"You know I love you, don't you, Florence?" She started toying with Marshall's ring on her left hand, but when she looked into his eyes, her backbone suddenly turned to jelly. "I want to marry you someday," he continued.

"Stephen, there's something I must tell you before you go on," Leslie interrupted him. She felt like she had to let him know. "You see this ring? It belongs to Marshall. I made him a promise I wouldn't marry anyone until he returns."

"Why did you do that?" he asked irritably.

"I don't know, honey. We were all so upset over the war and their having to leave so soon. At the time, it seemed such a little thing to ask."

"You aren't going to marry him, are you?"

"No, I know now that I couldn't do that,"

and she really did know. All her doubts and uncertainties were suddenly resolved and she knew she loved Stephen. "I'll always love Marshall. He was my first real beau, but I know now that what I feel for him is very much like my feelings I have for my brother. I'll work things out with him when he gets back."

"Well, it looks like we both have some fences to mend," he said thoughtfully. "I have a similar situation with a girl back home. Nothing definite, but more or less expected by our parents."

For the first time in her life, Leslie felt a sudden pang of jealousy. Stephen had never mentioned another girl and he'd never dated anyone at the university except her.

"Does she know about us?" Leslie felt like an ice cold hand had suddenly closed around her heart.

"No, I haven't seen her in over a year or written, either, but I will write and tell her as well as my parents."

"What is she like?" queried Leslie.

"Beautiful—one of the most beautiful girls I ever saw. We grew up together, but our friendship is more of a habit than desire," answered Stephen looking in the fire. Leslie felt another knifelike pain around her heart. She was actually jealous! There was no doubt in her mind now. She knew she loved Stephen.

"I've just let things drift along because there wasn't anyone else until you came along and even then, we spent our first few dates at each other's throats."

"Then we're both committed for a while," said Leslie, trying not to show how upset she felt over the knowledge that all along Stephen had a girl and hadn't even told her. He had known about Marshall from the beginning.

The music stopped and other couples came over and joined them by the fire. In a short while, they had to make preparations to go back to town. The girls had "late leave" but still had to be in by midnight.

The next night they gathered in Helen's room for what the students referred to now as the "night report," and Sharon made a startling announcement.

"Girls, Bob and I are getting married as soon as he graduates this spring."

"What!" they exclaimed in unison.

"You heard me." She then showed them a beautiful diamond solitaire she had on a chain around her neck. They weren't allowed to wear jewelry on duty.

"But, Sharon, you won't be finished school yet," protested Leslie.

"I don't care. I'll resign. I've decided a career isn't so important to me after all."

"But you only lack a year. Can't you wait until then?"

The students were not allowed to marry and remain in school. Some of them had been known to marry secretly and then announce it when they were safe after graduation.

"I don't want to wait!" Sharon was getting impatient. "Bob will join the army as soon as he graduates and I want to be with him as long as possible."

"Oh, of course you do," agreed Leslie. "Life is so complicated. I want to get married and have my four little boys, but I also want to work."

"It's awful to be a girl," complained Helen.

"Men can get married and have their careers too," agreed Leslie. "There's no justice."

"Well, anyway, I'm giving it all up," said Sharon emphatically.

"Honey, please forgive us for all this useless palaver! We're so happy for you." Leslie and the other girls put their arms around Sharon and laughed and cried at the same time.

"You're the first to go," murmured Alice sadly.

"Wedding bells are breaking up that old gang of mine," sang Helen, making everybody laugh again.

Graduation for Stephen and Bob

In May 1918, Stephen and Bob graduated from Medical School, and Stephen's parents came down from Boston. Leslie had looked forward to this meeting and dreaded it also. She wondered if Ann would also be present but she need not have worried.

Stephen was diffident as he made the introductions. His mother immediately assumed "command" and Leslie felt completely dwarfed by her. She towered above everyone. Sharon and Helen could almost look her in the eye, but she seemed to look down her nose at the other girls as she talked.

"Stephen tells me you're from the South." Mrs. Southall turned her steely blue eyes towards Leslie and made the comment as though she was referring to a foreign country. "We have a winter home on the Keys." She went right on talking before Leslie could answer. She was a big-bosomed dowager with her blond hair combed into an upswept hairdo, coiled on top of her head, which made her look even taller. When Leslie thought of her own dainty, beautiful little mother, who was charming and gracious to everyone, she wondered if she could ever feel any closeness to Mrs. Southall. Mr. Southall was also tall with dark hair and eyes and Leslie could see a marked resemblance to Stephen.

"My son will, of necessity, join the army now, but I'm sure we can arrange for him to be stationed in the Boston area. I want him to be near home. He *is* engaged, you know."

"I have already joined the army, Mother," interrupted Stephen impatiently. He looked so embarrassed. "I will be stationed here in Stanton at the new Veteran's Hospital. This time can also serve as part of my internship."

Mrs. Southall fairly bristled. "We could have done the same thing in Boston."

"I don't want to be in Boston! I want to be here near Florence. And you are right about *one* thing, Mother! I am engaged—to Florence." He was fairly glaring at her. Leslie had a feeling that these battle scenes were frequent with them. She looked at Stephen, thinking how handsome he was in his cap and gown, and wondered why his mother couldn't just relax and enjoy being with her son and stop trying to run his life. Stephen looked at his watch. "I have to get in line now. I'll see you later, Florence." He leaned over and kissed her on the cheek and then walked towards the group of students without so much as a glance at his mother.

"I thought your name was Leslie." Mrs. Southall looked almost accusingly at Leslie.

"It is." Leslie didn't bother to explain.

"Well, don't count on Stephen staying here. My son has never known what's best for him. I'm still going to try and convince him that he should come to Boston."

Sharon was outraged over Mrs. Southall's rudeness and utter disregard for everyone around her, so she couldn't resist this remark: " Mrs. Southall, we've come to know Stephen quite well these last two years and I can assure you he *is* capable of making his own decisions. Come with me, Leslie. The Harpers are waiting for us." With that the two girls excused themselves.

"Thank you, Sharon." Leslie breathed a sigh of relief. She could see now that Mrs. Southall would be a powerful adversary. "The only consolation I have is that I remember how, at first, we didn't like Stephen, but after we got to know him, we found out what a fine person he really was. Maybe underneath that big bosom beats a heart of gold." They found their seats next to the Harpers and settled down to watch the processional.

The graduation ceremony had a solemn, somber note. Each graduate knew he was facing an uncertain future. Many of them would enter the armed forces and all of them felt they must serve their country in some capacity.

After all the degrees were conferred, Leslie was busy congratulating her friends. She was especially pleased to see Dennis get his Engineering Degree. They had become such good friends over the past two years. He introduced her to his family and they immediately assumed she must be his girl friend and welcomed her warmly. She couldn't help but contrast this reception to the one she'd just received from Mrs. Southall. She and Sharon were so busy mingling that it was easy for her to steer clear of the Southalls.

That evening the Harper and Southall families went out for dinner. Stephen's mother had calmed down by this time, evidently after a good dressing down from Stephen, and she made a genuine effort to be congenial. Leslie was thankful for Mr. Southall who was most charming and considerate.

Summer passed with the war still raging. The case load in the hospital continued to be very heavy. Many of the wounded soldiers were being shipped back and the hospital was filled with surgical cases as the Veteran's Hospital was not yet in full operation. Now Leslie could get some firsthand information and she talked to as many soldiers as she could, hoping to get some news of her brother and Marshall.

Hers and the family's letters from the boys were few and far between, but they were always hopeful and one could only guess at the hardships they must be enduring.

The students had only a week's vacation and Leslie, along with Alice, Helen, and Stephen traveled to Charleston for Sharon and Bob's wedding. Leslie was maid of honor and Stephen was best man. It was a sweet wedding and, seeing Sharon and Bob so happy, made Stephen and Leslie realize how very much they would like to proceed with their own wedding plans.

Charleston was such a beautiful seacoast city and they enjoyed their stay. Getting away was good for them. On their return after the wedding, they made a brief visit to White Haven.

Stephen had always been somewhat awed by the South, but he was completely won over in a short time. Also he, as well as Alice and Helen, fell hopelessly in love with Janie and White Haven.

"And it's all for real!" exclaimed Alice looking around as though she was trying to take inventory. "It's everything you said it was. You didn't exaggerate one bit."

Stephen couldn't get over the charm and hospitality everyone extended to them. "Florence, you don't know how lucky you are! I've never seen such beauty and tranquillity—your parents, relatives as well as your home."

"I do know too, Stephen," she said earnestly. "And I thank God everyday for my blessings." Her heart went out to him. After having met his parents, she realized how impoverished his life must have been—a domineering mother and a father who was charming and gallant to strangers, but always too busy to give much attention to his son. The most expensive gifts and the most exclusive private schools could never atone for the loneliness he had known.

The visit was brief, but enjoyable, especially for Stephen. He had a better understanding of Leslie now after meeting her family and seeing White Haven and the little community called Denmark.

The months dragged by and September arrived with the war news sounding more promising. The Allies' victory at St. Mihiel Sept. 13 on General Pershing's 58th birthday, was a boost for everyone.

Two weeks after St. Mihiel, however, the Muese Argonne proved to be the toughest and costliest fighting the Americans had encountered. Each bit of ground won slowly and at high cost dragged on for 6 more weeks. Leslie just knew that Mack and Marshall had to be in the thick of it. "Please God bring them home safely," was her fervent prayer.

During all the turmoil and struggle, time did pass—not only the war, but school with graduation getting closer with each passing month and exam. Leslie looked forward to graduation. Like all young students, she could see so many improvements that needed to be made in the profession and felt like she was the very one who could bring about these changes.

She found her feelings hard to analyze. When on duty, she could completely lose herself in her love for her work. Yet when she'd return to the dormitory, her heart would almost turn a flip at the mere sound of the telephone ring, to say nothing of actually seeing Stephen in person.

Leslie sensed that Stephen definitely resented her work. Although he never mentioned it, she knew in her heart that marriage to him would mark the end of her hopes for a career. In this, however, he was actually no different from Marshall. Neither one of them had yet reached the point of accepting women in the business and professional world.

Armistice!

November 11, 1918! The whole world rejoiced and Leslie was delirious with joy. Her boys would be coming home!

All classes were dismissed and everyone was celebrating. Factory whistles, fire engine sirens and church bells were ringing simultaneously and people were dancing in the streets. When the news reached Leslie, she started searching frantically for her friends. Alice and Helen were still on duty and she was unable to reach Sharon when she called her apartment. Stephen called and she went out to meet him. After all, he was really the person she wanted most to share this happy time.

Stephen was ecstatic as he grabbed Leslie and kissed her. They made their way through the crowd to the Campus Drug Store.

Over their cokes, Stephen took Leslie's hand and said simply:

"It's all over, Florence. Surely now we can get on with our lives."

"That's what I want too."

"I want us to marry as soon as possible. You'll have to give up your plans for a nursing career, that is except for those four boys you talk so much about."

"As soon as Marshall returns and I can talk to him." Big tears welled up in her eyes. Conflicting emotions surged through her. Less than a year until graduation. Fulfilling one dream meant giving up another one.

In spite of the celebration, Stephen had to report back to the hospital. As he escorted her to the dormitory, her joy and happiness returned. The war was over, she was in love, and everything was beautiful. Leslie went immediately to her room. She was standing by the window looking out at the student's merrymaking when Sharon came in.

"Oh, Sharon, I tried to call you." She ran towards her friend with outstretched arms. "I have so much to tell! Stephen and I are going to be married! The War is over and Brother will be coming home." Sharon put her arms around Leslie. "Yes, darling. Please let's sit down. I need to talk to you." Leslie sat down, bewildered.

"—But, Sharon. Didn't you hear me?" She was so happy. Please God, don't let anyone take this away from me, she prayed.

"Leslie, I, er—" Sharon's eyes filled with tears. "Your father called me." Her voice broke as she tried to continue. "He didn't want you to hear such sad news over the telephone." She swallowed hard and continued. "The war is over, honey, but Mack won't be coming home. He was leading his battalion in the Muese-Argonne offensive when a land mine exploded."

All the color seemed to drain from Leslie's face and she swayed to the side. Sharon made her lie down and elevated her feet. Lucy Jones and some of the other students heard the commotion and came in to help. They bathed her face and worked over her. Someone gave her a whiff of amonia and she was brought around.

When Leslie's numbed brain could grasp the awful truth, her first thoughts were of her parents. She just must get home!

Sharon took charge of everything. First, she sent Bob to the hospital to relieve Stephen so he could return and be with Leslie. Then she informed Dean Miller and it was soon arranged for Leslie to go home to be with her family.

Stephen returned almost immediately. He offered to accompany Leslie home, but then they both decided perhaps, at a time like this, she should be alone with her family. He was very helpful in other ways and his presence seemed to give Leslie the strength she needed. He left her with Sharon and the other girls to pack while he obtained information about train schedules. Later he drove her to the station. She had tried to remain stoic until time to say goodbye and then Leslie sobbed on his shoulder. It was a relief to cry and feel the comfort of his arms around her. If she ever had any doubts about her feelings for Stephen, they were gone now. "Florence, I love you so much. It just kills me to see you suffer and not be able to stop it."

"Stephen, you've been wonderful. I don't

know what I would have done without you." He held her in his arms until the train arrived.

When Leslie arrived in Jackson, Mr. Chadwick was waiting at the station. She felt a new sense of guilt when she greeted him, knowing that he was bound to recognize the ring she was still wearing. She wondered how much Marshall had told him.

"Thank you for meeting me, Daddy Chad. How are Mother and Father?" she asked as she kissed him on the cheek.

"Absolutely crushed, but bearing up as you would expect them to."

"I'm so thankful Marshall is safe."

"Thank you. So am I. He's all I have, you know."

They were nearing home and Leslie knew she had to brace herself to meet her mother. She laid her head back on the seat, closed her eyes, and did not open them until Mr. Chadwick stopped in front of the house.

Jim and Sam, two of Mary's sons, came out and carried her bags in. Mr. Chadwick helped her out of the car and then started to leave.

"Won't you come in, Daddy Chad?"

"No, thank you, Leslie. You need this time alone with your parents. I will come over later. If you need anything, please call me."

As he drove off, Leslie stood a while in the drive. Looking up at the tall white columns of White Haven, she stifled a sob and her eyes filled with tears as the thought ran through her mind that White Haven would have gone to the son named "Thomas." Now there wasn't a son! There would never by any more Lee children at White Haven. *Oh, why did it have to be Brother*? she was thinking. *Four Tyson boys*! *Three McBryde boys*! *Why couldn't it have been one of them*? Then she was so ashamed of herself for having such thoughts.

"Forgive me, Lord!"

Knowing she couldn't put it off any longer, Leslie walked up the steps and across the wide veranda.

As she opened the door, the smell of flowers filled the parlor—mute reminders of the love and sympathy of many dear friends. The pink bowl on the hall table was filled with cards of friends who had called. Mary came out of the kitchen then and Leslie threw her arms around her old nurse. They were both crying.

"There, there, chile, don' let you mama see you lak this," sniffed Mary.

"Where is Mother, Mae Mae?"

"She's bak in the kitchen wurking lak a field han'. Yo Aunt Margaret had to go home, but she comin' bak and I'se glad. Maybe she can mak her res som."

Leslie quickly dried her eyes and powdered her nose. She must brace herself to face her mother. Aromas of freshly baked bread, beans and ham hock boiling on the stove greeted Leslie as she entered the kitchen and saw Janie bending over the ironing board, ironing a shirt as though her life depended on her finishing it.

"Oh, I didn't hear you come in, dear." Janie put the flat iron back on the stove and came over and put her arms around Leslie. "It was sweet of Chad to meet you for us. Come now, I'll help you unpack."

"Where's Father?" Leslie couldn't trust herself to say more.

"He's out on the farm somewhere." Janie moved as if in a trance. "I'll go and ring the bell for him." She went out on the back porch where the big iron bell hung. The bell ringing was a signal for dinner or to return home.

Leslie felt so depressed. She had been bracing herself, expecting to find her parents utterly devastated, but instead they were going on as usual. She entered the hall just as Mary was opening the door for her Aunt Margaret. Leslie rushed towards her aunt and threw her arms around her. What a relief it was to have a responsible member of the family around.

"Auntie, I'm so glad you're here."

"I've been with your mama all along, Leslie. I just had to go home and get some clothes."

"Aunt Margaret, I think Mother's gone crazy! Brother's dead and she's in the kitchen ironing as though it was just another day." Leslie was sobbing hysterically.

"There, there, honey," her Aunt comforted her. "That's not the way it is. When we first got the news, I thought Janie would die also. Dr. Miller stayed with her all day. After the initial shock, she's been in a state of constant motion ever since. She feels like she must keep busy and not allow herself time to brood over what has happened. Having you home will be a great comfort to her."

Leslie calmed down somewhat. Aunt Margaret's reassurance was what she needed.

"Now, Mary, please take Miss Leslie up to her room and see that she gets a nice hot bath. We'll come up later."

Leslie allowed herself to be piloted upstairs where Mary drew a tub of hot, steaming water for her. She was really exhausted not having slept much the night before and then the long train ride today. It was soothing to have Mary fuss over her and tuck her in bed just as she did when Leslie was a little girl. Mary sat down beside the bed until she drifted off to sleep.

When she awoke, it was dark outside and she was surprised to see her mother occupying the chair where Mary had been.

"Why, Mother, what time is it?" she asked, raising up on her elbow.

"It's after ten, darling," answered Janie. "Your father and Betsy have both come in, but I wouldn't let them disturb you. Now you stay right there. I'm going to get you something to eat." Janie tripped off downstairs.

Leslie sat up in bed and looked around. Yes—everything was the same—the white organdy curtains, the white organdy canopy over her antique maple bed had been freshly laundered. There were fresh flowers on her dressing table. It looked the same, yes—but would never ever be the same again.

Janie returned shortly with a large silver tray filled with tempting food and a pot of hot chocolate. Leslie had hardly eaten anything for the last two days and she found she was actually hungry. Her distraught nerves had been strained to the breaking point, but now she was home! The strong, sturdy walls of White Haven seemed to enfold her and give her security once again. As she finished eating and was sipping her chocolate, Leslie looked at her mother. She had on a light blue wool dressing gown and her blond hair was tumbling down her back. As always, she looked beautiful, but there was s dejected slump to her usually straight back. Leslie's keen eyes now observed the despairing, crushed expression in Janie's big blue eyes. How could she have been so blind and stupid this afternoon? She reproached herself. "That was so good. Thank you, Mother, but you shouldn't have waited up for me."

"I wasn't sleepy and besides, I rather enjoyed sitting here watching you sleep. You looked like my little girl once again. I can hardly realize that you're a grown young lady now and will soon be a graduate nurse." Janie moved the tray over to the table.

"Mama, I'm not going to graduate." Leslie startled even herself with the finality of her words. "Stephen wants me to marry him right away."

"In that case, then, I'll have to accept the fact that you're no longer a child." If she felt any disappointment or disapproval, it wasn't apparent.

"Mother, I know you and Father are disappointed that I won't be marrying Marshall. It's been such a hard decision for me to make. Please try and understand," she pleaded. "I love Stephen so much and you will too, once you get to know him."

"All we want or have ever wanted is for you to be happy, darling," said Janie gently. "If he's the one who can give you this happiness, then we'll just have to love him."

"Mother, you're so sweet." Leslie reached her hand out to Janie. "Tell me, have you heard from Virginia?"

"Yes. She will be here tomorrow to attend the memorial service for Mack. We'll have to help her through this tragic time. They were so much in love."

"Let me ask you one question, Mother. Do you wish Brother and Virginia had married before he left?"

"Well, er—yes, I'm very fond of Virginia," Janie mused. "But I could understand how Mack felt and I respected his decision."

"But, don't you see, Mother? Now he's gone! If only he had a child, we'd have something of him left." *A son, maybe, to carry on the Lee name*, she was thinking wistfully.

"I know, darling," soothed Janie. "It breaks my heart too, but we can't brood over what might have been. To those of us who loved him, Mack will never die. He will live forever in our hearts and memories."

"I have to tell you this, Mother." Leslie blinked back the tears. "I've had such mean, hateful thoughts today. You'll be so ashamed of me. I even found myself wishing it could have happened to Bill, Tommy, Greer or anyone except Brother. I just hope the Lord will forgive me."

"Of course He will forgive you!" Janie patted her hands. "Because you really didn't mean it, honey. Feelings of resentment and anger are natural reactions to personal tragedy. The good Lord will give us strength to bear this burden. Your brother would want us to continue our lives as usual and that's what we're going to do. Now let's go to bed. I'm going to sleep in here with you tonight."

Margaret and Virginia arrived, and the next day was full with friends and relatives calling, bringing in food, and offering condolences. Receiving these friends brought comfort and strength to Leslie and the family.

The whole clan gathered and there was enough food for everyone. That afternoon a Memorial Service was held for Mack at the Presbyterian Church. Reverend Stone's simple eulogy was a consolation to Leslie and the family.

After her visit home, Leslie was able to regain, in some measure, her strength and courage. After her initial shock at seeing her family carrying on life as usual, even though

91

their hearts were breaking, she resolved to do the same. She understood now that this was the only way to handle grief.

It was only a matter of time now until Stephen would get his discharge from the army. Then he could pick up his interrupted career plans and start his residency in some civilian hospital. He was off duty almost every evening and came to see Leslie at every opportunity. He repeatedly begged her to marry him and seemed fearful that further delay of their marriage might result in him losing her.

Since Stephen's proposal, their relationship was happy, yet frustrating. His desire for her was so great, he wanted more from her than she was willing to give. The fact that they were unofficially engaged was his justification for wanting to make love, but Leslie was adamant. She couldn't bring herself to compromise any of her ideals even though she felt the same frustrations he did. Stephen was able to stir a desire and passion within her she'd never known before and sometimes after one of their heated arguments, she was almost persuaded to give in. Then she would remember the look on Marshall's face when he slipped the emerald ring on her finger and she knew she could never break her promise to him. The fact that they were both under a great emotional strain at the time the promise was made did not matter. She'd given her word and she intended to keep it.

Stephen informed Leslie he'd written Ann about their wedding plans, even though he maintained it wasn't necessary. "We were never engaged. It was mostly my mother's idea." He couldn't understand why Leslie wouldn't do the same. "Florence, he would understand."

"I know, but I just can't do it and you know I can't," she answered impatiently.

"I'm sorry Flo." He was contrite as he put his arms around her. "I shouldn't pressure you like this. We'll just have to hope that Marshall will get his discharge soon.

Another contention was Leslie's pending graduation from Vale. Since it was only months away, it seemed logical for her to finish school and then marry after he was established in his residency, but Stephen wouldn't hear of it.

"No! We're getting married the day after Marshall returns."

In spite of it all, they were happy. They were young! They had each other and their hopes and dreams for the future.

Kidnapping the Kaiser!

November passed and still there was no word from Marshall as to his expected discharge. Leslie did receive a letter early in December telling her that he planned to call on a "prominent person" before coming home. She could only speculate as to whom that might be.

Her relationship with Stephen was becoming more and more strained. She would try repeatedly to reassure him that they wouldn't have to wait much longer and then, to her amazement, she opened the paper one morning and read this headline: "A GROUP OF TENNESSEANS ATTEMPT TO KIDNAP THE KAISER"—then, "Adventurous soldiers get inside Holland in the bold effort to take the Kaiser."

The article went on to explain that the desire to capture the Kaiser was shared by every doughboy in the army. It seemed grossly unfair to them that now the war was over for the Kaiser, who had caused the world so much misery, to be exiled and living in apparent luxury in a palace in Amerogen.

Colonel Luke Lea of the 114th Field Artillery, a former U.S. senator and publisher of *The Nashville Tennessean*, devised the plan to kidnap the Kaiser.

Actually, according to Colonel Lea's memoirs,[3] the idea was conceived over a cup of tea, June 11, 1918.

At this time the 114th Field Artillery, the only volunteer American regiment in the world's war was paraded before His Royal Highness, The Duke of Connaught. After the parade the field officers were invited by the British and ordered by the American Command to have tea with His Royal Highness.

During the conversation over tea, the Duke of Connaught boasted of his close relationship—Uncle—to both "His Imperial Majesty, The Emperor of Germany and his August Majesty, The Emperor of Great Britain and India." Thus the plan to kidnap the Kaiser was conceived by the Duke's boast.

Time seemed to drag after the cease-fire and the colonel requested the time off due him. His five days of leave requested "permission to visit any place not prohibited by the orders from General Headquarters American Expeditionary Forces."

The request for leave was presented to General Spaulding who read the order over twice. Finally he said: "Colonel Lea where do you intend to go?"

"Nowhere forbidden by orders of G.H.Q. I don't want to tell you where. I do not wish you to be responsible for the trip," answered the colonel.

The general finally signed the request "since it violates no general order." The next move was to recruit some brave, adventurous soldiers.

After the Armistice, Marshall, chaffing under the inactivity, was very receptive when Colonel Lea approached him to go along as their legal council. Two other officers and three enlisted men (all fellow Tennesseans) were selected to go. None of the other soldiers knew the nature *or* the destination of the trip. They were told "that it might be dangerous. It would most certainly be exciting."

Colonel Lea hoped that by a surprise visit to the Kaiser, he could persuade him that "his place in history would be larger as a brave man facing his accusers—the Allies in Paris—than a coward afraid of his own people as well as the Allies."

It was his intention to deliver the Kaiser to President Wilson at the Paris Peace Conference.

The first attempt was aborted because of confusion over passports and requisitioning cars, gas, and food. Since Colonel Lea knew the United States Minister to Belgium, they were able to cut the red tape and obtain visas and a laisser-passer granting them free passage within Holland.

The authorization requested "the Custom and Excise Officers in Holland to give, when passing custom examination, all facilities permitted by the existing regulations, to the most honorable Senator Colonel Luke Lea, who is proceeding to Holland on official duty from the U.S. Government—"

When they were within sixteen kilometers of Amerogen, the colonel stopped the cars, assembled the officers and enlisted men on the road side and revealed the purpose of the trip. Each man was given permission to return and wait at the border if they chose not to participate in the daring attempt.

Every member of the party wanted to go on but doubted that they would ever be able to get into the castle.

In spite of a washed-out bridge and having to cross the river on a ferry, they were able to make their way to the palace at Amerogen. Later this missing bridge would make their escape even more difficult.

Once outside the palace, Colonel Lea strode up to the amazed sentry and ordered him to let them inside. They were taken to Count Von Bentinck, the Kaiser's host who asked the purpose of their visit.

"I can reveal the purpose of our visit only to the Kaiser," answered Lea.

The Kaiser's aides were perplexed over this group of American soldiers without credentials and argued back and forth with them.

The burgomaster of Amerogen was summoned and he, too, demanded to know their purpose. Lea produced the laissez-passer.

"You are here then on official business of the American Government?"

"Oh no, we're here on a journalistic investigation."

Following Marshall's advice they refused to elaborate and continued to insist that their business was with the Kaiser. The count and burgomaster conferred back and forth with the Kaiser.

Although the Tennesseans could hear the Kaiser's voice in the next room, they never got to actually see him.

Time was of an essence and it seemed to be

slipping away from them. Colonel Lea became suspicious that they were being delayed for a purpose. Fortunately, Marshall looked out the window and observed a horde of Dutch soldiers and a German military guard setting up machine guns. It was then the group decided to make a hasty withdrawal. They were so frustrated over having to give up seeing the Kaiser, but realized further delay might endanger their lives. As they were leaving, Marshall looked around the room and grabbed an ashtray. He was determined not to go back empty-handed.

They were able to slip by the astonished Dutch soldiers and in spite of several close calls made it safely across the border. Two weeks after they arrived back at the base, the American High Command was receiving heated protests from Holland and Germany over their unauthorized intrusion. For appearance sake and to placate the Germans, a full-scale investigation was promised. The group would be detained until the Inspector General's office could make their study.

Leslie laughed and cried at the same time. "Oh, how could Marshall have risked his life like that? To think he made it safely through the war and then goes off on such a wild goose chase." Then as if the full impact of that daring mission dawned on her, she shuddered and covered her face with her hands. "Why he could have been killed," she said fearfully.

Stephen couldn't help but show his envy and irritation. His military service had been spent entirely at the Veteran's Hospital with long hours, hard work, and no recognition, praise, or acclaim whatsoever and now just to think how this band of nuts and that country lawyer had suddenly become world famous! "Florence, can't you see you don't owe him a thing now? Marshall has forfeited his chance to come home. He'll probably be thrown in jail after his court-martial. I think we should go on and get married."

"Stephen, honey, the paper didn't say anything about a court-martial. Besides public opinion would be so strongly in their favor." She paused and said wistfully, "If my brother were alive, I know he would have been right in there with them."

Leslie was finally able to soothe Stephen's ruffled feelings and persuade him to be patient for just a little while longer.

After a detailed interrogation of all the participants of the daring Kaiser kidnap attempt, the soldiers were finally convicted of having used army cars without the proper authority and then released with a reprimand.

General John J. Pershing told the group they had been "amazingly indiscreet" and added his severe reprimand. It was learned later, however, that the general had confided privately to one of his friends, "I'm not a rich man but I would have given a year's pay to have been with those boys on that trip."

Marshall's Return

Word finally came that Marshall had his discharge and was sailing. He'd been one of the lucky ones and would be home for Christmas. The timing was perfect as the senior students were getting a week off for Christmas. Since Leslie would be going to White Haven, Stephen decided he might as well go to Boston for the holidays although he disliked being away from her.

Stephen drove her to the station and they clung together as he kissed her goodbye. He seemed apprehensive and in spite of Leslie's assurances otherwise, he felt a strange premonition that Marshall's return might somehow separate them. Leslie also hated the idea of a week's separation and some of his fears transferred to her, but she knew she had to go and, besides, she told him, and herself, there were so many other things to do at home besides seeing Marshall. Getting together with her mother to plan her wedding, select bride's maids' dresses, silver and china patterns—all the happy, fun things a bride must do. But somehow her impending confrontation with Marshall overshadowed everything else and she wished it could be over.

The train puffed in and Stephen even came aboard to help her settle in, "You must promise to be back here for the New Year!"

"I wouldn't miss it for the world!" Leslie smiled happily. Now at long last she and Stephen could look forward to their wedding, but she recoiled at the thought of facing Marshall.

Stephen left the train and then stood by her window outside, "Florence, we'll be together New Year 1919 and I promise you, we'll never be separated again."

As the train pulled off Stephen walked along beside her window until the train gained momentum and then he stood on the platform waving to her. Leslie would never forget how alone he looked.

By the time Leslie reached home, she had worried herself into a sick headache and had to go straight to bed. Janie and Mary fussed over her and tried to alleviate her pain by keeping hot towels on her head. Mary warmed the sheets with bed warmers and made hot tea, all of which were very soothing and she'd feel better until she thought about facing Marshall and then all the pain would return.

Leslie couldn't understand herself. How could she be so happy and miserable at the same time? She shared her ambivalent feelings and fears with her mother and asked what she thought.

"I don't have to think, baby girl. I know exactly how you feel," soothed Janie as she placed another hot towel on her forehead. "I was sick for days trying to make up my mind between your father and Robby Miller."

"Robby Miller!" exclaimed Leslie raising up in bed, dropping the towel from her forehead. "Why Mother, I didn't know there was *ever* anyone besides Father."

"But of course, darling, there were several others besides your father," teased Janie.

"But you made the right decision, didn't you?" Leslie settled back on her pillow. Maybe she wasn't so abnormal after all. "You've never regretted marrying Father?"

"Yes, I made the right decision and No, I've never had a moment's regret," answered Janie. And I know you'll make the right decision too."

Leslie momentarily forgot her splitting headache. Robby Miller! Why he was the son of Dr. Miller who had been their family physician and dear friend all her life. Robert Jr. was also a physician but had left Jackson after a very bitter divorce and child custody suit. He had never remarried.

"Mother, could you help me tell Marshall? He loves you so much."

"My dear child, there's not many things in this world I wouldn't do for you, but this is one of them," Janie said gently as she changed the towel.

"I know. You're right, of course. This is

something I have to do for myself, but I dread it so much."

"Try and get some sleep and maybe your headache will leave."

Leslie smiled. It was amazing how much better she always felt after talking to her mother. No matter what was troubling her, Janie seemed to understand and give advice or comfort.

Leslie slept late the next morning. She felt better physically but when she thought of Marshall, she'd feel sick all over again. Marshall and his father were arriving from New York that morning and Janie had invited them over for lunch. Since she didn't feel like eating breakfast, Leslie called Jim, the stable boy and had him saddle her horse. Maybe a ride in the cold morning air would do her good.

As she was riding along looking at the familiar scenes of her childhood, she found herself near the Presbyterian Church which she'd attended all her life. As a child, Leslie remembered how she would come to the church on rare occasions during the week, slip in and say a prayer. There was something inspiring and elevating about being alone in church. After such a visit, she always felt better.

Back of the church a little iron fence enclosed the cemetery. Leslie dismounted and tied her horse to the gate post. She decided to walk through the cemetery. Her great grandparents as well as her grandparents were buried there. Pausing for a moment at her grandfather's grave, she couldn't help but wonder how he would have felt if, upon his return from the Civil War, the beautiful Laura Hutcherson had decided not to marry him? She brushed this thought away and then went on to the graves of her three little brothers. She couldn't remember them because she was so young when they died, but the heartache was still there. A memorial marker was already in place for Mack even though his body was buried at Flanders Fields along with his fallen comrades. On each grave in the family plot, her mother had already placed a Christmas wreath. Janie never forgot her family, even in death.

101

Leslie then went around to the front of the church and tried the door. It was unlocked. As she entered the chapel, Leslie felt, as always, an awareness of the presence of God and she knew that before she left, somehow she would have the strength to face the day.

Leslie knelt at the chancel rail where she'd knelt so many times for communion. How long she was there, she did not know when she heard someone enter the church. Quickly finishing her prayers, she prepared to leave. As she looked up, she saw Marshall, also kneeling in prayer. How inspiring to see a strong man unashamed of his religion. When he looked at her, she was smiling through her tears.

"Hello Marshall."

"Hello, little Lessie Lou. I called your mother and she told me you were out riding, so I decided to try and find you." He came over and stretched out his hands. She extended hers, and he pulled her up into his arms and kissed her tenderly. It was so good to see him and feel the security of his arms about her. Leslie started crying and couldn't stop as she remembered what she had to do—what she had to tell him—and quickly, as he continued to kiss her—hungrily now. Their long wait was over. He had survived the war but fate would yet deal him a cruel blow. The girl he hoped to be coming home to had fallen in love with someone else. The home and family he'd dreamed of would not be his. Leslie tried to regain her composure as she looked at him. He looked older and his eyes had a hurt, haunted look, all of which made her task even more difficult. He kept his arms around her as they left the church and walked towards the horses. "Marsh, I, er—" she faltered. "There's something I must tell you."

He gently placed his finger over her lips. "You don't have to tell me, Les. I think I already know."

"How did you know?" Her cry was anguished. Surely no one had told him! "Who?"

"You did, honey, in every letter you wrote. You were sweet to keep your promise. Maybe I should have released you, but I wanted to talk things over one last time. I kept telling myself that since you waited for me you must still care." He clenched his fists together in helpless frustration. "Oh God, Leslie, you don't know how awful it was! As I was lying in the trenches, cold and miserable, the only thing that kept me going was the hope of coming home to you."

"Oh, Marsh! I could just die." She was weeping openly now as she sat down on a small bench. If only she could roll these two boys together and come out with just one, because she knew now she must love both of them. Marshall with his Southern ideals, background and traditions so like her own, his tenderness combined with Stephen's dash and excitement.

"Leslie, I love you so much. I just couldn't give you up without at least trying."

"I love you too, Marshall. I'm so sorry. I never meant for this to happen."

"Then you're really going to marry that damn Yankee?" he asked bitterly. "I guess I knew it all along. Probably the reason I risked my life to capture the Kaiser was that I didn't care if I did get killed. I was afraid to come home."

"Please forgive me." Her body was racked with sobs, and Marshall gently pulled her towards him. "There, there, little Lessie Lou, don't cry. We won't talk about it anymore."

"I'll give you your ring—" she sobbed as she started tugging at her glove, feeling like she was losing another old friend.

"No, Les," he protested. "I really don't want it. Suppose you keep it until he puts one on that finger. Then later, if you accidentally have a little girl instead of the four boys, give it to her." He handed her his handkerchief. "Now dry your eyes. We don't want Mother Jane to see you like this."

Leslie dabbed at her eyes and blew her nose. She was thankful their ordeal was over but she felt completely drained. She didn't know it would be so hard.

"Let's go now. I'm anxious to see Mother Jane and your dad." He helped her mount her horse and then mounted his. They raced over the fields and Leslie could almost forget her heavy heart as the peace and tranquillity of the countryside enveloped her. A light snow was falling and the sky was a kaleidoscope of changing white and grey clouds over the blue sky. With Marshall at her side, her mind was flooded with so many memories—this was the "big" boy she'd adored as a child; the shy kid who stuttered and fumbled for words trying to explain roosters and hens to her. She might marry Stephen, but Marshall would forever be a part of her.

When they arrived at White Haven, Daddy Chad was already there. Marshall's meeting with the Lees was a very emotional one. Janie felt like at least one son had been returned to her. Since lunch was ready, they went on to the dining room where Mary hovered over him. She had prepared all his favorite foods. Afterwards, back in the living room, Marshall was able to answer some of their questions and fill them in on the details of Mack's death. It was comforting for them to learn that Marshall was the first to reach Mack after the explosion and cradled him in his arms until the corpsmen removed him. Mack died on November 9, 1919. Years later, Leslie learned that the defeated Germans had actually asked for a cease fire on November 8, but the Allied leaders had already decided that the war should end at 11 a.m. on the 11th day of the 11th month, thus more German and Allied soldiers had to die, among them being Mack.

Marshall was happy to be back with his family. He told them he had no immediate plans except to rest, relax and enjoy being home with his father. His long range plans would include boning up for his Bar exam and then making a decision where he would practice law. He preferred to remain in Jackson with his father, but his Uncle John in Memphis needed him badly.

He promised Janie he would come over everyday. He treated Leslie with the same tenderness and love he'd always shown her and only the two of them knew the agony he must be suffering. Leslie's heart ached for him and for herself. Certainly the war had taken its toll, and it would take a long time for the scars to heal. She couldn't help but feel that she was a civilian casualty. Anyway the dye was cast and she prepared to return to Vale—and Stephen.

Making her wedding plans was a bittersweet experience for Leslie. It should have been the happiest time of her life but she cried frequently and so did her mother as they thought of Mack dying in Marshall's arms, of Marshall's heartache and disappointment over losing her.

March 11th was chosen as her wedding day as this would mark the 27th anniversary of her parents' wedding.

On her return, she would resign from the school of nursing, stay a few days with Sharon and Bob before going to Boston for a brief visit with the Southalls, then return to White Haven to wrap up the final details of her wedding. She'd just as soon have dispensed with all the prenuptial parties but these rituals were such an ingrained custom among Denmark people she knew she'd have to comply.

Bob Harper would be best man and Margaret Reid maid of honor with Sharon, Alice, Helen, Virginia Neal, Laura McBryde and Betsy as bridesmaids. Dennis Raymond, Dr. Curtis Howard, Dr. Walter Hammond, and Leslie's cousins, Jerome and Tommy Tyson, and Bill McBryde would complete the wedding party.

Janie was planning the traditional White Haven wedding. The bridesmaids would come down the curving staircase to be met at the foot of the steps by one of the groomsmen to escort them. Leslie, wearing her mother's wedding gown and her great grandmother, Sarah Birdsong's wedding veil, would descend the stairs with her father waiting to escort her into the parlor where an altar would be improvised before the fireplace. Brother Stone, their longtime pastor would perform the ceremony.

New Year 1919

Leslie arrived back at the University on New Year's Eve. She was so anxious to see Stephen. After her emotional encounter with Marshall, she needed the security of his arms around her and the reassurance of his love. She called the army base but he had not returned. This puzzled her as he had stated emphatically that he would be back early to celebrate New Year's Eve with her. She waited an hour and called again, but to no avail. All day long, she was restless and had a curious sense of foreboding evil. It was quite lonesome in the dormitory as the other students would not return until tomorrow. She was afraid to leave for fear of missing Stephen's call. She busied herself about the room, unpacking, cleaning and then wrote some letters. In the evening some of the students started getting off duty and dropped by to chat and this helped pass the time away. About nine p.m. she was getting so panicky that she tried to call Sharon and Bob but they had already gone out for the evening. Still no word from Stephen. As much as she disliked calling his home, she decided to anyway. Something dreadful must have happened to him. When she finally got through, a maid answered the phone and informed her that, "Dr. Southall was out with his fiance." Leslie gasped. She felt like someone had just thrown cold water in her face! Her emotions were mixed—anger, uncertainty and bitter disappointment over their not getting to celebrate New Year's Eve together. Then she stopped and tried to rationalize. None of it made any sense! She thought she knew Stephen well enough to know he'd never break a date without calling.

Surely Stephen could explain everything when he returned. Finally, there seemed nothing else to do so she retired and spent a miserable night.

When the dawn finally came, Leslie prepared to go on duty. It was a relief to go to work as she felt she could not stand another idle day.

The seniors were working on obstetrics now and the delivery room was even more exciting than the operating room. There was a heavy schedule all day long and she didn't have must time to think. The news photographers were on hand to make pictures of the first New Year's baby and there was lots of excitement.

In the afternoon, as she was finishing her charts, Catherine Case walked up to her. Catherine was now a graduate and worked as a staff nurse in the hospital. Leslie had disliked the girl ever since the time she had frightened the entire class with her dire predictions of so many freshmen being doomed to failure.

"Here's a little item in the Boston paper that might interest you," she said, thrusting the paper towards Leslie.

Leslie took the paper with a puzzled expression. The Society Page contained several pictures. As she scanned through the announcements, the name Southall caught her eye, then her numbed brain began to comprehend the words, "Mr. and Mrs. Woodrow Hughes Howell announce the engagement of their daughter, Ann Hughes, to Captain Stephen Horatio Wainwright Southall III, U.S. Army Medical Corps.

"Miss Howell is a graduate of Smith College—"

Leslie looked at the picture. The loveliest face she'd ever seen looked at her from the newspaper. The hair appeared to be very light and lay in soft curls around her oval face. She had thickly fringed eyelashes under delicate brows. "Beautiful—really the most beautiful girl I ever saw—" were Stephen's exact words, Leslie recalled. Realizing that Catherine was watching her with malicious pleasure, Leslie struggled to retain her composure. She looked up, giving Catherine a sparkling smile, and said, "Thank you, Miss Case. Ann *is* very beautiful, isn't she? Stephen didn't exaggerate one bit."

The girl was obviously disappointed, but if she could have penetrated the look on Leslie's face, she would have felt more gratified. Leslie felt as though she was standing all alone on a precipice and the whole world was tumbling down around her. Her one thought was to escape to the safety of her room where she could try and think things through. She completed her charting hurriedly and then fled to the dormitory. Behind closed doors, she read and re-read the announcement and studied every detail of the picture. It must be true. The maid was right! "Why that low-down varmint!" she was thinking. How could he have done this to her? She had fulfilled her promise to him by going home and facing Marshall. Why couldn't he have done the same? His mother had won after all. She'd always felt that Mrs. Southall was determined to have her way and would stop at nothing to get it.

She laid down wearily on the bed feeling nauseous and frustrated over her nescience of what had really happened.

She had no idea of the time when suddenly Alice came in and turned on the light.

"Hi, Les! I just got in. Looks like we're all running late. Why aren't you getting ready for the school banquet?"

"Banquet?" repeated Leslie blinking her eyes.

"Yes, dear. The all school banquet. You're the toast-mistress—remember?" laughed Alice.

"Oh horrors," wailed Leslie. "I can't go! I feel so sick." She handed Alice the paper. Helen came in at that moment and together they read the announcement. Helen went immediately to the phone and called Sharon who could always advise Leslie better than anyone else. She then returned to Leslie's room where she and Alice tried to console Leslie and comprehend what had happened.

Sharon arrived in record time. Helen had already briefed her so she lost no time looking at the paper. "Leslie, you've got to go to that banquet tonight. Everyone will know why you stayed home. You just can't let them see you beaten!" She was very persuasive.

"I don't care what they think," bawled Leslie. "I want to go home to my mother."

"Leslie, you're a big girl now," said Sharon

sternly. "You can't run home to mama every time something happens to you."

"But you don't understand," protested Leslie. "I've got to stop her. She might have already sent my picture and engagement announcement to the paper. My wedding invitations are being engraved—"

"Now just don't panic," soothed Sharon, trying to conceal her own emotions. "Let's try and reason this thing out. Today is a holiday," she was thinking out loud, "which means she can't get anything done today. Now why don't you start getting ready for the banquet. I'll wire your mother to stop all wedding plans. I'll tell her that you will write tomorrow."

The girls were deeply shocked and were probably thinking of worse names to call Stephen than Leslie had, but for the present they felt they must help her pull herself together. Through the combined efforts of all three, Leslie was finally dressed and whisked off to the banquet. She never knew how she was able to struggle through the evening, but, somehow, some reserve strength took over and she presided with poise and dignity. No one was aware of her anguish and the effort it cost her to join in the festivities.

Helen and Alice spent a miserable evening for fear Leslie would be unable to carry it off. Neither of the girls could eat a bite of the delicious food that was placed before them. They watched Leslie's every move and she did not let them down. To all appearances, she was having a marvelous time. Sharon, who was no longer a member of the school and could not attend the banquet, paced the floor at home much to Bob's consternation. Bob, who was supposedly Stephen's closest friend, was as shocked as the girls when he heard the news.

As Leslie ably discharged her duties as mistress of ceremonies the thought kept running through her mind, *if I can just get through this banquet, I can go to my room and have a good cry.*

When the ceremonies were over, Helen and Alice formed a protective shield around her and they were among the first to leave. When the last goodnights were said and Leslie started for her room, the phone rang. It was for her.

The night supervisor was calling to say that Miss Hanse had cut her hand and was unable to scrub for deliveries that night. Could Miss Lee possibly take the calls? Leslie changed into her uniform and went immediately to the hospital where she worked the remainder of the night. In the excitement of her work, Leslie was able to bury her troubles and enter wholeheartedly into the task of assisting the doctor. She had helped with any number of deliveries by now, but she still experienced the same feeling of awe and reverence each time a new life was ushered into the world.

When she returned to the dormitory the next morning, she was completely exhausted and went directly to bed and was soon asleep. As she drifted off, she kept thinking dazedly, *My heart is broken, my life is ruined and I haven't even had time to cry about it.*

It was late in the afternoon when she awoke. Sharon was sitting at her desk writing a letter.

"Oh, Sharon, how sweet of you to come over—"

"Leslie, I wired your mother last night like I promised. I have written this letter telling her what little we know, and I will enclose the picture and newspaper clipping," she said.

"Thank you," said Leslie, getting up and putting on her kimono. "Tell her I'll write tomorrow."

"I feel like we've done everything possible. I'm sure the message reached your mother in plenty of time. Now, I want you to take a bath and get dressed. You're going out to dinner with Bob and me.

The next few days were agonizing for Leslie and her friends. It had been awfully hard to remain here at school and face people day after day, but in the long run that had probably been the best solution. Also the busy times in the hospital and the numerous school activities had helped. If her wedding plans had materialized, Leslie would be resigning about now and leaving

110

a lot of extra work for someone else. That would really have been quite unfair, she realized.

Leslie acted her part out so convincingly, that if Alice and Helen hadn't known her well, they would have thought she wasn't hurt so badly after all, but they could tell her gaiety was forced and a bit too animated.

It was only when she went to bed at night that Leslie could release the tears that had welled up all day and ask herself over and over: "Why? Why has this terrible thing happened to me?" Her hopes and dreams had been centered around Stephen for so long that any future without him was a complete blank.

She thanked God she had not resigned from the school and that the only persons who knew of her intentions were Helen, Alice, Sharon and Bob. Sharon's telegram had reached her mother in time to stop the formal announcement of her engagement. She was, therefore, spared that humiliation.

Gossip and speculation were rampant at school. Everyone assumed that Stephen had jilted Leslie. After all, they said, it wasn't at all uncommon for a medical student to date a nurse during school when it was convenient and then scurry back home after graduation and marry his hometown sweetheart.

The upcoming school dance had them all concerned. Stephen had escorted Leslie to the dances for so long that none of the other students even thought about asking her. By now, everyone had learned of Stephen's marriage, but still no one called Leslie and she felt reluctant to ask anyone. As Helen so aptly expressed it: "If a man gets jilted, the girls pounce on him like vultures going after raw meat, but just let a poor girl get jilted, all the men leave her strictly alone."

Bob offered to ask one of his friends to escort her, but Leslie refused. She'd rather stay home than feel like she was imposing on anyone. She couldn't help but feel disappointed as were Helen and Alice. The solution came unexpectedly in the form of a telephone call from Marshall stating he would be in town "on business" and would arrive the day of the dance.

Leslie wondered if he really had business or if he was responding to the letter she had written him about Stephen's sudden marriage. Whatever the reason, Leslie was happy to go ahead and plan to attend the dance. Being entirely human, she couldn't help but feel satisfaction over being able to attend afterall, and with a handsome man at that.

Marshall stayed several days and Leslie had dinner with him every night. They either went over to Sharon and Bob's apartment or double-dated with Alice and Helen. They had a good time just being together and Marshall never once mentioned Stephen nor did he try to revive their romance. He seemed to sense her confusion and unhappiness and was unusually sweet to her. Leslie would always be grateful to him.

The gossip mongers began to wonder now, if perhaps Leslie might have been the one to break off with Stephen. They recalled that Marshall had been her steady beau before Stephen. Now he was back from the war—she was still wearing his ring—and so the talk went on.

When it became apparent that Leslie was not entirely destitute, some of the medical students started calling her. This unexplainable phenomenon of male psychology was a revelation to Leslie. When she really needed a friend, none appeared. This was just too much and she, therefore, decided to rely solely on Marshall. At every function if an escort was needed he was always there and very attentive. His constant devotion was a soothing syrup to her wounded pride, and did much to stop the flow of gossip.

Marshall's decision to join his uncle's law firm in Memphis surprised her. He explained that his uncle was in failing health and he felt obligated to help him and his father agreed. John Marshall was a prominent Memphis attorney. He and his wife were childless and he made Marshall his sole heir.

Also the two brothers-in-law already shared legal responsibilities in several large corporations and Marshall could coordinate these programs. Since Memphis was only 80 miles away and

Marshall had the use of a monoplane, he could still see his dad two or three times weekly. His long-range plans would be to help his uncle until retirement, and then return home.

Graduation

The months continued to slip by and June arrived and graduation day was fast approaching.

During all this time, Leslie had not received one word from Stephen nor had she tried to contact him again. Bob did write him at his home address but never received a reply. The only information they could get from the army was that he had been discharged and his footlocker shipped home. Bob also learned the university officials had mailed his transcripts and credits to a Boston hospital and apparently Stephen was to start his residency in surgery there. It looked as though Stephen had deliberately cut himself off from all former friends and associates. Gradually, Leslie was able to accept the fact that she had lost Stephen and to push her thoughts of him to the back of her mind. She knew, however, that he would remain forever a part of her innermost being. Sometimes, she would still find herself rushing off duty, and then would pause in her mad rush when remembrance returned as she realized that never again would she find Stephen waiting for her at the dormitory door.

As graduation day approached, Leslie was eagerly looking forward to seeing her family. She had not been home since Christmas and she missed her mother dreadfully. When the day finally arrived, only her father and Marshall appeared. Leslie was delighted, of course, but inquired anxiously for her mother and Betsy.

"Mother didn't feel well, and Betsy decided to stay with her."

"What's the matter with Mother?" cried Leslie. Sudden panic seized her.

"Now, nothing serious, honey," soothed her father. "She's been a little tired lately, but I think she's saving her strength for the surprise we have for you."

"Surprise?"

Her father smiled, hoping her attention had been diverted. "Now if I tell you, it won't be a surprise, but I will anyway. We have decided to go abroad for your graduation present. Betsy is old enough now to enjoy it and Mother and I would like to visit Mack's grave."

"Oh, Father, how wonderful." Leslie would have preferred to wait a while before making such a trip but she could sense it was important to her parents. "What do you think of the plan, Marshall?"

"It's fine for you, but this side looks good to me. I don't care if I never see Europe again!" answered Marshall emphatically.

In spite of her disappointment over not having her mother present, the day went off well. Leslie and a few of her friends were receiving the degree of Bachelor of Science in Nursing and wore caps and gowns. The other students who were receiving a diploma in nursing wore starchy white uniforms and their nursing caps. They made a striking picture in the processional. Leslie's grade point average was the highest in the class. She also received The Founders Medal.

Graduation day was like a dream come true. Was it possible that once she had considered giving it all up? She had entered Vale an enthusiastic child and now she was leaving as a mature woman of 21.

She had known both happiness and heartbreak here. It was all over now. Never again would she gossip with the girls until dawn as they kept the lights out; never again would she rush off duty to meet Stephen; never again would she experience the thrill of assisting with a first operation or delivery. Leslie was both happy and sad.

Recalling Catherine Case's dire prophecy that "only half would graduate," Leslie had to admit she was almost correct as only 28 of the original 50 did graduate. Not all left because of poor grades, however. Some left voluntarily after deciding nursing just wasn't for them, some left for health reasons and three, like Sharon, decided to get married.

Some things she was glad to be leaving, such as: never again would she have to endure Dean Miller's wrath or be humiliated by insecure head

115

nurses. Leslie looked forward to the opportunity of working with students because she knew she'd never forget how a student felt. If she lived to be a hundred, she'd never forget! She made up her mind even if she remained an old maid for the rest of her life, she'd never let her frustrations thwart her in dealing with younger, more beautiful girls.

When Leslie returned to Denmark with her father and Marshall, she felt as always, a sense of well being. As long as she had her family and White Haven, she could face the uncertainty of the future.

Betsy was twelve years old and getting lovlier with each passing year. She seemed to be one of the fortunate few who was escaping the awkward age. Poor Leslie had looked like a young colt at that age—all arms and legs—and Mack and Marshall had always been ready to remind her of it. Betsy was an almost exact duplicate of their mother. Her blond hair fell in soft curls around her face and down her back. Her big blue eyes looked expectant and questioning at the same time. What a difference a few months could make! Leslie smiled as she remembered how Marshall had fallen so completely in love with her at the Spring Cotillion just before she entered Vale. She knew now how he must have felt—the little girl he had known suddenly grown up. Leslie experienced that same feeling as she looked at Betsy.

"Mother, I can't get over Betsy! She's so sweet and pretty. I know now how you must have looked at age twelve."

"What a sweet thing to say, darling," smiled Janie. "Betsy is a joy to us. We've been extremely fortunate to have such a dear family." Leslie thought she detected a fleeting look of sadness on her mother's face. She let the moment pass, however, and attributed it to her own feelings. Ever since the shock over Stephen, she had harbored a numb, uneasy feeling.

This was the first time Leslie had been with her parents since her broken engagement. She had talked to her mother once from Sharon's apartment since it was impossible to talk privately on the dormitory phone, but the conversation had been mostly about canceling the wedding plans. Since her arrival home, there was a reluctance on both sides to broach the subject. Finally, Janie did ask, "Honey, have you learned anymore about Stephen?"

"No, only that he's probably started his residency in a Boston hospital. No one knows anything for sure and I certainly wouldn't think of calling his home again. I must have been wrong about him, Mother, but knowing what we had together, it's still so hard for me to believe he could have deceived me like that." The thought ran through her mind it was as though Stephen had died on a foreign battlefield and no details of his death were available. She couldn't hate him.

"I'm just going to try and forget him, Mother."

She was deeply appreciative towards Marshall and not wholly unaware of his attractiveness, but for the life of her, she couldn't transfer her affections so quickly and she knew Marshall wouldn't want any rebound romance with her either.

Her parents did everything possible to help. They had never been too enthused over the marriage in the first place and after the way things had turned out, they felt relieved that Leslie wouldn't be marrying Stephen. Not only was he a Yankee, but a cad as well. It was heartbreaking and frustrating though for Janie and Tom to stand by helplessly and observe how hurt and crushed she was.

They talked enthusiastically about their trip to Europe, and suggested asking Margaret to come along, hoping this would please Leslie. Sensing a feverish haste on the part of her mother to make this trip, Leslie tried to react as happily as possible. She recalled her visit home after Mack's death and although they were all heartbroken, she was still able to regain a feeling of security just over being home with her family. Not so this time and she tried to understand why. Finally, she attributed it to her own selfishness. Stephen's betrayal was her

117

albatross and no one could really understand or share her anguish. She, therefore, determined to put these ambivalent feelings aside and show her parents how much she appreciated the vacation they had planned. It would really be nice if Margaret would go with her.

Margaret was easy to persuade. She and Leslie's cousin, Tommy Tyson had dated each other for years, but of late had mutually agreed to part company and try dating others, causing Margaret to be lonely and restless. However, her frequent visits to White Haven boosted both hers and Leslie's enthusiasm as they consulted maps and travel brochures.

They booked passage on *The President Wilson* for July 3, and would leave Tennessee June 25, which would allow them time for a short stay in New York. This only left a few weeks at home. Marshall came over every day and night during this time. Knowing she had hurt him once, Leslie couldn't bear the thought of doing so again. Finally, she broached the subject to her mother.

"Mother, should I let Marshall come over so often?"

"I don't see why not, Leslie Jane, if you enjoy being with him."

"Of course I do, Mother. He's so very special to me and all of us, but I just can't feel anything this soon—maybe never—"

"Well, as long as he understands, I can't think any harm will be done. Besides, we'll be leaving soon and this will give you both a breather." Janie looked thoughtfully at her daughter who was so young, yet mature beyond her years. Would she ever get over this lost love of hers?

Europe

The European vacation was just what Leslie needed and she was glad after all they had come. Putting great distance between herself and her troubles seemed to help her put them aside and concentrate on other things. The family toured England where Tom wanted to make a sentimental journey to the Lee Castle located just outside Nottingham. As it turned out, a distant cousin, Sir Archibald Lee-Reynolds still lived in the castle and had, in recent years, due to the depression, opened it to tourists (mostly Americans) who were flocking to England in droves. Tom recalled how his great grandfather had kept in contact with the English cousins but down through the years, they'd lost touch.

Sir Archibald and Lady Frances were most gracious to the Lees and invited them to tea. Leslie and the family were so thrilled over this unexpected pleasure. To think these people were actually their "kinfolks"! Southerners valued family ties and no matter how distant the relationship might be, they still claimed "kin." The English Lees, although more stiff and formal, accepted their American counterparts.

After leaving England, they went over into Belgium and found the town, Waeregham, where Mack's grave was located. They remained in the village a week and visited the grave daily, taking fresh flowers. The landscaping in the military cemetery, Flanders Fields, wasn't completed at this time, but the setting was beautiful. Janie gained some satisfaction in actually seeing and visiting the grave site and it gave all of them a sense of finality to the fact that Mack was really gone.

After leaving Waeregham, they visited other points of interest in Belgium and then traveled on to Switzerland, France, and parts of Northern Italy.

Upon their return to England, Leslie and Margaret suddenly conceived the idea of remaining there to attend the University of

London. They begged, wheedled, and pleaded with their parents. Margaret sent frantic cables home and Leslie continued to beg also, arguing that a Master's Degree would help them professionally.

Leslie's bruised feelings had healed somewhat during this summer vacation and she felt that, perhaps, a year of intense study in new surroundings would hasten her complete liberation from the past.

Janie was reluctant to give her consent, which was unlike her. Instead, she suggested a restful year at White Haven before going to work or back to school. Leslie, being wrapped up in her own problems, failed to notice anything unusual in Janie's attitude and continued to beg to remain in London.

Finally, the Lees gave their consent as did Margaret's parents. Late in August, Janie, Tom, and Betsy set sail for American leaving behind two very excited girls.

Both Margaret and Leslie were well pleased with the University program of study. Margaret's major was history and Leslie was able to take a course in midwifery along with obstetrics and gynecology.

During the holidays, they were invited to Nottingham to spend Christmas with Leslie's newfound cousins. This time, they met a daughter, Frances Ann and a son, Archibald Henry who were college age. It soon became most obvious to both Leslie and the Lee-Reynolds that Archie was strongly attracted to Margaret.

After Leslie and Margaret returned to the university, Archie became a frequent weekend visitor. He always brought along a friend for Leslie and thus the girls were royally entertained.

As their year of study was drawing to a close, Leslie became alarmed that Margaret might be persuaded to marry Archie and remain in England.

"Maggie, you just must return home with me. Aunt Margaret would kill me if I didn't bring you back."

"I can remember a time when you were perfectly willing to desert your dear old Southland and go off to Boston," Margaret answered sarcastically.

"I know," agreed Leslie, nodding her head. "You're right, of course, but at least Boston was in the United States! London is a whole ocean away from home and you're all Aunt Margaret and Uncle Jim have."

Finally as graduation day approached, Leslie's persuasive powers won over Archie's and Margaret agreed to return home for a "cooling off" period. Leslie was relieved. She wanted Margaret to be happy, but she felt a real responsibility to get her back home. She hoped Archie would come to Denmark, then her Aunt Margaret could be the judge.

"But Lessie, just think," Margaret said wistfully, "someday I might have been 'Lady Margaret.'"

"You can *still* be Lady Margaret, but please come back and be married at Forest Home. You do owe that much to Aunt Margaret."

Before leaving for America, Leslie and Margaret accompanied by Archie, returned to Flanders Fields for another visit to Mack's grave and to leave fresh flowers. She knew this would please her mother. As Leslie placed flowers on her brother's grave, she could see and understand the anguish Margaret and Archie were experiencing over their impending separation. She began to regret now her efforts to get Margaret to return home with her. She shouldn't have interfered in someone else's life.

They returned to Leeshire Castle to spend the last two days before their sailing date to America. On the eve of their departure, Leslie had already retired when she heard Margaret come in after being out with Archie. She got up, put on her robe, and sat down on the bed beside her cousin. "Maggie, please forgive me for trying to talk you out of marrying Archie. I can think back now and realize if I'd married Stephen when he begged me to, I would never have lost him. I try to tell myself that if he'd

121

really loved me, he could have waited, but it doesn't make me feel any better."

"Don't blame yourself, Les." Margaret was tearful. "I knew all the time I should return home before making such a momentous decision." It just tore Leslie's heart out to see her so unhappy. "I'm so confused, I do want to stay here, but you were right. I'd be so far away from Mother and Daddy. And Leslie, I also owe it to Tommy to at least go back and tell him."

"But don't you see? That's what happened to me!" argued Leslie. "I felt like I had to wait and tell Marshall. Oh, Maggie, if you love Archie—stay here and marry him. I'll go home and face the music alone." They were both crying now. Leslie could feel all the pain and heartache over Stephen return. She so much wanted Margaret to be spared these agonies. How she envied these people who could just fall in love and get married without complications.

The next day, Archie accompanied them to the pier where he and Margaret said a tearful farewell with promises to see each other again. Leslie had a sinking feeling that it was really farewell and that somehow, she was responsible for it.

It was June, 1920.

Janie

Leslie had only a short visit at home as she had already accepted a job in the Chicago area. She was determined now to follow Miss Webb's advice and work as a general duty graduate in the hospital before aspiring to a position of leadership.

Leslie's parents were pleased with the change in her. She had gained weight and had regained, to some degree, her natural sparkle and vivaciousness. It had definitely been good for Leslie to be separated from the past.

The new environment in Chicago was good for her too. She was able to find an apartment in the Edgewater Beach area which was also near the hospital. Working with patients again was very stimulating for Leslie and she asked for a rotation of services in order to get all kinds of experience. After all, she had spent three years preparing for her career and she certainly intended to learn all she could.

Now that she was back in the States, Marshall had renewed his courtship. It was as though he had waited a respectful interval following Stephen's "passing" to launch his own campaign.

Leslie almost hated herself for her attitude towards him. She enjoyed his company and felt so much security in his love but she still couldn't face the possibility of marriage. She knew she wasn't being fair to lead him on but she couldn't bear the thought of giving him up either.

Marshall's visits were infrequent however, because of the distance. She mostly saw him on holidays. She made many new friends and never wanted for dates. She was sure that Marshall had started dating others also. As the weeks stretched into months, Stephen's image receded more into the background and her heartache lessened somewhat.

Leslie had been working in Chicago one year when the urgent message came for her to come home at once. Janie was seriously ill. Leslie was so upset, she could hardly pack her things.

By the time she arrived home, her mother had already been admitted to the hospital. Leslie immediately sought Dr. Miller for an explanation.

"I'm sorry, Child. I'm not sure," he answered her. "I've sent for Robby. He'll be here this afternoon." Leslie had a feeling that Dr. Miller did know but wanted Rob Jr. to confirm his diagnosis.

Leslie found her way to her mother's room. The whole clan had gathered. Some were in the room, others in the waiting area. Janie looked as pretty and sweet as ever, but so pale and thin. "Oh," Leslie reproached herself, "why did I take that job in Chicago? Why didn't I come home more often?" She tried to hide her anxiety from her mother but it was no use.

"Now, darling, don't you worry about me," soothed Janie after their first greeting was over.

When Rob Jr. arrived that afternoon and made his examination and read the test results, he ordered an operation immediately. "It's cancer of the uterus, Leslie," he told her quite frankly. "I just hope to God it's contained in the uterus and hasn't spread."

During the operation, the family gathered in the waiting room. Leslie was terrified. Marshall had come from Memphis and was spending every possible moment with her. He felt almost like he was losing his mother for the second time. They tried to encourage each other but no one dared voice their fears.

After about two hours, Dr. Robert Jr., still wearing his operating cap and gown, entered. This was a surgeon's most difficult task and, as he looked into the stricken faces turned towards him, he felt like the villain. Robby found he just couldn't tell Tom, his old rival, the whole truth. He would tell Leslie privately that the cancer had metastasized and the prognosis was grave.

"Janie stood the operation fine, Tom, and is in stable condition. We were able to remove the tumor and insert radium which we will remove in 3 days. We'll just have to wait and see about the results."

When Leslie learned the awful truth, she felt as though life was no longer worth living. A week following the operation, when Janie was feeling stronger, she begged to return home. She, too, loved the sturdiness and tranquillity of White Haven. Since she had such a short time to live, Dr. Miller and the family agreed this was best.

Leslie prepared Janie's room and brought the necessary equipment to the bedside table. All her nursing skills would be put to the test now. She just must take good care of her mother.

Whenever Janie felt like listening, Leslie would read to her. Mary and Aunt Margaret hovered around and other relatives, friends and neighbors brought food and offered to help, but Leslie just couldn't bear to leave her for long.

Finally, when her father insisted that she must get away for a break, Leslie went straight to the little church, and it was there that Brother Stone found her.

"Excuse me, Leslie. May I pray with you?" He stood looking down at her as she knelt at the Chancel Rail.

"Oh, Brother Stone, please do." Tears were rolling down her cheeks. "Tell me, is it wrong for me to pray for my mother to recover? I know it's scientifically impossible, but I just can't give up! If only the radium will work and stop the spread."

"Oh course you can't give up, my dear," said the kindly old minister. As he looked at Leslie, he recalled how he had baptized her at almost the exact spot where she was kneeling.

"But Brother Stone, Mother's too young to die," sobbed Leslie.

"I know, child, but remember our Lord was only 33 when He died and He had a full and complete life," soothed the minister.

"What shall I do?"

"We'll pray for the Lord to give you and your family the strength to bear and accept whatever comes," he answered simply as he knelt down beside her.

Leslie felt better after her session with Brother Stone and she returned home with renewed strength. She would see this thing through as Janie would want her to.

When she entered her mother's room, Mary was dozing in the chair. Leslie gently kissed her on the cheek, "I'm back now, Mae Mae. Go and try to get some rest." Janie was wide awake and smiling. She had on a pale blue bed jacket and her blond hair was lying in two long braids in front of her.

"You're both completely exhausted." Her keen eyes observed Leslie's wet cheeks. "Honey, you've been crying."

"No, Mother, I've just been walking in the wind." She sat down beside the bed.

"You don't have to pretend to me, Leslie Jane. I made Robby tell me the truth."

"Oh, Mother," sobbed Leslie, laying her head on the bed beside her. "I'm so ashamed! I've been away taking care of other people and let my own mother get sick."

"Leslie you mustn't feel guilty. I should have known enough to consult the doctor sooner," answered Janie, gently stroking Leslie's thick black hair. "I just thought the symptoms I was having were related to the menopause."

"But Mother, cancer is curable in its early stages."

"I know, darling, but please try and pull yourself together. I must talk some things over with you," urged her mother.

"I'm sorry, Mother. You're comforting me and I should be comforting you."

"You've always been a comfort to me, dear. I've been so lucky to have such a sweet family. I guess I just wanted to live forever and enjoy my grandchildren."

"Remember how I used to talk about my four little boys?" Leslie smiled ruefully.

"Yes, but please don't say 'used to' like it will never happen."

"I know, but sometimes now I don't think it ever will."

"Another selfish whim of mine. I wanted so much to see you happily married."

"I just can't even think of such a thing now."

126

"Yes, of course, honey. I understand. You need more time. I know, however, and you must believe it too, that someday the right person will come along for you." Janie was so sincere that somehow, Leslie felt renewed strength and hope. Janie then asked for her head to be raised. After Leslie had positioned her comfortably in bed, she said, "Now Leslie, we need to talk. I wanted you to know that your father and I have agreed on the terms of our wills. As you know, I have some money and property my parents left me which Tom would never touch except to help me invest it. This will be divided equally between you and Betsy. Since she is not yet of age, we've decided to have you appointed her legal guardian in the event that something happens to Tom. Since there are no male heirs, we would like for you to have White Haven. Betsy will get "Arrowhead," the farm at Pinson."

They continued to talk and make plans. It was heartbreaking for both of them to acknowledge that Janie's illness was terminal. Finally, when Leslie noticed she was getting tired, she lowered her head rest and slipped quietly out of the room.

Janie died as she had lived—quietly, peacefully and surrounded by those who loved her. After that last conversation, there had not been much more time for talks. Robert Jr. left his practice in Memphis when possible to come and do what he could for Janie. He was present the night she died along with old Dr. Miller, Brother Stone, Marshall, and all the family. Although she knew it was inevitable and thought she had prepared herself, the shock of actually seeing her mother draw her last breath was almost unbearable. A lifetime of memories flooded through Leslie's mind as she gently kissed her mother and persuaded her father to leave the room with her. She turned him over to Dr. Miller. After making sure Aunt Margaret was with Betsy, she went in search of Marshall. He was talking to Robert Jr. who was preparing to leave. Leslie put her arms around him, remembering he had once been in love with her

127

mother. "Thank you so much, Dr. Robby, for being here. It means so much to all of us." Their eyes met and somehow he knew that she knew. "Everyone loved Janie. She was special."

"—And a very special mother, too," answered Leslie, smiling through her tears. Exhaustion overpowered her and she felt completely drained. It was all over and the battle had been lost. Everything humanly possible had been done and she had to divest herself of any guilt feelings. Marshall put his arms around her and it was comforting to rest against him. She was tired of being brave.

They stood alone in the hall, locked in each other's arms, and cried together for the gentle, sweet person they all loved so much.

After her mother's death, Leslie resigned her job in Chicago and returned to White Haven. She was determined to be courageous for her father's and little Betsy's sake. Outwardly she was calm and brave, but inside she had the most empty, lost feeling. With her mother's departure, she felt that all the strength and wisdom in the world had gone with her. In spite of her resolve not to brood over what might have been, Leslie couldn't help but reproach herself for her selfish blindness. Because she had been so wrapped up in her own heartache, she had failed to see some unmistakable signs: her mother's inability to attend her graduation; her feverish haste to make the trip abroad to visit Mack's grave; her reluctance to let Leslie remain in London.

Leslie and her father were especially concerned about Betsy. She was 14 now and a sophomore in high school. Thank God Janie had her during her formative years, but they realized the years ahead were important also. Leslie recalled with a lump in her throat how much fun it had been coming home from a date to find Mother waiting up for her with a cup of hot chocolate ready and how they would "talk things over." Betsy would miss all this as she was just beginning to go out on boy and girl parties and had not had any real dates as yet.

The more Leslie thought about it, the more

she worried. Betsy needed someone during her adolescent years. She knew Mae Mae would take good care of her and that Aunt Margaret and her other aunts would help but it wouldn't be the same as someone being in the home. After talking things over with her father, Leslie decided it would be best for her to remain at home. Tom was delighted, of course. He really needed her as much as Betsy did. Dr. Miller offered her a part-time job as office nurse two days a week. This would enable her to keep in touch professionally and yet be at home with her father and to supervise Betsy's social and religious training. Leslie felt like in this small way, she was repaying her mother for all the love and devotion she had bestowed upon her.

After the first year, when members of the family were gradually becoming adjusted to Janie's absence, Leslie accepted a position as head nurse at the Memorial Hospital in Jackson.

Betsy blossomed into a lovely young girl and Tom and Leslie marveled daily at her likeness to Janie. Leslie recalled her mother's remark that "having children is like life renewing itself." Yes, indeed, Janie would never die as long as either of them lived.

Leslie determined to follow Janie's policy of making their home attractive and inviting to the younger crowd. Betsy frequently had overnight guests and her friends felt free to drop by anytime. Like Janie, Leslie would wait up and have hot chocolate ready when Betsy came in from a date. She had a few dates herself, but most of her old crowd were married. Marshall had slipped back into his custom of dropping in on holidays and vacations.

Leslie found herself enjoying her mother role and she could relive so many of her own little triumphs and heartaches as she guided Betsy through the Girl Scouts; playing forward on the basketball team; becoming a cheer leader; her first prom; her installation into the Cotillion Club; even capturing the leading role in the Senior play.

Leslie tried to be objective and accept
129

Betsy's friends, most of whom she really did like. Emily Bennett was the exception, however, and she'd almost have to bite her tongue to keep from saying something to Betsy. Whatever Betsy had, Emily wanted it or something better. If Betsy got a new dress, Emily would get two. If they double-dated, Emily would spend the evening flirting with Betsy's date. Betsy hadn't settled down to any steady boyfriend as yet but Leslie's favorite was Timothy Marshall, who was Marshall Chadwick's cousin. When Timothy became Betsy's most frequent date, Emily's interest in him seemed to perk up. Leslie elected not to interfere.

Before long, Timothy started dating Emily, and Leslie had to grind her teeth and say nothing. Betsy would learn to fight her own battles she was sure. In spite of all her extra curricular activities, heartaches and triumphs, Betsy still managed to graduate as valedictorian of her class. Tom and Leslie beamed as they sat in the audience on graduation night. Much to Leslie's relief, when the colleges were chosen, Emily decided Radcliffe was a more prestigious college than The University of Tennessee where Betsy chose to go. Timothy would attend Cumberland Law School. Leslie just hoped the separation would be good for them.

When Betsy left for college and was more or less on her own, Leslie felt her obligation had been fulfilled. These three years at home and been enjoyable and rewarding and at the same time she had gained some valuable professional experience. She felt like she'd earned her "wings" and was now qualified to teach. Several tempting offers were considered, but she finally decided to return to Vale University. Enough time had elapsed now that she no longer felt any reluctance about facing the past. Besides, Sharon and Bob Harper were there and she would see other friends.

She easily slipped back into the professional and social life at Vale. It was gratifying to her to be teaching student nurses and to be able to implement some of her beliefs and ideals. In spite of her busy schedule, Leslie made it a point to return home for holidays and vacations. She still felt responsible for Betsy and wanted to be there for her when she came home with her friends. One Thanksgiving holiday, Allen Long visited and the family instantly liked him. He was an amiable, handsome youth from Kentucky. When he became a frequent guest, Leslie and Marshall gave up hope that Betsy and Timothy would ever get back together.

Betsy graduated in 1928 and returned home to teach school. Allen returned to Kentucky to work with his father on their race horse breeding farm. When the Long family invited Betsy to the Kentucky Derby and to be their house guest for a week, Leslie's heart sank. It seemed that Betsy and Timothy were drifting farther apart and she was definitely committed to Allen.

Leslie was amazed therefore, when about a month following Betsy's visit to Kentucky, she called to announce that she was engaged to Timothy. Leslie was delighted, of course— "But what happened to Allen?"

"Oh I let Emily take him away from me," Betsy laughed.

"Well, this is one time I'm glad she did, but how did you manage it?"

"Big Sis, if I were Catholic, I'd most surely have to go to Confession."

"Then why don't you just confess to me?"

"Well, it's a long story," giggled Betsy. "I really do like Allen and we'll always be good friends. But when I was in Kentucky I met Judy Taylor, Allen's former girl friend. It didn't take me long to realize he was still carrying the torch for her. When I confronted him, he admitted it. Then I told him about Tim and we decided to use each other to get what we really wanted. The next time he came to White Haven, we double dated with Tim and Emily and as usual, she latched on to my date and Allen led her on. I think Timothy saw right through her. Tim and I got back together, Allen went back to Kentucky and he called today to tell me he and Judy are engaged. When Emily realized she'd been 'had,'
131

she was furious and now won't speak to any of us."

"That's the best news I've heard. I can't wait to tell Marshall."

"Tim is going to practice law with Daddy Chad. Now we call all be together here at White Haven. Anyway, I don't think I would have liked living in Kentucky.

It was 1929 and Betsy's engagement announcement occurred simultaneously with the stock market crash! This tragic failure cast a pall over America and the depression that followed affected everyone whether they were investors or not. Cotton and other farm prices dropped to an all-time low. Tom had never invested heavily in stocks but his losses were bad enough that he was forced to mortgage "Arrowhead," the farm at Pinson in order to keep White Haven solvent.

In spite of the gloom and doom, both Tom and Leslie were determined that Betsy's wedding should be joyful and carefree. Leslie took her vacation time and came home to help.

Between shopping tours and the numerous parties they attended, Leslie managed to help Mary get the house and food ready for the wedding and reception. Two long tables were placed in the library to display the wedding gifts. By the time the wedding day arrived, they were all exhausted but happy.

On the eve of Betsy's wedding after they had returned from the rehearsal dinner, Leslie knocked at her bedroom door.

"May I come in, Betsy, Baby?"

"Sure, come on in, Big Sis."

Since Janie's death, Leslie had easily assumed the mother role with Betsy but tonight for the first time, she felt totally inadequate. She sat down awkwardly on the love seat. So many sweet things she wanted to say, no many memories and so much love she wanted to share, but she choked up as the lofty remarks she had planned left her and all she said was: "I can't believe my baby sister is getting married."

"Neither can I, Big Sis." Betsy sat down beside Leslie and reached for her hand. "I want you to know I really do appreciate all you've done for me. When Mother died I was so young and could think only of myself. I realize now you gave up three years of your life to be here with me and Father," she said earnestly. "And you've worked hard putting this wedding together—Thanks."

Leslie was so touched. Betsy had never expressed herself like this before. "Thank you, darling, but I really didn't 'give up' anything. I thought it was important for us to be together after Mother died. And I loved working on the wedding. I tried to do everything like Mother would want it to be," she said, blinking back the tears. She glanced over to see Janie's wedding dress all sparkly white and great grandmother, Sarah Birdsong's wedding veil carefully spread out on a chair. Everything in readiness.

"I know." Betsy's big blue eyes looked at her expectantly. Leslie knew, in spite of Betsy's seeming sophistication and assurance, she could use some encouragement now.

"Honey, I wish I could prepare you for your wedding night but I can't." Leslie was fumbling for words.

"I wish mama was here." Betsy's voice trembled as she laid her head on Leslie's shoulder like she was a little girl again. Leslie put her arms around her, kissed her on the top of the head and said: "I like to think she is here watching over us and I know she's so proud. I don't know what Mother would say to you because my marriage never took place. The only thing she ever told me was that marriage would be the culmination of our love, which really doesn't tell you anything.

"I doubt, however, that Mother or anyone for that matter would go into much detail, because there are some very intimate, sacred moments in a person's life that they just simply can't share with anyone. Even my dear friend Sharon has never told me anything other than she is divinely happy and being able to share love with her husband has brought a completeness to her life she'd never known before. With the love you and Timothy share,

133

there's no doubt in my mind that you'll be able to work out your marital relationship in a loving and giving way. You are going to have a wonderful life together."

Betsy raised up and looked gratefully at Leslie. "Thanks, Big Sis. For someone who didn't know what to say, you said it beautifully and," she paused, "I like what you said." Betsy's eyes misted as she looked at Leslie. "You know, Mama and Daddy wanted so much for you to marry Marshall."

"Yes, and maybe someday I will—but this is *your* wedding eve—" Betsy quickly forgot her serious moment and in a bantering tome, said: "Tell you what! When you do get married, I'll talk to you."

"And I'll just hold you to that," laughed Leslie, leaning over to give Betsy a goodnight kiss.

The wedding was beautiful. Everything Leslie had hoped for, and she was so happy.

After Tim and Betsy departed on their honeymoon amid a shower of rice and good wishes, Marshall put his arm around Leslie and guided her towards the little gazebo in the rose garden. It was private there as the rest of the crowd had shifted back towards the house. Leslie was feeling very sentimental and tearful over the wedding and didn't resist when Marshall took her in his arms and kissed her.

"All your obligations are fulfilled now, Leslie. Don't you think it's time now for us to get married?"

"Marshall, I love you dearly, but I'm not ready to get married—not just yet." In a way, Betsy's wedding had revived all the heartache and uncertainty over Stephen. She couldn't help but remember that this wedding should have been enacted for her ten years ago. Another deterrent was her work at Vale, which had reached an exciting and crucial stage. Real progress was being made on the educational standards she was trying to establish. Vale University did have a Baccalaureate program now, but the students were required to have two years of college on admission, then receive their B.S. degree after three years. Leslie was determined to get a four year program. Why should it take a nurse five years to get a degree when other students got one in four years? Also, she had just been elected president of the American Nurses' Association and now she could carry her fight for higher standards nationwide. "I just need more time, Marshall."

He released her. His hurt was overpowered by his anger. "I might as well give up! We're both getting older, you know. I still want a family and I thought you did, too." He was finding it difficult to continue. They were sitting on the bench now. "I've met a girl in Memphis—"

"I understand, Marshall," she interrupted him. She laid her hand gently over his. "You've always been so patient and sweet to me." She was trying hard to be understanding but she felt completely abandoned. He was right about her getting older and his reference to a "family" hurt to the quick. It might already be too late for her four little boys. "Please don't ever stop being my friend and counselor." As Marshall walked away, his usually snappy gait and military-like bearing seemed altered and his shoulders sagged. Leslie wanted to call him back, but she just slumped against the lattice work and cried silently. Her father found her there later. "Honey, the guests are leaving. You need to come in." He put his arms around her and they walked to the house. He didn't have to ask because he had seen Marshall leave.

When she returned to Vale, Leslie poured her heart and soul out to Sharon whom she'd turned to more and more since her mother's death as her confidant and counselor.

"Oh Lessie Lee! Why couldn't you have fallen in love with Marshall instead of that stinking Stephen?"

"I keep asking myself that same question, Sharon. I do love Marshall in a very special way and I do want to marry someday, but there's still so many things I want and *need* to do. I won't

135

rest until the Nursing School is an integral part of the university equal to the other schools. I resent having the school and hospital separated from the rest of the university."

"Then you've answered your own question. Your career is more important to you than your 'four little boys.'" Sharon knew she'd found a touchy spot.

"There's nothing more important to me than my mythical family, but I had wanted to be madly in love and at this point I'm not madly in love with anyone."

"You know, of course, you've embarked on a long hard road to convince the doctors and even some of the faculty. There are still those who believe that hospital training is all a nurse needs. Bob will help anyway he can."

"Good. I'll need all the help I can get. When I presented my paper on a proposed four year Baccalaureate program for nurses, you should have heard some of their remarks. One old geezer actually had the nerve to say, 'instead of all those high stepping thoroughbreds you're talking about, what we actually need is some more old plugs to do the work.' I could have throttled him."

Sharon laughed in spite of herself. She wasn't worried about Leslie though, who she knew could match wits with the best and that she actually enjoyed a good round with the doctors. It might take a while and some doing, but she knew eventually Leslie would outsmart them all and achieve her goals.

"Thank you, Sharon. Talking this out with you had helped me to realize just how important my career is to me. I can't abandon it just yet. I'll try to give Marshall up gracefully." She did feel better but she knew there would be a void in her life forever without Marshall.

Betsy sent her a clipping from the Memphis paper of Marshall's engagement announcement. Leslie still subscribed to *The Jackson Sun* and she had already seen the picture in that paper. She couldn't stop the tears that welled up. "Cornelia Catherine Foster" a Memphis
136

debutante, recently presented at The Cotton Ball, a lovely girl. Leslie wondered what she was really like.

The newspaper picture looked vaguely familiar, but Leslie couldn't remember ever having known any Fosters.

Ambivalent feelings surged through her as the finality of the actual engagement seeped through. She felt like a child whose security blanket had suddenly been snatched away. Her career was important to her yet another part of her wanted to dash it all, call Marshall and tell him she wanted him more. She wondered if their relationship would be strained now. Would he continue to do her legal work and manage her and Betsy's inheritance? People did change after marriage.

The wedding was scheduled for November 19, but on the afternoon of October 4, Betsy called her. Marshall's father had died suddenly of a heart attack. Leslie was badly shaken. "Daddy Chad" was yet another link to her childhood she was fast losing. She knew she would have to return home and do whatever she could to help Marshall. He had his fiance, of course, but, she reasoned, he needed someone from home; someone besides the servants, who was familiar with the house; someone to receive guests and help with the arrangements. She caught the first flight out and arrived in Jackson at 7 a.m. Betsy and Tim met her and they drove on to Denmark. After stopping off at White Haven long enough to leave her bags, Leslie went immediately to Inglenook, Marshall's home. Callie, the maid opened the door.

"Oh, Mis Leslie, I'se so glad to see you. Mr. Marshall's so pitiful—you know, jus' the two of 'em so long—"

"Yes, I know, Callie." Leslie patted her shoulder. "Where is he?"

"Him an that girl is in the study," sniffed Callie, pointing to Mr. Chadwick's office.

Leslie's Aunt Elizabeth and the McBryde kin were milling around and neighbors were bringing in food. Marshall had very few close relatives. Tim and his sister were second cousins.

Leslie knocked gently at the door with a feeling of nervous anticipation knowing she was about to meet the future mistress of this house, but for now, she felt she was the one who could help Marshall the most.

Marshall opened the door and the sight of Leslie completely unglued him. They were suddenly in each other's arms, comforting and giving comfort as they were both suffering almost the same loss. They were completely unaware of anyone else in the world. "I was afraid you wouldn't come." Finally Leslie was able to talk between sobs, "But of course, I'd be here for you just as you've always been for me." She then extricated herself from his arms and waited expectantly for him to introduce his fiance.

Instead he walked over and sat down on the couch as though in a trance. Leslie turned towards Cornelia and extended her hand—

"I'm Leslie Jane Lee. I'm sorry we had to meet under such painful circumstances. Marshall and I grew up together and I feel like I've lost a member of my family also." She hoped Cornelia would accept this explanation.

"Yes, I understand," she answered as she clasped Leslie's hand. "I'm Cornelia Foster. It's good you're here. I'm afraid I haven't been much help." She was a pretty little thing. Leslie suddenly had the eerie feeling that she was looking in a time mirror and seeing herself of about ten years back—straight black hair, green eyes— "Oh," she realized with a shock, "this is why her picture looked familiar. She looks like *me!*" Cornelia seemed to be reeling with the same realization.

"—Er, it's too bad you didn't get to know Daddy Chad better," she stammered. "He was so sweet."

"Yes, I met him only once." Cornelia had regained her composure. They tried to make small talk and not reveal the fact that they were each keenly aware of their striking resemblance.

Marshall finally recovered enough to discuss the arrangements, but he left the details and finalizing up to her. Leslie set the funeral for

138

the next afternoon as she saw no reason to prolong the agony for Marshall. It was heartbreaking for her to see him so completely crushed. She remembered how strong he had been for her when Janie died. Now he turned helplessly to her rather than Cornelia.

After the funeral, Leslie, feeling she had officiated enough, returned to White Haven with her father, Betsy and Tim. She was anxious to return to Vale as soon as possible. Once there, maybe she could plunge back into her work and put her grief over Daddy Chad and Marshall out of her mind. Marshall only needed her during the early shock over losing his father. Cornelia could take over now and give him the love and comfort he would need to adjust to life without him.

Back home, a restless, uneasy feeling gripped her and she felt the need to get out. She asked Betsy to go horseback riding with her. It felt good to ride along and feel the tingly fall breeze. Everything on the farm looked so beautiful and peaceful. The leaves were turning their colors.

"Betsy, do you remember the little poem Mother used to quote us at this time of year?"

"Come little leaves, said the wind one day

"Come over the meadows with me and play

"Put on your dresses of red and gold

"For summer is gone and the days grow cold—"

Betsy smiled wistfully, "Yes, it was almost like a ritual every year." They rode on, enjoying the beauty of the late October afternoon. The blackeyed susans and golden rod were blooming in profusion and the leaves of the dogwood trees had turned a deep scarlet.

"Betsy, it's good that you and Tim are here with Father. He's so upset over Daddy Chad."

"We both love White Haven," Betsy said. They rode on until Betsy startled Leslie with this declaration: "Big Sis, Marshall is still in love with you. And did you notice?" She reined in her horse and looked at Leslie intently. "That girl looks like you! That's why he was attracted to her."

139

"You mustn't say that, Betsy!" Leslie protested. Then it *was* true. Her imagination wasn't playing tricks on her after all. "Don't even think it. I'll be returning to Vale early in the morning and I won't be back until the wedding—if then."

"*If* there is a wedding. I saw the way he looked at you."

"Please, Betsy. Let's ride back home—" Leslie spurred her horse and rode on ahead of her sister. She was moved more than she cared to admit. Maybe she shouldn't have come home after all—but she couldn't have stayed away either. It seemed she was always unintentionally hurting Marshall.

Two weeks after Leslie returned to Vale, Betsy sent her another newspaper clipping:

"The marriage of Miss Cornelia Catherine Foster and Mr. John Marshall Chadwick has been canceled by mutual consent of both parties."

Cornelia

Cornelia had used her key to let herself in and was busily preparing dinner in Marshall's apartment. She wanted everything to be perfect, because tonight she intended to tell him good-bye.

After seeing Marshall and Leslie together, she knew she could never go through with their wedding. She'd had a vague feeling all along that he wasn't totally committed to her, but had been flattered by his attentions and her family was ecstatic over their engagement. After all, he was considered the best "catch" in Memphis—young, handsome, a firmly established law practice, sole heir to a rich uncle and father—everything a girl could want.

When Marshall arrived, dinner was ready. He kissed her and looked around, "My something smells good." It was amusing to see her stack of cook books and he appreciated her efforts to please him. He knew she'd probably never cooked a meal before in her life. The table was attractively set and they enjoyed a candlelight dinner.

Her intentions were to wait until after dinner before returning his ring and explaining her reasons, but the evening had been so pleasant she hated to spoil it. Maybe she should wait, but then shortly after dinner Marshall guided her towards the bedroom.

She really hadn't intended to go to bed with him tonight, but he seemed so restless and unhappy, she couldn't deny him. They had been sleeping together since the engagement was announced. She had accepted it as the natural thing to do and he had reasoned that the wedding would take place soon, so why not? He knew Leslie would never have gone to bed with him, but Connie was of a younger generation.

Later, when Marshall was sated and relaxed, Cornelia turned to him and said, "This has to be our last night together, Chad."

"What?" He was completely unprepared.

"I'm saying I can't marry you. You're still in

love with Leslie." There was no acrimony or reproach in her voice. She was simply stating a fact. "Oh!" he gasped. It was like he'd been punched in the stomach. Denying it would be useless and he felt like a first class heel. He had honestly thought they could have a good marriage. They could have, if she hadn't seen Leslie. "Connie, we can make it work," he pleaded. "I know we can. We're so compatible, both in and *out* of bed."

"But that's not enough for me. I want the man I marry to love me for myself, not because I look like the person he really loves."

Marshall groaned inwardly. This child had far more perception than he'd given her credit for. "I'm so sorry, Connie. I never meant to hurt you."

"I know you didn't. Don't worry. I'll get over it."

"What will your parents say?"

"I'll convince them it was by mutual consent."

"Will I see you again?" In a way he was relieved. He'd fairly ached for Leslie since he saw her last.

"No, because we'd continue sleeping together and I can't do that. I've got to save something for the man I'll eventually marry."

"Well, he'd better be good to you. If he's not, I'll kill the bastard."

"That's probably what my father will want to do to you," she laughed. He took her in his arms. Ambivalent feelings of relief and regret surged through him. He felt a warm protective feeling for Connie. She represented youth and the family he'd longed for and now probably would never have. "Connie, you're wise beyond your years. I respect you more than any person I've ever known. Please don't shut me out entirely. Let me see you occasionally. We'll go out for dinner. I need you and want you as a friend and I promise not to lay a hand on you."

"Friends then, forever." She kissed him and pressed her body closer. She knew she would miss him. Their relationship had been so

142

satisfying. "Please make love to me the rest of the night. Tomorrow will be time enough to start our platonic relationship."

1939

The years slipped by so fast Leslie couldn't realize where they had gone. She had been dean at Vale for the past five years, but was now in New York on her second year of sabbatical leave at Columbia University working on her doctorate. She had already completed all her college credits and was now putting the finishing touches on her dissertation. As a part of the requirements for her Ph.D., she was teaching a class on research to undergraduate students. In a matter of weeks now, she would be through and could have a nice visit at home before returning to Vale.

Betsy had four children and Leslie felt like a grandmother. In fact she was godmother for all four and Marshall was their godfather. The children were named, Leslie Jane "Janie," Elizabeth Lee "Lee," Timothy Jr. "Timmy," and Thomas McKay "Mack." Leslie marveled at how perfectly Betsy "fit the mold" her parents had planned for her, but No, she had been the maverick who had to go out and seek a career. Once she had been willing to give it all up, but fate had settled her ambivalent feelings about marriage vs. a career and then her career became the most important thing in her life.

Leslie and Marshall had continued to see each other through the years, but it was different now. Since his aborted engagement to Cornelia he had more or less played the field and was sought after by every eligible female in Memphis. Leslie often heard of some of his affairs, but never mentioned it to him. She felt somewhat responsible for his conduct. If years ago, she had given him a definite answer, maybe he could have found another nice girl and settled down. Instead she had let matters drift on. They were bound together by a strange bond. He still loved her but sometimes, he almost hated her. He never mentioned marriage anymore. He was probably having too good a time, she thought.

The APHA (American Public Health

Association) was having its annual convention in New York and Leslie was invited to present a paper to the Nursing Section on her successful efforts to advance nursing education. These meetings were always very inspirational to her as well as a lot of fun. She had checked into the convention hotel and resolved to forget all about her dissertation and research.

On the 3rd day of the convention, Marshall came up to escort her to the dance at the Astor Hotel. He had phoned from his hotel and would call for her around 8 p.m. As she dressed, she felt a twinge of excitement and the thought ran through her mind that she would like to get married. When she completed her doctorate, more career opportunities would be available to her, but she had already achieved most of her goals. Her articles had been published in all the professional magazines. Her books on *Curriculum Guidelines*, and *History of Nursing* were used as text books in most of the major schools of nursing as well as her book on *Nursing Care and Procedure*. One of the publishing houses had already contracted for her dissertation on research. Nursing, to her, was still an exciting and rewarding profession and there was so much more still to be done, but for now, all she wanted was to complete her doctorate and then pass the grail on to someone else. She felt like she had helped pave the way. Let the next generation take on the dragon of requiring a Baccalaureate degree as the first level for the professional nurse. She had planted the seed and done some groundwork. They could take it from there.

She made up her mind that if Marshall showed any interest at all, she was prepared to encourage him. She surveyed herself in the mirror and was satisfied with what she saw. Her straight black hair was parted in the middle and falling loosely around her shoulders in a page boy style. Her aqua evening dress accentuated her green eyes. A wide gold belt and an aqua evening bag completed the ensemble. Her antique bracelet, emerald ring and gold chain were her only ornaments.

Marshall gave an appreciative whistle as she came towards him in the lobby.

"It's good to see you, Marsh." She lifted her face for his kiss. "How's everybody at home?"

"Fine, and you should see our godchildren. They are growing by leaps and bounds," he answered her proudly.

"They are sweet, aren't they? And Betsy and Tim are such wonderful parents."

"You and I would have been 'wonderful parents' too," he said pensively. "And your dad never ceases to amaze me. He still works in the garden and oversees the farm," he added hastily as though to nullify his first remarks.

"Yes, he's a very special person. I really need to go home soon," she said wistfully. Ever since her return east, Leslie had made it a practice to fly home at least every two or three months. Since her mother's death, she couldn't bear the thought of letting anything else slip upon her. "Now what was that you just said about us being such wonderful parents?"

"Of all sad words of tongue or pen,

"The saddest are these: 'It might have been,'" he countered.

"Well, since I'm not Maude Muller and you're not the judge, why don't we check that dance out? After all, that's why you came, wasn't it? To keep me from being a wall flower?"

"We'll resume this conversation later," he promised.

"Let's do." She couldn't decide how serious he was. It had been years since he'd shown any real romantic interest in her. When she was in need of an escort, he was there. He still spent his holidays with them at White Haven. Tonight, however, she sensed a difference.

The ball room was decorated as a southern mansion with tall white columns and murals of magnolia trees painted on the walls. The orchestra was marvelous. Leslie and Marshall had not lost their love of dancing. At the dinner preceding the dance, they were seated at the table with other nurses and doctors. Leslie was always so proud of Marshall. He could hold his own in any situation whether he was conversing with doctors, lawyers or farmers. Leslie was glad though when dinner was over the floor was cleared for dancing and she could have him to herself.

As they danced, he held her closely and seemed tense as he pressed her body close to his. Maybe the time has come, she thought. He continued to hold her even after the music stopped.

"Why don't we leave?" he asked. "I have something I want to ask you."

"Why not?" She was feeling reckless. She just knew he would ask her to marry him and she would say "yes."

"I'll go and get your jacket," he offered. She was standing alone waiting for Marshall to return when she seemed to feel a presence, even though the room was full of people, of someone behind her.

"Florence?" She recognized a familiar and beloved voice. It had been years since she'd heard it but it seemed like yesterday. Leslie stiffened all over. Her heart raced so, she could hardly control herself. Not but one person in the whole world had ever called her Florence. Finally, mustering all her courage and strength, she turned around to face him, praying that her expression wouldn't give her away.

"Florence, I knew it was you." There he stood—tall, handsome, and nattily dressed in white tie and tails. Still the same snapping black eyes, black hair, graying at the temples. He was so handsome it hurt. Leslie couldn't speak. She didn't realize that she must look just as beautiful and desirable to him. They looked at each other, their hearts showing through their eyes like two people time hadn't changed.

Finally, Stephen said: "Florence, please come with me. I want you to meet my wife."

All the joy and illusion she first felt left her and Leslie was suddenly filled with rage. How dared he? She'd never had such a strong desire to stamp her feet and throw things. *Go on and see this thing through*, she kept telling herself. *Don't let him know how you still feel*.

147

"Of course, I'd love to Stephen." She spoke for the first time. Looking around frantically wondering where Marshall was, she allowed Stephen to escort her across the room.

As they approached, Leslie recognized Ann's profile from the newspaper print as she had memorized every detail. She was talking to one of the doctors. The Ann she was seeing now was older, but still lovely. Her blond hair was curling loosely around her shapely head. Her profile was almost cameo perfect and Leslie thought to herself that it was little wonder she had lost out.

"Ann, Dr. Edwards, I want you to meet an old and very dear friend of mine, Leslie Jane Lee."

Leslie almost fainted when Ann turned to face her. It was only her years of experience as a nurse that enabled her to keep an expressionless face. The beautiful profile she'd just seen left her totally unprepared. The whole left side of Ann's face was an ugly, hideous scar! She wore a mantilla cleverly draped so as to cover most of the side of her face, but Leslie had a full view as she turned to greet her. Leslie's trained eye could detect the evidence of many plastic operations but the result was still pathetic. The left eye was entirely gone. A new lid had been constructed over the artificial eye, and her reconstructed cheek bone failed to cover the cavernous appearance of her face. The scar tissue extended down her neck and even her hand was badly scarred. She wore a long-sleeved dinner gown and Leslie guessed the entire left side of her body must be affected.

"It's nice to meet you."

"Thank you. Stephen has spoken of you," Ann answered simply.

At that moment, the music started and Dr. Edwards turned to Ann and said, "May I have the pleasure?"

"Why yes," she answered, first looking at Stephen for approval. They danced off leaving Leslie and Stephen alone. "Florence?" He held out his arms and without a word Leslie slipped into them. She didn't even notice when Marshall

148

appeared with her jacket over his arm.

All the years in between seemed to vanish in one short moment and once again they were students at Vale University. A happy couple so much in love. Leslie felt the weight of the world drop from her shoulders. As they held each other, they knew their hearts were the same. All the years, doubts and fears left her. Everything could be explained. Ann had had a horrible accident and Stephen had somehow felt obligated to marry her. MARRIED! Just as one weight slipped from her shoulders, another was added. The fact remained that he was married and nothing could ever change that.

"Florence, I must see you," Stephen whispered urgently in her ear as they danced. "Will you have lunch with me tomorrow?"

"Yes," she answered as if hypnotized.

"Meet me at The Commodore at 1 p.m."

The music stopped, Ann and Dr. Edwards returned and it was then she saw Marshall. Feeling a guilty pang of remorse, Leslie quickly made the introductions. The two men sized each other up immediately, remembering that once they had been bitter rivals. Marshall could still read Leslie like a book and he knew she was badly shaken. After a few polite exchanges, Marshall adroitly maneuvered her away. They danced one more dance but his mood had changed and he reverted back to his polite and cynical attitude. They had lost their magic moment. The past had returned to haunt them.

As they left, he suggested an all-night restaurant for breakfast. Marshall lingered over his food but their conversation was strained, almost in monosyllables. Leslie knew he was guarding against the possibility of her having a late date with Stephen. Back at the hotel at four a.m. she felt almost like a school girl coming in late, as the doorman eyed them suspiciously. Marshall all but locked her in her room and ordered her to get some sleep and then meet him for tea at three p.m. She knew he thought he'd taken every precaution to keep her away from Stephen. Well, he just didn't know how wide awake she was!

The final session of the meeting would be that morning and she wanted to attend. After a hot shower, she felt refreshed.

The meeting was over at noon. As she was leaving several people stopped Leslie to compliment her on the paper she had presented and to request copies. She finally got away and hailed a cab to take her to the Commodore. In spite of her excitement, Leslie felt a certain sense of guilt also. This was the first time in her life she'd ever had a clandestine date.

Stephen was waiting for her in the lobby and guided her to a secluded table he'd reserved in the back of the dining room. During the next two hours, Stephen bared his soul to her. She had never seem anyone so emotionally upset as he told her the whole story without bitterness.

After having seen Ann, she had been able to guess at parts of the truth. What she hadn't known was Stephen's mother's determination for him to comply with her wishes and marry Ann. Although she had ostensibly accepted Stephen's decision to marry Leslie, his mother had planned to somehow force him to change his mind. After being pressured by Mrs. Southall, Ann's mother agreed to have Ann's picture and engagement announcement published in the Boston paper.

Mrs. Southall assured Mrs. Howell that once the announcement was made, Stephen wouldn't humiliate Ann by not going through with the engagement that had been planned for years. Stephen learned later that Ann had been so upset when her picture appeared in the paper without her knowledge or consent, she threatened to have a retraction published but the two mothers persuaded her to wait for Stephen.

Due to some last minute emergencies at the hospital, Stephen did not arrive in Boston until after Christmas. By this time the announcement had been made and before he could do anything about it, the accident happened. After confronting his mother with the picture and making her admit that she had engineered the whole thing, Stephen stormed out of the house to find Ann and have it out with her. He felt like if he could get her alone and explain what had

happened, she would understand. When he
arrived at the Howell home, he rudely brushed
aside the congratulations of some well-meaning
guests and asked Ann out for a drive. Because he
was so upset, he knew he was driving too fast
when the car rounded a curve, he lost control
and careened into a light pole. Stephen was
thrown clear, but Ann was trapped inside when
the car caught on fire.

Stephen had suffered a concussion and did
not regain consciousness for four days. Ann was
badly injured and burned over 60% of her body.
For days her life hung in balance.

When Stephen awoke and asked the date, it
was January 2nd.

"Oh how I agonized over our New Year's
Eve date—"

"I tried to call you," Leslie interrupted.
"The maid informed me you were out with your
fiance. You can imagine how that made me feel!
Then the next day, I read your engagement
announcement in the paper and presumed it to
be true."

"That was Mother's order. She forgot to
rescind it after the accident." He swallowed hard
and forced himself to go on: "Florence, I was
almost crazy. Even after I regained
consciousness, I was in the hospital, my leg in
traction for two more weeks. I felt imprisoned.
My father left town—as usual—and I certainly
wouldn't ask Mother to call you. One of the
nurses did try to call for me, but you were out.
Also, we didn't know if Ann would live or die,
then I guess I just gave up!"

He went on to tell her that it was after
weeks of hospitalization when the doctors finally
decided Ann would live, she first learned the
truth about her beautiful face. She was not really
a vain person but was so accustomed to being
beautiful that the shock of realizing suddenly she
was not only not beautiful anymore, but was
hideously scarred and ugly, was more than she
could bear. Stephen felt so responsible. He knew
her very sanity was in danger and probably he
was the only person who could save her. He had
to convince her that the loss of beauty would

have no effect on his feelings for her. His leg was still in a cast, but he stayed at the hospital constantly and tried to forget his own anguish.

Now that Ann was so horribly scarred, Stephen's mother was repulsed. She felt that having such a disfigured wife would be a handicap to him and she urged him to break off the engagement. She was beside herself with guilt and shame and confessed how she and Ann's mother had intercepted his letter telling Ann of his intention to marry Leslie.

If it was possible for a man to hate his mother, Stephen guessed he must hate his. Ann was an innocent victim as was he. He had a great decision to make: either wreck two lives (his and Leslie's) or destroy Ann completely. Stephen sometimes wondered how he retained his own sanity during that time.

"I tried several times to write, but what could I say? I thought if I could just buy some time, maybe when Ann improved I could show her the intercepted letter." It just didn't work that way though. Ann's faith in him was so great and she became so dependent on him he just couldn't tell her. She was still far from well and the psychiatrist told him that only thing that had pulled her through was her assurance of his love.

A year after the accident in 1920, they were married.

"That was the year Margaret and I went to school in London."

"Never a day has passed that I haven't wondered about you; where you were; what you were doing; if perhaps, you had married your Marshall. I wanted to return to Vale and find out but I just couldn't. I was married! I had forfeited my right to you."

Over the years, Ann had undergone over 20 plastic operations and skin grafts. She was greatly improved but still so disfigured. Her injuries had been so extensive that she was unable to have children. Thus their marriage had lacked even that fulfillment.

"Florence, if you only knew the gosh awful hell I've been through. You know I wanted you more than I ever wanted anyone. When we were together at Vale, I was able to restrain myself only because I thought we would soon be married. After I married Ann our relationship was a disaster. Her extensive injuries and contractures prevented any normal relationship. It was painful and almost impossible for her to make love. I always felt like a monster when I—er—"

"Stephen, you shouldn't be telling me this," begged Leslie.

"Florence, I've had a mistress for years. I just couldn't force myself on Ann. It's only in recent years that her contractures have been corrected so that we could er—"

"Honey, please!" Her heart bled for him, but these intimate revelations made her very uncomfortable. His misery had been much greater than hers. At least she hadn't spent the last 19 years living a lie as he had done.

After his marriage, Stephen had thrown himself wholeheartedly into his work. He had a large practice and was also teaching and doing research at the medical school in Boston.

"My work has been my salvation. I would have died without it. We've perfected the heart valve operation. I remember you telling me your baby brother was a 'blue baby.' We are able to save most of those babies now. Our research has paved the way for further heart surgery. I can visualize so many possibilities." He looked at her longingly. "I can see that your career has been important to you also. Not many nurses have achieved a doctorate degree. I'm impressed."

He continued to talk about his life and his work and Leslie listened as though mesmerized. A redemptive joy surged through her. It was as though a life sentence had been lifted and she was free again—free of that feeling of insecurity and rejection she'd harbored so long. Stephen still loved her—he always had.

Before she left, they agreed to have dinner the following night. Ann was meeting with some of her Smith College classmates. Leslie finished her rendezvous with Stephen and then hurried off to meet Marshall. My! What a day she had had. She hadn't slept for 24 hours yet she was

153

strangely exhilarated. Leslie had never felt old, but seeing Stephen again had seemed to erase all the years. She refused to look beyond the present. Stephen loved her and nothing else mattered. Somehow they would work things out.

Marshall was waiting for her in the lobby and together they went into the coffee shop and ordered tea and sandwiches. Leslie certainly wasn't hungry but she had to keep up a pretense. Strange how her entire life had seemed to center around these two men.

"Did you have a nice nap?" Marshall asked, eyeing her quizzically.

"Well, er—no. I just couldn't sleep," she answered truthfully.

He let the matter drop, and then said, "Did you finish your meeting today?"

"Yes, the closing session was this morning. I return to the university tomorrow."

Marshall had an appointment with a client so after he helped Leslie check out of the hotel, he left. They planned to have dinner and see a play that night.

The next day Marshall came over to the university to have lunch with her before he left. She was so preoccupied with her plans to see Stephen that evening, she scarcely spoke during the meal. They ate at the table with some of the other instructors and Marshall kept up a lively conversation, making himself charming to them. Leslie couldn't help but be amused at him—the eternal flirt, she thought.

After lunch they returned to Leslie's office. Marshall sat down and made himself comfortable. She wished he would announce his plans so she could either see him off or bid him goodbye here.

"What time shall we have dinner tonight?" He surprised her.

"Why, I thought you were leaving today!" she exclaimed.

"No, I haven't finished with this client yet."

"Well, I've made another engagement," she said flatly.

"Not with Stephen Southall, I hope?"

"Yes," she gasped. There was no need to lie about it now.

"What time are you meeting him?"

"Eight."

"Then I'll call for you at seven. You're not going to keep that date," he said emphatically.

"Oh, yet I am!" stormed Leslie, sudden anger filling her. Marshall had been playing a cat and mouse game with her all along and she'd not realized it.

"No, you're NOT! I'll not allow you to make a fool of yourself." She had never seen him so angry. "You see, it so happened that I also had lunch at the Commodore yesterday and I saw you walk in switching your tail like a prostitute!"

"Why, how dare you talk to me like that!" Leslie thought she would explode. "And don't you assume any self-righteous attitude around me either. As if I, and everyone else at home, haven't heard about your affairs in Memphis."

"And that's exactly the reason I'm qualified to recognize a gal on the make when I see one," he answered bitterly. "You really dressed yourself up just to impress him, knowing all the while he was a married man and you had no right to him."

"Aw, shut up!" wailed Leslie. She was deeply hurt as she realized the truth of his words. Surely he didn't really believe those awful things about her. "Marshall, this is different." She tearfully tried to explain, "Stephen still loves me, We're entitled to some happiness."

"Leslie, you won't find any happiness or peace of mind if you are a party to wrecking that girl's life."

"Marshall, please try and understand. Stephen has spent twenty years helping Ann. She's no longer sensitive about her scars. She owes all that to Stephen."

"Lessie Lou, you're still a dumb little girl. Can't you understand anything? The minute she loses Stephen, she will lose all that self-confidence. Yes, she holds her head up and looks the world in the face, but do you know why? Because she thinks that bastard loves her. If she

155

ever finds out differently, she's lost."

"I don't care what you say. I love Stephen and he loves me," she stormed. "I've been good all my life and where has it gotten me?" She was almost hysterical.

"Little Lessie Lou, I know you too well," Marshall said tenderly, putting his hands on her shoulders. "You can't mean what you're saying. You're Janie Lee's child and you could never intentionally hurt anyone."

"You leave my mother out of this," said Leslie furiously, backing towards her desk.

"She can't be left out. You know what she'd think of your home-wrecking intents. I'll call for you at seven," he said angrily, reaching for his hat and walking towards the door.

"I'll not be there."

"You'd *better* be."

Leslie was so angry, she grasped the first thing her fingers touched on her desk and hurled it across the room at him. Marshall dodged through the door just as the object shattered against the wall. He stuck his head back in long enough to say:

"I'll see you at 7 o'clock," and slammed the door again.

Leslie was trembling as she walked across the room to investigate the object of her fury. It was then, for the first time, she realized what she had so ruthlessly destroyed!

"Oh," she sobbed, kneeling down trying vainly to piece together her precious little paper weight. The four little boys the girls had given her for Christmas the night Stephen had proposed to her. As she held the little broken pieces in her hand, she leaned against the wall and slowly sank to the floor, weeping bitterly. It was as though, with one swift blow, she'd destroyed forever all her hopes and dreams. Her four little boys.

Marshall knew her even better than she knew herself. For one wild, reckless, idiotic moment she had thought she could turn her back on everything she'd stood for all her life, now sanity had returned and she knew what she must do.

Slowly, she got to her feet, carefully carrying the broken pieces of the figurine back to her desk. She bathed her face and prepared for her class. She finished the day with remarkable calm and poise.

That evening, she dressed very carefully, smiling to herself as she recalled Marshall's words, "You really dressed yourself up." Well, she was determined she would spend as much time and effort dressing to look beautiful tonight. She must hurry if she was to be ready for her 7 o'clock date!

It was a pleasant evening. Marshall had recovered somewhat from his anger and they both chose to pretend their bitter argument had never occurred. After dinner they opted to see the opera Aida at The Metropolitan Opera House. It was late in the evening when they returned to her apartment. At the door, she turned to give him a goodnight kiss, but Marshall brushed past her and came on in.

"It's rather late, honey—"

"I know, but I'm staying a while anyway."

"Please don't worry about Stephen. I promised you I wouldn't see him again and I won't. I must have been out of my mind to think we could erase all those years and start over."

The mention of Stephen's name seemed to infuriate him and her soothing voice had an adverse effect. Marshall gave her a cynical look as he deliberately removed his coat and tie and unbuttoned his collar. She watched him with mild curiosity and was totally unprepared when suddenly he seemed to lose control as he grabbed her and started kissing her roughly, forcing her lips apart, almost bruising her with his passion.

Leslie was so dumbfounded and frightened she was almost paralyzed. Then she rallied and tried desperately to fight him off, but the more she struggled, the more determined he became. He flung her on the couch and stretched out on top of her continuing his hard, brutal kisses. This beast couldn't be her sweet, gentle Marshall. She'd always felt so secure and safe with him but now she was fighting him off like a tiger.

His mouth stifled her scream as he ripped her blouse open and caressed her breast. In spite of herself, she felt a thrill of response. She'd often dreamed of her first sexual experience, but please, God, not like this. She suddenly stopped struggling and started crying, "Oh, Marshall—"

The sound of her tearful voice suddenly jolted Marshall back to reality. "Oh, my God! What have I done?" He got up as though dazed and stared at her, then looked away in embarrassment as she struggled to a sitting position on the couch and tried desperately to cover her bare breasts. He almost staggered into the bedroom, found a robe and brought it back and helped her put it on.

"I'm so sorry—" He gently touched her bleeding lip. "Let me get some ice for that lip." He went to the kitchen and opened the refrigerator. Now he was the Marshall she knew, but he had revealed a self, a demon she never dreamed existed.

"There now. Is that better?" He was gently pressing the ice to her lip.

"Yes, that's fine, thank you." She had the robe securely around her now. "I'll make some coffee. I think we could both use it." Her hands trembled as she held the ice compress to her lip. She went toward the kitchen and he followed her.

"Little Lessie Lou, I'd give my right arm if I could undo what just happened." His voice was hoarse and he looked devastated.

She felt sorry for him. "I know. Please don't be too harsh on yourself, Marshall. I had it coming to me," she said thoughtfully. "I've held you off for years and then the minute Stephen reappears, I toppled over completely. You have every right to be angry."

"But, Leslie, you must know I've never done anything like that before in my whole life—to anyone—" He was pleading.

"I believe you, honey." She gently caressed his cheek. "Now let's not talk about it anymore. The coffee's ready." She was the calm one now and in control. They sipped their coffee in silence, both preoccupied with their own

158

thoughts. She knew she should be outraged but she wasn't. She felt a strange tingle of excitement and when he gave her a goodnight kiss, she wanted to fling her arms around him and beg him to stay, but she felt a sense of shame and let him leave.

The next morning, a dozen yellow roses were delivered to her door. The card read: "I'm sorry. I'll always love you, Marshall."

Leslie had good intentions of not seeing Stephen again but she found he was not to be dismissed so easily. She was able to evade him at the university as her calls came through a secretary, but at home it was a different situation. When he finally reached her and she heard the sound of his mellifluous voice, she found it very difficult to be firm. He wanted to come to her apartment but she wouldn't allow that. She knew she'd promised Marshall she would not see Stephen again, but she felt like their traumatic encounter should nullify any promises made prior to that. Besides, she reasoned, it would do no harm to meet Stephen and hear him out and then reiterate her feelings about divorce. Finally, she agreed to meet him in Central Park that afternoon at 2:00 p.m. Her class lasted till 1:00 p.m. so she left hurriedly. Marshall certainly couldn't accuse her of dressing carefully this time. She didn't realize though that the result was just as pleasing. Leslie had a knack for wearing clothes. She had on a grey skirt and a wine-colored sweater as the days were still a little chilly. Her hair fell loosely around her shoulders and she looked like a school girl. Leslie arrived first and watched Stephen as he approached. He was so handsome, she could almost forget her resolve to give him up. His face lighted up when he saw her. He walked over and held out his hand to help her from the bench and into his arms. Her lips met his almost magnetically and she was thankful they were in the park rather than her apartment. The park looked beautiful with the early spring flowers blooming. White frothy clouds shifted back and forth across the blue sky. Hand in hand, they wandered around the park, stopping at the pond to feed the ducks. To the casual observer they appeared to be a happy couple without a care in the world. Leslie felt she must crowd a lifetime of happiness into this one, brief afternoon because it would be all she would ever have. As she looked at Stephen, she thought how little he had changed and yet so much. The years of his unselfish care of Ann had given him a tender, protective bearing he'd lacked before. Fine lines were etched around his eyes and mouth but this only enhanced his charm. She could just imagine how the young student nurses must all have a crush on him.

"You're smiling." He tightened his grip on her hand.

"I know. It's like turning back the clock. I didn't know it was possible."

"Florence, I'll never give you up. You must know that by now."

"When are you returning to Boston?" she asked, not answering his question.

"Ann is returning tomorrow. I'm staying here until we get something settled."

"You must go back with her, Stephen. I'll never marry you."

"And I'll never give you up. I know you love me. Why else haven't you married? Certainly not the lack of opportunity with old, faithful Marshall still hanging around. —And after all these years of yearning and doubt, we're together again by pure chance. Why I'd be insane to let you go now, Florence."

"Oh," exclaimed Leslie, her backbone suddenly turning to jelly. She had intended to be so firm with him. Life was unfair. She had to make him understand quickly because she knew she couldn't resist him for long.

"You know, Stephen, my family doesn't believe in divorce unless there's a Biblical reason. Ann has never given you any cause for divorce," Leslie explained earnestly.

"No one 'believes' in divorce, Florence!" he said impatiently. "It just happens. Divorce is an accepted fact of life."

"But Stephen, you have such a great
160

responsibility as a doctor. Why my father would never have allowed Dr. Miller to attend my mother or any of us if his character hadn't been above reproach."

"Great Balls of Fire, Florence!" he exploded. "You select a doctor for his knowledge and ability, not his moral standards. Doctors are only human and some of them are regular—"

"I know, darling," she interrupted, unconsciously letting the endearment slip, "but they are in the minority. Most doctors, like most nurses, take their pledge and responsibility seriously."

"Florence, how on earth could you live to be grown and work in New York City of all places, and continue to have such impossible, impractical ideals?" He was becoming frustrated.

"One must have standards to live by and my mother set ours very high."

"I love you, Florence. You and all your quaint, old fashioned ideals. It's not wrong or sinful for two people who love each other to seek happiness."

"It's wrong if there's a third person or maybe a fourth who would be hurt."

"A fourth person? That means Marshall is still involved."

"He's been a part of my life so long, he's definitely involved."

"Oh, my God!" Stephen groaned. "To think how many times we quarreled over that dolt. If it hadn't been for him, we'd have married before you finished Vale."

"Honey, it's useless to look back and wonder what might have been," Leslie said miserably. It was so hard to be strong when you loved someone so much.

"Florence, I love you now and I'll love you until the day I die." They were sitting in a little pagoda and Stephen took her in his arms and kissed her. Just as when they were dancing, Leslie felt the years between fall away. Momentarily she forgot everything except that she was with the man she loved.

"I must go, Stephen," she said, pushing away from him. She had to escape now or she was afraid she'd agree to almost anything.

"I'll see you tomorrow."

"If you really love me, catch that plane for Boston tomorrow," begged Leslie.

"It's no good, Florence."

"Goodbye, Stephen," Leslie rushed out of the pagoda into the park. She was so blinded by tears, she could hardly see her way back to the car. Her one thought was to put distance between herself and Stephen.

When Leslie reached her apartment, the phone was ringing. She refrained from answering it, thinking Stephen might be calling. She was so upset. She just had to pull herself together. Leslie laid down across the bed and longed for her mother and White Haven.

The buzzer sounded shrilly but Leslie decided not to answer.

"Leslie! Are you there?"

Then she recognized Miss Rhea's voice. Miss Rhea was one of her instructors at Columbia University. She got up and opened the door.

"Leslie, I've been trying to reach you, but you weren't in. Then as I was passing by, I saw your lights and decided to try again."

"Oh, I'm sorry," she said, feeling very guilty about not answering the phone. "I just came in."

"Leslie, we are in a most difficult position," continued Miss Rhea. "You know, of course, that Nina Bates was supposed to present a paper and represent our school at the International Council of Nurses in London. Well, she had an acute attack of appendicitis and has had emergency surgery, and can't possibly go. Do you think there is any possibility that you could take her place? I know this is very short notice," she went on to apologize, "but it's most important for this paper to be presented and our school represented. She has a flight reservation on American for tomorrow at 1:30 p.m."

"Yes, I can go," Leslie answered instantly. "My passport is still valid." This must be the answer to her prayers. She had thought of resigning her position and completing her dissertation back at Vale. However, ethics did require that she give proper notice. Now she could leave immediately and still be in good standing with the school. "I'm so sorry about Nina, though," she added, trying not to seem too elated over this trip.

Marshall and Connie

When Marshall arrived in Memphis, he received a telegram from Leslie: "Leaving for London this afternoon to attend the International Council of Nurses." He immediately wired back: "So you had to run away. Bon Voyage."

Since his return he'd had such a let down, abandoned feeling. Certainly a contrast to the ebullience he had felt on the plane flying to New York four days ago. In recent months he'd thought he sensed a change in Leslie; less concentration and intensity about her career and therefore he had hoped maybe at last they could work things out and she would marry him. Now he felt like he was back at Square I.

His work had piled up during his extended absence and he was very busy all morning. After dictating several letters and reviewing some briefs for the next day's trial, it was time for lunch and he didn't want to eat it alone. On an impulse, he decided to call Cornelia. She was married for the past five years now to Jason Thornton, a wealthy banker 20 years her senior, a widower with grown children. They had two small sons. Her family had been pleased with the marriage as Jason was one of the wealthiest men in the nation, far richer than Marshall would ever be. Marshall seldom saw Cornelia now except at the Club or parties, but a strong bond still existed between them and she was the one person in the world he could unburden himself to about Leslie.

She agreed to lunch and he named a small restaurant in Germantown where they'd likely not be recognized and she met him there.

After they were seated, the waitress gave them a menu and left. "You've been to see Leslie?" Cornelia asked.

"How did you know?"

"Because you look as though you've been torn apart. Also, when you said you wanted to talk, I knew."

He hesitated a moment, beginning to feel a little foolish over his need for a sounding board, but them he plunged into it: "The New York visit was a disaster to say the least. When I first got there, it looked for a while like we could get things worked out. We both know there's something lacking in our lives. Leslie's had all the career and acclaim she'll ever need or want. Everything looked good until—well, would you believe that Southall son of a bitch turned up again?—After twenty years?"

"What!" She was aghast. "Surely she wouldn't ever trust him again?"

"Oh, he explained it all away." Marshall was bitter. He then proceeded to give her an account of the whole visit including Leslie throwing the paper weight at him. "She did go out with me and not him that night but then I blew it. I was so crazy with jealousy when we returned to her apartment, I almost raped her."

"Well, why didn't you? That might be just what she needed."

This blunt remark shocked him. "Oh no! Not Leslie—You just don't know her."

"Maybe you don't know her either, Chad. During all these years you've treated her like a fragile doll—like she might break or something," she argued earnestly. "Why you even speak her name with a kind of reverence. I have a feeling that she would enjoy the Chad I know—the bold, aggressive lover."

Before he could answer, the waitress appeared and, realizing they hadn't even looked at the menu, they just ordered the house special which was creamed chicken on egg bread and apple pie. When the waitress left, Marshall continued: "And today I get a wire that she has bolted off to London. She was afraid to face him, I'm sure."

"You'd better be glad she did leave. It's awfully hard to say 'no' to someone you love, or in her case thought she loved. If you remember, I couldn't ever refuse you."

"You refused to marry me."

"And," she continued, ignoring his remark, "you will recall how we agreed to end our relationship, but we didn't. We couldn't resist each other."

165

"I would have married you anytime you said the word," he said again defensively.

"I know, but I didn't relish spending the rest of my life watching you go into a tail spin whenever you saw Leslie. If Jason has any lost loves, at least I don't know about them."

"I just hope you're happy, Connie." She still reminded him so much of Leslie.

"Oh yes, I guess." She shrugged her shoulders. "Anyway, Jason is a fine person. He gives me everything I could ever want, but he's so involved with civic and political affairs, the conglomerate, his bank, and being 'King Cotton' that sometimes I feel like I'm just another one of his prized possessions to show off at parties and conventions. But, I keep telling myself, I chose this life, since I couldn't have you. I actually enjoy being married to one of the richest men in America."

"I wonder how many people are lucky enough to marry the person they really love," he said wistfully.

"I have a feeling you will be, Chad," she said tenderly, placing her hand over his. "When Leslie returns from London, my advice for you is to go after her."

"No, I'll let her lick her wounds over Southall for a while. In the meantime, I won't be lonely." He looked at his watch. It was time to leave. He got up and helped her with her coat.

"Chad, I know I'm the nearest thing you've ever had to your Leslie. Let me help you." She was practically offering herself to him. He looked at her fondly. There was still so much chemistry between them but he knew he shouldn't take advantage of her friendship. He caressed her cheek with his knuckles: "You have helped already. I just needed to talk and you're the only person who knows about Leslie that I feel free to talk to—"

"But Chad, I need you as much as you need me," she pleaded. Marshall hesitated, thinking of all the work left at the office. He certainly hadn't intended for this to happen but being with Connie again had rekindled his desire for her and the frustration he always felt after being

166

with Leslie had increased his need. After all there was just so much a man could resist. "I'll have to call my office." When he returned he asked, "Are you sure this is what you want?"

"Yes, I'm sure."

"Then drive around to the back of the apartment. I'll be waiting for you." He paid the check and left the restaurant first. In a few minutes, she followed.

At the apartment, Cornelia quickly undressed. She was so completely uninhibited as she stretched out on the bed and opened her arms to receive him. Marshall's pent-up passion was so great by this time, he entered her almost immediately. "I'm sorry, Connie. I just couldn't help it."

"That's what I wanted you to do," she said soothingly.

Then he slowly made love to her making sure she had an orgasm. It was good for them to be together. Connie confided how frustrating her relationship with Jason was. "He satisfies himself and I am always left hanging."

"Have you ever told him how you feel?"

"No, he just rolls over and goes to sleep." She pressed closer to him. They made love again. Finally, Cornelia looked at her watch. "I must get home. It's 5 o'clock. Please, Chad, I can meet you here next Thursday—"

"Connie, No!" He stopped her. "What we have done is wrong. It must never happen again." Then he added, "I don't regret today. We needed each other. It was beautiful, but we can't let it happen again."

"But I haven't felt this good in five years," she protested.

"Connie, if you'd respond to Jason like you did to me today, he couldn't help but like it—Promise me you'll talk to him. Tell him what pleases you," urged Marshall.

"If you'll stop having all your silly affairs and tell Leslie how you feel," she said petulantly.

"Leslie knows how I feel. The next move is up to her. Please promise me you'll talk to Jason. You're so young and viable, you mustn't let your

167

frustrations continue. He loves you and would want to please you if you'd only tell him how."

Cornelia arrived home just minutes before Jason. She panicked as the full impact of that afternoon dawned on her. She was mid-cycle and had not used any protection. It was imperative for her to be with Jason tonight. This would be a different role for her as she had never initiated the love making. She had always remained passive and let Jason do his thing. Maybe Chad was right. It was probably as much her fault as his that their relationship was not satisfying to her.

She was clad only in her chemise when he came into their bedroom. His pulse quickened as he surveyed her slim, scantily clad body. She felt a pang of guilt as she put her arms around him and kissed him. It didn't take much to arouse Jason and he quickly laid her down on the bed. She was still so keyed up after Marshall's lovemaking that Jason's slightest touch sent a thrill through her. "Darling, that feels so good!" She held him close. "Please keep doing it." For the first time in their married life, Jason made love to her slowly making sure she was satisfied before he entered her. She had started out to be calculating and lure him to bed for his usual quick lovemaking but this was for real and she was enjoying every minute of it.

"You've never made love to me like this before," she sighed happily as they finished.

"You've never made love to me like this before, either."

"You're always in such a hurry."

"I'm not in a hurry now," he said, kissing her and relishing her response to him. Exultation mixed with guilt assailed her. Being with Chad today was wrong, she knew, but he had made her aware of her own inadequacy. For the first time, she had talked freely to Jason about their lovemaking and her needs, which had resulted in her discovering what a dynamic lover her husband could be.

London, 1939

Leslie cabled Archie she was coming to London. She was looking forward to seeing him again. It had been almost twenty years since she and Margaret had attended school in London. Over the years, she had kept in touch and had returned one time for a visit. Archie and Frances had also visited White Haven in 1922, the year after their return. Leslie had taken her vacation and made an all-out effort to entertain them because she knew the situation might be awkward between Archie and Margaret.

Somehow, things hadn't worked out for them. After her return, Tommy Tyson had renewed his courtship in earnest. He was quite upset over almost losing her. In fact he had already booked passage to London when word came they were returning. Margaret was also being pressured by her parents to marry Tommy. The thought of their only child marrying an Englishman and living overseas was totally unacceptable to them. By the time Archie arrived, Margaret was so emotionally torn between her parents' pleading and Tommy's cajoling that their reunion was less than perfect. Here on her own turf, she viewed him in a different light and trying to recapture the magic was difficult especially with Tommy around constantly. Maybe theirs had just been a rebound romance after all, and both agreed that perhaps it had all been a mistake. Neither one was willing to give up their homeland. It was a heartbreaking decision and Leslie would always remember how, later, she and Margaret had cried over what might have been. Margaret waited another year before she finally gave in and married Tommy. Several years later, Archie married an English girl.

Archie was at the airport when Leslie arrived, helped her through customs and then drove her to the hotel.

"Now tell me about Meg?" was his first question, as she settled back in the car.

169

"Maggie's fine, sweet and beautiful as ever. She's a busy little homemaker and involved in all sorts of school and civic activities. She seems to be happy with my cousin, Tommy. They have a son and daughter—my double second cousins, you know." Leslie hesitated a moment and then said: "But Archie, I have a feeling there's a part of her that will always be in love with you. Neither of us will ever forget our wonderful year over here, and the lasting friendships we made."

London was in a bevy of excitement over the war situation. Mr. Chamberlain had made a valiant effort to secure "peace for our time," but English prestige was at an all time low after the treaty at Munich. British cartoonists made Chamberlain, with his ever-present umbrella, the symbol of appeasement. However, the British people were hopeful that Hitler would abide by the treaty and be content with Poland and the Sudetenland but then the usurpation of Czechoslovakia had stunned the world.

This unrest and uncertainty about the future served as the background for the conference which lasted a week. If war should come, then nursing would be an important part of it. This made the international meeting even more meaningful. Leslie presented Nina's paper and then took voluminous notes of the other reports to take back to the school.

When the meeting was over, Leslie made a short visit to the university, visiting old school friends, then on back to visit with the Lees.

Leslie was anxious to return home, but felt she must fly over to Belgium and visit her brother's grave one last time. Sir Archibald offered to accompany her, but she refused since Hitler had not made any move in that direction yet.

She arrived in Belgium and had to take a bus from the airport. All the trains and buses were filled with soldiers and there was an air of excitement and tension everywhere. When Leslie reached Flanders Fields she couldn't help but weep as she placed flowers on Mack's grave. To think that hardly a generation later, the world was once again in an upheaval. Had his death, then, been in vain? Would other fine boys also have to give up their lives?

Leslie returned home in June before England declared war in September of 1939. In the meantime, her class had been completed by another instructor, leaving her free to return to Vale and resume her duties as dean. She was allowed time to complete the final details of her dissertation before assuming full control. It was so good to be back "home" with her friends. Each year at homecoming, many of her classmates returned for class reunions. During the years she had managed to keep up with most of them.

Alice and Helen were married and raising families in distant cities. Alice had married an architect she met at Vale. Helen had returned to Dallas and married her high school sweetheart and was living on a ranch. Leslie had been a bridesmaid at each of their weddings. Her other friends who had not married had attained high positions in their profession.

Sharon was the only one who had married a doctor. Sharon and Bob were most interested in Leslie's account of her meeting with Stephen. They had been surprised to receive a letter from him trying to explain away the past and asking if they knew of Leslie's whereabouts. They hadn't answered the letter. Bob had, of course, heard of Stephen professionally due to his widely publicized operations and research in the heart field.

Leslie had always thought she was happy with her life and her career, but seeing Stephen again followed by her traumatic encounter with Marshall had left her confused and unhappy. If only Stephen had stayed lost, she thought, maybe she and Marshall would be on their honeymoon by now. Whenever she felt dissatisfaction and self-pity, she always used Sharon as her sounding board.

"Sharon, I've made such a complete mess of my life. I feel like a failure! I've lost Stephen forever and Marshall never bothers to ask me to marry him anymore. And because I've been such a puritan virginal fool all my life, I've driven two good men into frustrating affairs with other women and now, I'm being paid back for it all."

"Now, now, Les, you're just feeling sorry for yourself," soothed Sharon. "Suppose we just face the facts and do a little soul searching. After you lost Stephen, you really didn't want to get married, did you? Didn't your career become the most important thing in your life?"

"At that time, maybe yes, but now—I don't know."

"But you've brought about changes that will affect future generations. Because of your persistent courage, nursing educational standards have been raised. You have your four year Baccalaureate program—"

"Other schools also have it," she interrupted.

"But you spearheaded it," insisted Sharon. "And look at your personal accomplishments! Why you have a PhD! How many nurses have achieved that level? And by so doing you have paved the way for future nurses." Although Sharon did not finish nursing school, she had never lost interest in her once intended profession.

Sharon put her hands on Leslie's shoulders and gave her a gentle shake. "Don't you ever let me hear you say you're a failure again."

Leslie smiled as she put her arms around Sharon. "Oh, Sharon, you can always make me feel better. Thank you."

Three months had passed now and she was far away from New York. Apparently Stephen had accepted the fact that there could never be anything between them.

One day as she was hurrying from school to her parked car, Leslie was almost electrified as she heard a familiar voice say, "Florence, wait for me."

She turned around to see Stephen walking towards her. He was dressed in the uniform of the Royal Air Force.

"Oh, Stephen, you shouldn't have come."

172

"Florence, didn't you know you couldn't keep running?" he said gently as he slipped in the seat beside her. "Sometime, somewhere, I'd be bound to find you."

"I know, Stephen, but it's all so wrong," she said sadly. "What do you have on?" She became aware of his uniform for the first time.

"I've volunteered as a flight surgeon to the Royal Air Force for a special mission. Our research team will monitor the pilots and crew during air raid missions for heart reactions under duress."

"Won't it be terribly dangerous?"

"All war is dangerous. My assignment will be only for two months."

"But why on earth did you have to get involved in a war that isn't even ours?" she protested earnestly.

"It will be ours."

"Oh, no, no!" Leslie just couldn't face the possibility of another war.

"Well, Florence, don't worry your pretty little head now. I only came to say good-bye. I just had to see you one more time. I have been by to see Bob and we are invited to their home for dinner tonight. Please come with me. There can be no harm in a get-together of old friends."

"Are you alone?" She couldn't believe they were sitting together in the car talking so calmly.

"Of course. I came just to see you and bid you goodbye. I will give you up, but I'll always love you."

"How is Ann?" asked Leslie, blinking back the tears.

"Ann is as kind, sweet and patient as ever. You were right not to let me hurt her. When I returned to Boston after you so unceremoniously left New York, we learned that she was pregnant. That's why I will be gone only for a short time. I need to get back to be with her during the later stages of her pregnancy and during delivery."

"Why, Stephen, congratulations," said Leslie, momentarily forgetting her own anguish. "Will she be all right?"

"I hope so. Dr. Wilson told me that it did

173

happen sometimes for a woman to get pregnant during the menopause when she had apparently been unable to do so before."

"I'm glad for you, Stephen. It's so wonderful to have children." Leslie wept, thinking of her four little boys.

"Thank you." Stephen couldn't allow himself to say more.

That night, Sharon literally put "the big pot in the little one." The girls were home from college and they joined them for dinner as Sharon was anxious to have Stephen meet them. It was a pleasant, family gathering. The girls had dates and left soon after dinner.

As they settled down in the drawing room for coffee, Leslie was more relaxed and happy than she had been for a long time. She knew this was the end for her and Stephen. Always before there was a nagging doubt and uncertainty.

It was like old times as the friends laughed and talked together. The two doctors enjoyed comparing their schools and programs of study. They were all enthralled over Stephen's accomplishments and his plans for the future. Stephen and Leslie sat on the couch together. Being together even for such a short while was a bonus they both treasured. Leslie was content to just listen.

At a late hour, Bob made ready to drive Stephen to the airport. He requested the girls not to come. "I'd rather remember you as you are here," he said smilingly, surveying Sharon in her red velvet evening gown and Leslie resplendent in black. "I'm going to kiss your beautiful wife, Bob," he said, pulling Sharon towards him. Then he turned towards Leslie. Bob and Sharon turned awkwardly away, not knowing what they should do. Sharon went out into the hall to get their coats and Bob followed.

"Florence," whispered Stephen, taking Leslie in his arms. "I'll love you till the day I die. May the good Lord bless and keep you always." He kissed her tenderly at first, and then as though their will suddenly yielded to their desires, he was kissing her passionately, almost forgetting Bob and Sharon in the hall. Leslie was the first to recover as she gently pushed him away. "Goodbye, Stephen." She couldn't trust herself to say more. He kissed her again and then went out into the hall where Sharon was waiting. Bob was already warming the car up in the driveway. Stephen, tears streaming down his cheeks, gave Sharon a final kiss as he rushed out.

As Sharon closed the door, Leslie felt as though she was closing the final chapter on her life with Stephen. Sharon was leaning against the door sobbing as though her heart would break. She had known such great happiness with Bob that it hurt her to know her dearest friend had not been so blest.

Leslie, however, could feel nothing but relief. She knew Stephen would keep his word and not try and see her again.

Strangely enough, it was she who was consoling Sharon, instead of vice versa.

Florence

"Really, Stephen! I've never known anyone in either of our two families named Florence." Mrs. Southall was standing beside her son looking through the viewing window at the small cuddly bundle of pink lying in a incubator. She had just been delivered by caesarean section and appeared to be in good condition.

"I'd appreciate it, Mother, if you'd just shut up! Her name is Florence Ann. She will be called Florence." Stephen was in no mood to argue with his mother. He'd spent the last two days and nights at Ann's bedside. When it became apparent she would be unable to deliver her baby, the decision was made to perform a caesarean. Stephen couldn't help but reproach himself for ever allowing this pregnancy to happen, but he knew how much Ann wanted a baby, as did he. It was as though she felt that by giving him an heir, she could repay him somewhat for all his years of entrapment. He'd just been informed by the obstetrician that his wife had had an adverse reaction to the anesthetic and had lapsed into a coma. She was brain dead but her life could continue for months—even years.

Stephen squeezed back the tears as he tried to ignore his mother's constant babbling. Would there never be an end? He should never have left on that overseas mission. He knew that now, but because of the months of planning and research involved he'd gone on, thinking he would be back in plenty of time. However, Ann developed complications and Stephen had to rush back and barely arrived in time for the premature delivery. He thanked God that Ann was still in her room and semiconscious and was aware he was there and cared. "I do love you, Ann. Please get well so that, together, we can raise this baby we're about to have." He was holding her hand to his lips and she opened her eyes and smiled. This was the first time Stephen had ever actually voiced his love her her. "I love you too," she answered happily. "Our baby will be the most wanted baby ever born. He's just bound to be perfect."

Shortly afterward, Ann was rushed to the delivery room. Feelings of guilt and regret assailed Stephen as he realized that he must have loved her for a long time, but his stubbornness and deep hatred for his mother had blocked his acceptance of this marriage he felt had been forced on him. During all their years together, he recalled, Ann had never once complained or reproached him about the accident. The medical community had accepted and admired Ann for her durability and refusal to indulge in self-pity. Stephen was made keenly aware of her popularity by the stream of visitors and the outpouring of love for this brave little mother who had literally given her life to have this baby. It was a well known fact among the old-timers that during her coming-out year, Ann Howell had been one of Boston's most beautiful and popular debutantes and could have had her choice of any number of eligible bachelors—until the accident.

In spite of her scars and handicaps, she had ably fulfilled her duties as the wife of a distinguished doctor and dean of the medical school. She hosted innumerable dinner parties for his colleagues and visiting doctors. Her scars were cleverly concealed by mantillas that matched her gowns.

Stephen had always respected and appreciated her and now he thanked God that she never knew about Leslie. She probably suspected his involvement with various mistresses during her many operations and convalescences but had never let on that she knew.

He could understand now how Leslie had been so torn between her love for him and her loyalty to Marshall. It was possible to love two people. He knew that now.

Feeling both physically and emotionally exhausted, Stephen left the hospital. His mind was busy trying to think things through and decide what would be best for all concerned. Some arrangements would have to be made for

Ann's care in a nursing home and a nanny to care for the baby. He would resume his teaching and research work at Boston University Hospital, where he would be near his child.

Ann's younger sister had small children and Stephen felt like she would help him. Florence could be a frequent visitor to her cousins and this would give her life some normalcy.

Stephen resolved to devote the rest of his life to his little Florence. Under no circumstances would he ever allow his mother to have any role in her upbringing.

He had a daughter now and he'd named her for the two women he loved and he'd lost both of them. Remembering his own bleak childhood, he was determined that hers should be happy and fulfilling.

1941

Once again the years slipped by. Dean Lee was still a dominant figure at Vale University and a nationally recognized leader in nursing. She had frequent requests for speaking engagements and seminars. Several interesting positions were offered to her, but she saw no reason to change. Besides she enjoyed being near Sharon and Bob and sharing the love of their two daughters who called her "Aunt Lessie."

Sharon was very much the society matron, entertaining frequently for the faculty and visiting doctors. Whenever she had an extra man, Leslie was persuaded to fill in. Except for these occasional dates, Leslie's social life was absent of men. Church and school activities kept her very busy, but she had to admit she missed Marshall terribly.

Sharon sensed that something must have happened because Marshall hadn't been to Vale in over a year. On her persistent questioning, Leslie finally broke down and told her about their last date. Sharon wasn't the least bit shocked. "That's wonderful, Les! I'm so glad to hear it! I was beginning to think he wasn't human."

"Sharon!"

"Les, I think it's up to you to make the first move," Sharon said thoughtfully. "He's probably so ashamed of himself, he'll never call you."

"But wouldn't I just be asking for it, if *I* called him?"

"Would you mind so much?" Sharon questioned her seriously.

Leslie was stunned into silence.

"Be honest with yourself, Les. Wouldn't you like to go to bed with him? The man loves you. He wants to marry you."

"I know I miss him terribly," Leslie admitted. "Sometimes I want to call him and propose myself, but what would he think?"

"He'd think you were the warm, human, passionate woman he's been in love with so long. Now go call him immediately! Just try being yourself, for once."

Leslie opted to write instead. She couldn't trust herself to talk. She invited Marshall to White Haven for Thanksgiving and concluded her letter with this: "Please come, Marshall. Father has missed you terribly. He can't understand why you haven't been around in so long, and," she added, "I miss you too. I really do. Love, Les."

Marshall accepted immediately and wrote his apologies for neglecting her father so long. Political activities, which was partly true, and a heavy case load was his excuse.

Tom was so happy to see Marshall, and Marshall was just as happy to be "back home." He gave a whistle of approval as he saw Leslie. He had always been so complimentary of her and she did look beautiful in a simple winter-white dress with a red sash. She seemed to have inherited Janie's quality of perpetual youth. At age 42, her hair was still black with a tiny streak of grey through the center. Her weight was still a slim 125 lbs.

Mary and Betsy had prepared their usual sumptuous dinner. Mary was "crippled up with rheumatism" but still managed to help Betsy when she needed her. All in all, it was a happy holiday and everyone enjoyed it. The children were so glad to see their "Uncle Marshall," they hardly left his side. It was a family oriented day, leaving little time for Leslie and Marshall to be alone and talk. A pre-trial conference and an interview with a key witness necessitated his immediate return to Memphis. Leslie accompanied him to the door.

"It's good to be back, Leslie."

"I can't begin to tell you how much I've missed you," she answered.

"What a hellava time for me to have to leave," he said as he kissed her. "I'm coming to see you next weekend."

"I'll look forward to it." She blushed in spite of herself.

He smiled, kissed her again, and left.

180

Marshall arrived on the late Saturday afternoon flight and Leslie met him at the airport. It was easy to spot him in the crowd as he towered above most of the passengers. When he saw Leslie in her maroon, hooded coat and fur-lined boots, he gave his usual whistle of approval.

"Does this mean I'm forgiven?" he asked as he leaned down to kiss her.

"I'll forgive you, if you'll forgive me."

"For what?"

"For being such a goose for so long."

"Oh, but I love gooses!" It was so good to have him back. She was trying to act natural like old times, but she knew there was no turning back now and that things would never be the same between them again. The first snow of the season was falling and the dreary buildings of the city were transformed into a fairyland. The sidewalks were slippery and they laughed as they made their way through the parking lot and found her car. She handed him the keys.

"Shall we stop somewhere for a bite to eat?" he asked as he slid under the wheel.

"I've already fixed something at the apartment."

"Looks like you're a jump ahead of me."

"Unless you'd like to stop by Sharon and Bob's."

"No, let's go to your place. I rather like that." He drove slowly through the heavy traffic. When they reached the apartment, he drove the car in the garage. He brought his bag in, saying that he'd call a cab later.

The tension between them was obvious as they ate the dinner Leslie had prepared. Their conversation centered around Marshall's plans to return to Jackson and practice law with Timothy in his dad's old law firm. The death of his uncle and aunt had released him from his obligation, although he had strong ties in Memphis, he still preferred to return home.

When they finished dinner, Leslie poured their coffee and suggested going into the living room. Marshall followed her.

"You'd make a perfect wife, little Lessie

181

Lou."

"Yes, I know—" She grinned at him.

Marshall settled down on the couch and, looking at her sternly, said, "All right, Les, game-playing time is over. I warn you before I say anything more that this will be the last time I'll ever ask you—"

"In that case the, the answer is 'yes.'" she interrupted him.

He continued as if he were reciting a prepared speech. "Will you mar—WHAT!" he shouted, knocking the coffee cup off the table.

"I said yes, I thought you'd never ask—" she laughed, dropping to her knees to clean up the spilled coffee.

He was down beside her. "Let it go! I'll buy a new rug." They were laughing and crying as Marshall crushed her to him. Suddenly they were lying on the floor and she was responding to his ardent embraces. All her doubts and fears were gone. After so many years of waiting, loving, hating, yearning, restraints and frustrations, it was almost impossible for Marshall to halt now.

In spite of his ardor and desire, Marshall remembered their last date and felt he just mustn't let anything mar this moment for them. He wanted their first experience to be a happy one for her.

"You know how much I love you and want you, Lessie, but are you sure?" he asked huskily.

"I love you too," she answered, squeezing his neck. "I'm just sorry we've waited so long." He kissed her again and then gently picked her up and carried her to the bedroom. As he helped her undress, he continued to show remarkable restraint. He felt that he must blot from her memory forever the night when he'd completely lost control.

Later, as they were lying in bed, Leslie felt complete fulfillment for the first time in her life. She still couldn't believe she'd actually gone to bed with a man and not be married to him and surprisingly enough, she didn't even care anymore.

Marshall was almost apologetic as he kissed her. "I love you, little Lessie Lou. We'll get
182

married in the morning."

"On Sunday?"

"December 7th, 1941—A day to remember."

They slept late the next morning. Their discovery of each other had been so exciting, neither one of them could sleep but wanted to make love again and again.

Leslie awakened first and watched Marshall as he slept. She had known him all her life but really hadn't known him at all. She felt so content and comfortable. Not the wild tumultuous feeling she always had with Stephen, but she knew their marriage would be happy and exciting. Marshall turned over, opened his eyes, stretched contentedly and kissed her.

"Are you hungry?" she asked, returning his kiss.

"Yes, for you." Leslie had thought she would be embarrassed, but she felt only exultation and satisfaction as she allowed Marshall to explore her body and love her.

Later on, she slipped out of bed and went to prepare breakfast. Marshall came into the kitchen in his shorts. "Seems like I had a bag last night. Have you seen it?"

"Over by the door. You were going to a hotel. Remember?"

"Oh, yes. I do remember now having a change of plans." He found his robe in the bag and put it on. Leslie brought the paper in and they sat at the table, eating, reading and talking. She marveled at how much fun they were having and reproached herself for not allowing it to happen long ago.

After breakfast, she curled up on the couch. Marshall turned the radio on and sat down beside her, putting his arm around her shoulders. It was as though he had to keep touching her to convince himself it was for real. The radio music was soothing and they were content just being together until suddenly the program was interrupted by a grave-voiced announcer who said:

"Ladies and gentlemen, we interrupt this broadcast to bring you a special news bulletin

183

just received from Washington: 'Pearl Harbor has been bombed by planes from a foreign power, presumed to be the Japanese—'"

They were both so stunned. Of course they knew the war situation was serious but had hoped against hope that the United States would not get involved. It was almost a repeat of a bad scene they'd played before. He took her in his arms and she laid her head on his shoulder and cried. "I'm so sorry, sweetheart. Looks like we're being cheated again."

Marshall was so tense. "Leslie, I'll have to report to my commanding officer. I still have my commission in the Reserves." He went to the bedroom and started dressing. "Honey, please call the airport and see if I can get an earlier flight out."

Leslie was able to get his reservation changed and then she dressed hurriedly to drive him to the airport.

The scene at the air terminal was more like pandemonium than a station. Some people were hysterical, others in numbed shock desperately trying to get return tickets to the safety of their homes. "I shouldn't have allowed you to come down here," said Marshall, concerned over her driving back alone.

"Don't worry about me, I'll be fine. Besides, I need to be here. Every minute with you is precious." She was being brave again but inside she had the most empty, miserable feeling. How could this happen when her life was just beginning to have such wonderful new meaning? They clung together until the flight to Memphis was called. "Leslie, I'll call you just as soon as I've reported in." He kissed her and then was gone.

The next day, Leslie went immediately to the president of the university and stated her wish to join the army. If Marshall was going, she might as well go with him.

The kindly old dean heard Leslie through before he asked: "Dr. Lee, pardon me for being so personal, but how old are you?"

"Er—43." She had to stop and think.

"Well, my dear, can't you see that you would be of much more value to your country right here?"

"But I stayed home during the last war. I've just got to get in this one!" she pleaded.

"I know how you must feel. There will, of course, be a great demand for nurses, but you, as head of a large university school of nursing are invaluable in the preparation and education of young nurses into the profession. We don't know how long this conflict will last, but there will be a constant need for trained personnel. You duty is right here," he finished apologetically.

"I guess you're right," conceded Leslie, blinking back the tears.

"Please don't look so downcast, child," begged the dean. "It will be harder to stay home than to go. You'll not receive any of the honor or glory that you might in the army, only the satisfaction of a job well done. I won't tell you not to go, but by continuing in your teaching role, you can send Uncle Sam one hundred young graduates, whereas if you go yourself, there will be only one. Why don't you think it over and come back tomorrow and we'll talk about it some more."

"All right," agreed Leslie. She knew he was right, but it was so hard to stay home again.

Marshall called that night and said he had reported to the base. He would be given time to straighten out his affairs and transfer his law practice to his partners, before being sent to Washington for his assignment.

She agreed to meet him at White Haven for Christmas.

This proved to be another sad homecoming and so reminiscent of 1917 when Mack and Marshall had left together. When he came over, Marshall tried to comfort her as he had long ago at their first parting.

"I'm so sorry, sweetheart. It's just not fair."

"Marshall, I wanted to enlist but Dean Brown convinced me that I should continue as dean of the School of Nursing."

"He's right, of course. Besides, I want you here when I return."

"And when will that be?"

"I'm hoping to be back within six months. I've been promised a position in Washington with the Joint Chiefs of Staff. My overseas assignment will consist of a firsthand evaluation of our bases and installations."

"Then we'll have to wait again?"

He kissed her on the nose. "It won't be like last time—"

"—But we're being separated just as we finally got together."

"Les, do you want to get married before I leave? I only have two days."

She thought that was what she wanted but—"Yes, I do, but maybe we should wait. While you're gone, I'll get someone lined up to replace me as dean. There's a lot to be done and I can make my contribution to the war effort by doing what I do best—teaching students to become responsible nurses."

"I want you waiting for me in New York," he said, kissing her. "We'll get married the minute I return."

"I'll also be there when you leave," she said emphatically. Suddenly she was assuming the role of aggressor. Now that she had experienced love, she wanted and needed every chance to be with him and enjoy the intimacy she had waited for so long.

Mrs. Marshall Chadwick

Marshall returned from his tour of duty in December 1942, and true to her promise, Leslie resigned from her position as dean and met him in New York.

They had planned to have a very quiet and private wedding but Betsy wouldn't hear of it. If she couldn't get Leslie to come home to White Haven, then she would bring White Haven to New York. Leslie was finally able to persuade Marshall to wait for the family and have a "proper wedding."

"Sweetheart, it's not as though we were missing anything," she said. "We'll be together every day and night."

"You know you're a little hypocrite, don't you?" he said with mock seriousness. "Wearing your grandmother's wedding veil when all the time, you're a fallen woman." He loved to tease her.

"I know, but you're about to make an honest one of me." Now that she had found the fulfillment of loving someone, her values had changed but she still felt some pangs of guilt over their premarital relationship and would be glad when they were actually married. "Honestly, Marshall, I believe it would break Betsy's heart if she didn't get to 'do' my wedding for me."

"Whatever you say, honey." He kissed the tip of her nose. "Two more days won't matter as long as we're together." He was serious now as he put his arms around her. "Leslie, I love you so much. I want you to know I didn't, er—do anything or go out with anyone the whole time I was gone. All I could think of was to get back to you as fast as I could." He kissed her tenderly. "I'll never let you go again."

She snuggled closer to him. "We're together now and that's all that matters and I intend to spend the rest of my life trying to make it up to you for being such an idiot for so long."

Betsy arrived the next day and Leslie was

busy scurrying around with her, consulting the florist, caterers and the minister. Margaret and Sharon spread the word and soon the hotel was filled with cousins, Alice, Helen and their husbands, even Dennis Raymond and his wife along with Marshall's law partners and several army buddies.

The Little Church Around the Corner was hastily decorated, and the results were pleasing. Leslie's 73-year-old father gave her away and she looked beautiful in her mother's wedding gown. Colonel Marshall Chadwick was a commanding presence in his army uniform. Betsy and Tim were their only attendants.

It was a lovely wedding and Leslie was glad after all, to be surrounded by family and friends. Betsy and Tim had engaged a suite at the Astor Hotel for the reception and Leslie and Marshall were toasted and "roasted" at the same time.

"Leslie Jane Lee, we've had to wait a long time for this. You surely couldn't cheat us out of being here," was Sharon's comment.

"I don't know how we could have ever thought of doing it without you," Leslie said as she kissed Bob and Sharon. "You are my dearest friends. Our reasoning for a quiet wedding, I guess was the war and also the fact that we're really not young anymore. Anyway, I'm so happy you're all here."

The city-wide blackout prevented too much of a celebration and so, at an early hour, the newlyweds were able to slip away. "Well, thank goodness!" Marshall heaved a sigh of relief as they reached their hotel room.

"I feel the same way, sweetheart, but wasn't it sweet of everyone wanting to be with us?" She kissed his cheek as she started to enter, but Marshall reached out his hand and stopped her. "*Mrs*. Marshall Chadwick." He made a pompous bow. "Since we've observed all the other traditions, let's not stop now." He then swooped her up in his arms and carried her over the threshold.

"Mrs. Marshall Chadwick," she repeated as big tears welled up in her eyes. "It sounds so beautiful. Thank you, darling." It suddenly seemed unreal—that her long wait was over. He put her down gently as he kissed her. "Mine at last." He crushed her to him and they forgot everything except each other. Finally Leslie called a halt: "Sweetheart, be careful! Help me out of this dress. Remember, Betsy has to pack it away for the next generation."

"Gladly, my dear. You know something? I've been wanting to undress you all day."

The next day, Marshall and Leslie left for Washington, where they finished out the war with Marshall serving with the Joint Chiefs of Staff and Leslie doing volunteer work at the hospital.

The war seemed even more real and sinister this time. During World War I, the only information available to the waiting world was news bulletins and newspaper stories bringing the battle news several days after the fact. Now the radio blasted out daily, giving almost on the scene news of campaigns, victories, and defeats. Each morning Leslie would tune in and agonize for the British people and the French underground. She wondered how they could continue to survive under such constant bombardment. She remembered how terrified she once was for fear the Kaiser would dominate the world. Now Hitler was the dragon and, she realized even more formidable than the Kaiser had ever been.

Being a member of such a large family, it was inevitable that she would become involved again. She thanked God daily that Marshall was home safely, but so many of her cousins were in the armed forces. Lee and David Tyson's sons were in the army. Jerome and Thomas's boys were still too young. Greer, William, and Archibald McBryde had draft-age sons so Leslie received frequent letters from Aunt Clara and Aunt Elizabeth informing her of the whereabouts of their grandchildren.

Early in the war, word was received that David Tyson Jr. had been captured at Bataan and after surviving the "Death March," was incarcerated in a Japanese prison camp. The whole family agonized over his plight but was helpless to do anything other than send care packages and messages through the Red Cross. Bill McBryde III was among the paratroopers who came tumbling out of the sky on D-Day. The air drop was badly scattered and Bill was shot down over the Channel and drowned. His body was never recovered. Leslie was also saddened over the the death of Jake Jones, Mary's grandson. He was one of the Marines taking part in the invasion of Iwo Jima. Leslie could remember all these boys as youngsters when they had romped and played on the lawn at White Haven.

They were lucky in that the other boys came home safely—even David Jr. who was a gaunt skeleton of his former self, but was nursed and coddled by his family and friends and within a short while regained his weight, but it would take years and years for him to recover and cope with his nightmares and fears.

Leslie grieved over her own family members, but when President Roosevelt died of a cerebral hemorrhage on April 12, 1945, she wept almost uncontrollably. "But victory is so near!" she sobbed to Marshall. "It's almost like Moses looking at the Promised Land."

When the war was over, Marshall resigned his commission and they returned to Denmark and reopened Marshall's home Inglenook. Marshall would resume his law practice with Tim who had maintained the firm since Mr. Chadwick's death. The firm was now known as Chadwick and Marshall.

Leslie found it surprisingly easy to settle down as a member of the community. Twenty-five years of her life had been devoted to the profession she loved, but now she was determined to be just as efficient as a homemaker. Being near Betsy and Margaret and their children was the happiest part. The children were at various stages: Janie was 15; Lee, 13; Tim Jr., 11; and little Mack was 6. Margaret's Meg was 16 and Tommy Jr., 20. They all loved Leslie and Marshall so much and would take turns spending the night at Inglenook. Leslie's life was busy and fulfilling and she marveled now at how her mother had devoted so much time to the family and yet was active in church and community affairs.

As Leslie grew older, the more nostalgic she became over family ties and the reunions that used to be such a bore to her. Because of the war and the family members being scattered, these get-togethers were a thing of the past but she had a strong urge to revive this custom. Aunt Clara lived with Margaret and Tommy in Jackson, and Aunt Elizabeth had moved to Medina with Laura and her family. Aunt Margaret insisted on remaining independent and lived alone at Forest Home. With their help along with Betsy and Margaret doing most of the work, all family members were contacted and a systematic reunion schedule was worked out. Leslie put her writing skills to work and compiled a family genealogy and wrote a charming history about the family. Each cousin was presented with a copy at their first reunion. A log would be kept at all subsequent reunions, thus starting a treasured heritage for future generations.

Since their marriage in 1942, Marshall and Leslie had never been apart. It was as though they felt they had to make up for a lifetime of separation. Their physical relationship was still as exciting and satisfying as it had been that first night in 1941.

"Lessie Lou, maybe it's just as well you made me wait so long for you. I believe we appreciate and cherish each other more than the average couple."

"I'm just lucky you were still there when I, as my father would say, 'finally came to my senses!'"

"Any regrets?"

"Only that it didn't happen sooner so we could have had our four little boys." They were lying in bed and Leslie could sense that something was troubling Marshall. She took his face between her hands so she could look in his eyes. "What is it, honey?"

"I can't seem to hide anything from you."
He hesitated a moment and caressed her face
with his hands. "Leslie, I know we both love our
tranquil life here at Denmark after so many
years of upheaval, but could you consider giving
it all up?"

"Whatever for?" Leslie was shocked. She had
thought she would be a suburban matron for the
rest of her life.

"I've been approached to run for the U.S.
Senate." He studied her face as he blurted it out.

"Why that's wonderful, Marsh—if that's
what you want." He'd always been active in
politics, but she never dreamed he would ever
consider becoming a candidate.

"Well, yes, I think I do and yet I'm not sure
I should put you through a political campaign.
They can get pretty rough and nasty." He
studied her face.

"Wasn't it President Truman who said, 'if
you can't stand the heat, get out of the
kitchen?'" She hesitated a moment as she thought
wistfully that she would be giving up forever
something very precious to her—her privacy, but
she could sense this challenge was very important
to him, so she said: "If you want to get in the
kitchen, then I'm willing to get in there with
you."

He was real pleased but felt he must make
her understand all the ramifications of such a
decision. "There'll be all sorts of charges. Do
you realize they'll probably drag up my
escapades in Memphis? Also, the Foster family is
very powerful in that part of the state and I
don't think they ever quite forgave me for that
broken engagement, even though it was actually
Connie who refused to marry me after she saw
you."

"But Marshall, that's so long ago."

"It doesn't matter. They'll drag up
everything! Politics is like that."

"It's not as though I didn't already know
about your 'escapades' as you call them. As for
Cornelia, she's happily married and I'm sure she
can think of us only with compassion and love.
Why can't our campaign strategy be focused on
192

your brilliant law career, all the cases you've won, your work and loyalty to the party and the fact that you've served your country through two world wars!" She raised up in bed, slapped her fist in her hand, and said, "What the heck! Let's get in there and fight."

Marshall laughed. She was so fired up and sincere. "Oh my God, how I do love you. You were worth waiting a lifetime for." He pulled her towards him. "Let's wait until tomorrow to start the campaign. We've got more important things to do tonight."

The Senator from Tennessee

For the first time since their marriage, Marshall and Leslie were forced to separate. The campaign trails took them in different directions, but as often as possible, they campaigned together. This was good for the cause as they made a handsome couple. She was 52 and he was 56 but both looked at least ten years younger.

Everything Marshall predicted came true. His affairs in Memphis were aired, but since most of the ladies involved were married now, it wasn't likely that any of them would come forward.

Betsy and Margaret suggested that Leslie organize the women for Marshall and they helped her plan tea parties and receptions. Marshall attended some of the functions, but mostly Leslie. She had nurse friends all over the state due to her activities in the ANA (American Nurses Association) and the TNA, the state organization. Margaret and Betsy had teacher friends, so help came from many sources.

When they were campaigning in Memphis, Leslie called Cornelia who offered her home for a reception, thus forestalling any gossip about the broken engagement. She and Marshall had remained friends over the years and she was glad to help him out now.

As the last guest departed, Marshall and Leslie were expressing their thanks to Cornelia when two little boys came bounding into the room.

"Mama, John broke my horn," shouted the younger child. "He wouldn't let me play with it—"

Cornelia, obviously flustered, separated the boys. "These are my sons, John and Ben. I don't know what happened. They were supposed to be at camp all afternoon." Then holding each by the hand she led them over to Leslie and Marshall. "Boys, I want you to meet Mr. and Mrs. Chadwick. Mr. Chadwick will be our next senator."

Leslie and Marshall were amused at the

antics. Marshall solemnly shook hands with the boys. Leslie smiled as she accepted John's hand. Suddenly all the breath seemed to leave her body as she found herself looking into Marshall's blue eyes! The little boy was the image of Marshall, even the dimple in his chin. She looked up and met Cornelia's pleading look and almost imperceptible shake of her head, as if begging her to forget what she had seen. Then as if in a trance, she shook hands with Ben. Marshall was playing with the boys, completely unaware of the by-play between the two women.

Why, he doesn't even know, thought Leslie! Not even after seeing himself as he must have been at that age. She mentally calculated John (Marshall's first name) to be about 9 years old. This would be about the time Stephen reentered her life and caused Marshall to leave her and seek solace elsewhere.

It broke her heart to realize Marshall had a son—a son he didn't even know about and could not acknowledge if he did know. A child she couldn't give him. This was a burden she'd have to bear alone. She couldn't tell him and betray Cornelia, who obviously hadn't intended for the boys to be around today. A power failure had forced the camp to close early.

"You have four boys now?" Marshall asked.

"Yes, Bob is 14, Bill 13, John 9, and Ben 7."

"How lucky you are." Leslie had regained her composure. "We just can't thank you enough for this reception, Cornelia. If we win the election, it will be because of all the support we've had from Marshall's friends."

As they were leaving, Leslie couldn't resist putting her arms around little John. She might never see him again and her heart was filled with sadness.

All during the campaign, as the gossip was leaked to the press and innuendoes were tossed about, Leslie and Marshall never answered or denied anything. They just discussed the issues. Marshall attacked his opponents on their voting records and the issues only. He never made any personal criticisms nor would he allow his staff

195

to do so.

Strangely enough, the public was tolerant and understanding. They couldn't see anything sinister in the amorous affairs and drinking bouts of a young bachelor. Anyway he seemed to be settled down now with a lovely wife. So the smear campaign failed and Marshall was elected by an overwhelming majority.

Being in Washington was stimulating and exciting. Some friends from World War II days were still around. Marshall was appointed to several committees and made such an impressive record that during his second term, he was elected Majority Leader. Because of her experience and background, the president appointed Leslie to serve on his health commission. Soon she was a prominent figure in her own right and became a champion of legislation in the health field and was instrumental in getting a bill passed for higher education scholarships for nurses.

During their tenure, both Timothy Jr. and Mack came to Washington on separate summers and served as Senate Page Boys. The girls, including Meg, Lee, Janie, came also for visits. Leslie was careful to do equally for all the children, but she and Marshall couldn't help their strong attachment to little Mack. He reminded them so much of Leslie's brother, Mack: the same blond hair and blue eyes, the same disarming smile and personality.

They remained in Washington for twelve years (two senate terms). Leslie had already lived through some historic and traumatic times but just as she thought the world would be at peace, the Korean War, which the president chose to term as a "police action" broke out. Regardless of the label used, lives were still being lost and families upset and disrupted.

The desegregation suits and racial unrest during the '50s and '60s were disturbing. Americans had gone blissfully along for years expecting to remain at a status quo, but World War II had changed all that. Even Mary tried to warn Leslie on one of their visits home. "Lessie, baby, these young niggers ain't lak we used to be." She moved her massive weight around the kitchen which was still her domain. "Dey thinks the world owes 'em a living and dey don want to wurk."

Actually, it was no longer necessary for Mary to work as Jake had bought enough land from Tom to have his own farm. Their eight children had turned out well. All had finished high school and the five youngest, with Tom's help, had attended Lane College. Sam, Jim, and Joe had chosen to remain at White Haven to help Tom and later, Tim, run the farms and also the horse breeding farm at Forest Home. Mary and Jake were understandably proud of their children. They gave her money on a regular basis which she stashed away in a savings account to "save for a rainy day."

Mary still came to White Haven daily. Ever since Janie's death, she'd considered Betsy her personal responsibility.

On this particular day, Betsy was having a luncheon for her club and none of her help had shown up, so Leslie was working frantically in the kitchen with Mary trying to get things together.

"Have you tried to call? Surely Susie or Katie, one could have come."

"It wouldn't do any good."

"This happens frequently," Betsy explained. "Just let you plan a big party, the extra help you've been counting on fails to show. They call it the 'disappointment' club! I don't know what I'd do without Mae Mae and, of course, when they pull one of these 'disappointments' stunts we always join in and help each other, but I'll tell you it's irritating."

Another thing Leslie couldn't understand was the hostility of some of the young blacks. She tried to talk to Susie, one of the girls who failed to show up for Betsy's party. "Jes don' you try sweet talk me. You can't treat me lak a slave lak you do po' old dumb Mary."

"Susie, if you could have seen Mae Mae bossing us around as children and even now, you

197

wouldn't ever think of her as a slave," snapped Leslie. "And let me tell you another thing; Mae Mae has worked hard all her life and still does—and do you know why? Because she has pride and character. You would never find her sitting at home with a house full of bastards drawing welfare!" Leslie could have bitten her tongue out the minute she said it, but the words just came out. Susie had four children and no husband.

"I'm sorry Susie. I shouldn't have said that, but it hurt my feelings for you to infer that Mae Mae has ever been mistreated when we all love her so much.

"Let me tell you this," she continued, as Susie regarded her in sullen silence. "Our president is dedicated to Civil Rights. My husband is a United States Senator and he is a strong supporter of Civil Rights. If you have a grievance and I'm sure you must have, I suggest that you go down to the court house and talk to him. He'll be there all day and I assure you, he is doing everything possible to better your situation."

"Big Sis, I can't believe you said that. She'll never come back to work now!" Betsy said when Leslie told her. Much to their surprise, however, Susie did work at Betsy's next party and did not participate in any more "disappointments" after that.

When Leslie reported her actions to Marshall, he smiled tolerantly at her. He still enjoyed seeing her get fired up over an issue. "Don't worry, honey. It's probably good that you brought it out in the open. We can't continue to bury our heads in the sand. Problems do exist and we both know the blacks have every right to fight for equality. As you know, we've been able to pass some important Civil Rights legislation. We need to do still more, but it takes time. It certainly won't happen over night. The answer is better education. Mary and Jake's children are good examples of what I mean. A doctor, a lawyer, three teachers and three good farmers. Tim and Aunt Margaret couldn't operate their

198

farms without them. Whatever those Jones do, they do it well and with dignity. Yes, they *are* fighting for equality too but are doing it peacefully and forcefully through their Civil Rights organizations. Dr. Jones and Tom, the lawyer are my best link to the black community. I have frequent conferences with them."

Leslie felt so much better after talking things over with Marshall. She was so proud of him.

Marshall's senate record was both controversial and distinguished. He supported the Medicare Bill but was opposed to National Health Insurance except for catastrophic illness. He continued to be a champion of Civil Rights, but was opposed to welfare give-away programs. Instead he advocated rehabilitation programs designed to get people off welfare and back to work. He was too liberal for some and too conservative for others. Thus he made both enemies and friends. His supporters urged him to seek reelection and according to polls, he would most likely win. However, he and Leslie decided another six years would be too taxing as well as the fact his law firm in Jackson was suffering without him. He declined to run for the third term, but promised his support for the nominee.

Denmark and life in a small community looked good to them so they packed up and returned to resume their lives where it all started.

The children were growing up. Janie, Meg, Lee were given the European tour on graduation from college and Margaret, with some misgivings, finally allowed Leslie to write Archie so the girls could meet the English Lees.

"But Maggie, it's only a summer vacation. Not a whole year like when we were there," Leslie argued.

When the girls returned home apparently unscathed, Margaret breathed a sigh of relief. "Les, I'd never have forgiven you if she had fallen in love with an Englishman! I know now how my mother must have felt when I was over there vacillating over Archie."

Meg did report that Archie had asked a lot of questions about her mother. "You two didn't have something going, did you Mom?" she asked half-seriously.

"Of course not, Meg," snapped Margaret impatiently. "Didn't I come right home and marry your father?"

"Well, yes." And she let the matter drop.

Both Lee and Janie had stunning White Haven weddings. Leslie and Betsy cried as they unpacked the wedding gown and veil. Janie dutifully wore both the veil and gown, but Lee balked over the dress. It was just too old-fashioned, she said, even if it did belong to Grandmother Janie. She did wear the veil of Brussels lace but a new dress was selected.

Meg's love life wasn't so smooth as she and her mother seemed to clash each time she became interested in anyone. Leslie gently tried to intervene but then decided Meg would have enough backbone to defy her mother if and when she really fell in love.

They were saddened by Tom's death in 1957 at age 88. He had remained active and healthy all his life and Leslie was thankful he had lived so long and had been privileged to enjoy his grandchildren and they him. Aunt Margaret died the following year, and as other relatives died, Leslie realized that she and Margaret and their generation were now the "old folks" in the family.

When Mae Mae died at age 92, it was like the end of their little world. Leslie was so touched when she read the obituary and found herself and Betsy listed among the survivors.

Upon graduation from law school, Timothy Jr. became a junior partner with his dad and uncle. Marshall still received numerous requests for public appearances across the country and having a junior partner freed him somewhat to accept some of the invitations. He and Leslie enjoyed these contacts even though they were no longer campaigning.

Timothy Jr. married his high school sweetheart from Jackson, and Betsy was gratified to have all her children nearby. Then to Leslie's delight, Mack expressed a desire to go to medical school. She urged him to apply to Vale as she still considered it to be the best medical facility in the country. Bob Harper was retired now, but he and Sharon still lived in Stanton and Leslie looked forward to some return visits to her alma mater.

1963-1964

The country was paralyzed with grief and shock in November 1963 over the assassination of President Kennedy. The whole world mourned.

The Vietnam War which had started out innocuously enough with our country supplying military equipment and a small contingent of "technical advisors" had suddenly turned into a full-scale war—an undeclared war—but war just the same. The controversy surrounding the conflict was disillusioning and confusing and suddenly we became a nation of cynics. All the patriotic fervor of World War I and World War II days was gone forever. The war had literally torn the country apart as more and more troops were sent over.

Luckily, Timmy and Mack had low draft numbers and were never called. However, Jerome's two boys were not so fortunate. Wallace dutifully reported to camp but Jerry Jr. left for Canada to join the ever-increasing army of draft dodgers.

"Wouldn't you just know that Jerome Jr. would go high-tailing it off to Canada?" Leslie fumed. "I can't believe a descendant of Thomas Lee could ever refuse to serve his country."

"All right, Leslie, don't try to be the judge and jury," Marshall said sternly. "This is a rotten war and we should never have gotten so deeply involved. Who knows? Jerry may prove to be the brave one after all. He gave up everything to stand by his principles."

Leslie was surprised to be so harshly reprimanded. "I'm sorry. Maybe I reacted too quickly," she said. "But Marsh, honey, it's just so hard for me to think that my country could ever be wrong!" She regarded Marshall thoughtfully. "What do you think will happen to Jerry?" She couldn't help but worry about the little rascal. He reminded her so much of Jerome when he was that age.

"I don't know." Marshall shook his head. "Let's just hope that some future president will acknowledge the futility of this war and grant amnesty to these boys." He stroked his chin thoughtfully. "Now I'm not saying it was wrong to try and contain communism to that part of the world, which was our original intent," he continued, "but now the war has gotten out of hand. It's a no-win situation. I just hope we can soon find a way to back out gracefully. Too many young men are being slaughtered and do you know the thing that bothers me most?" he said despairingly. "It's the cold shoulder treatment these returning soldiers get! Even after they've risked their lives for us. This attitude of some of our citizens is a disgrace!"

"Well, we can certainly do our part to welcome these boys." Leslie soothed. "Remember, you are still in demand as a speaker for political events. Why can't you express your views at every opportunity? People respect you and will listen." She knew another campaign had started for them and she intended to help him. Already the wheels of her mind were turning—she and Margaret would organize the ladies! Why they might even erect a Vietnam Memorial!

This would be far in the future, though. A lot of scars would have to heal, but she knew Marshall would guide her in the right direction.

John

When Leslie read of Jason Thornton's death, her first thoughts were of little John. It still hurt her to the quick—not because Marshall had turned to Cornelia after she had let him go, but because she had not let him have her that night. Then maybe she could have been the one to have had their child. The "child" must be 23 or 24 by now. With Jason dead, she felt Marshall had a right to know he had a son. However, it couldn't be her decision. Cornelia should be the one to tell him.

She handed Marshall the paper as he was sitting down to breakfast. "Marsh, I think we should go to the funeral."

He took the paper. After reading the headlines, he said, "Maybe you're right. 74 years old—seven sons," he was reading aloud. "And Connie's only 54. Why she's still young."

He continued to talk and read and Leslie couldn't help but think how good it was that their love was so secure, they could discuss an old flame of his with such ease. As though reading her mind, Marshall placed his hand over hers. "Connie was the only other person in my life besides you. And—" he added, "she was only a substitute."

After the funeral the next day, Leslie finally had an opportunity to be alone with Cornelia. She felt somewhat diffident as she didn't know how her suggestion would be received. After all, the woman had just lost her husband and now she was, in effect, asking her to give up her son also. Leslie was surprised and touched that Cornelia tearfully agreed.

"I've always felt that he should know, but I just couldn't do that to Jason." She looked at Leslie with such anguish. "I do hope you know I really did love my husband."

"Of course, I know. And I feel terrible to bring this up so soon. Please take time to think it through before you decide."

"Leslie Jane Chadwick, I didn't know there
204

were people in this world like you. No wonder Chad worships the ground you walk on."

Marshall had a client to see while he was in Memphis and Leslie decided if she returned home with some friends, it would give Cornelia an opportunity to be alone with Marshall. What she had to tell him was theirs and theirs alone. Marshall begged her to stay overnight with him because he always felt incomplete without her but she finally convinced him that she had a meeting that required her attendance.

The next morning Cornelia left an urgent message for Marshall that she must see him before he left Memphis. When he talked to her, she asked him to come to her home. He hesitated, feeling awkward not having Leslie with him. As if reading his mind, Cornelia said: "It's imperative that I see you, Chad. Don't worry about Leslie, In fact, she's the one who suggested we have a meeting."

Marshall's curiosity was really piqued now. He checked out of the hotel and drove over to the Thornton mansion.

Marshall was so shaken and totally unprepared for the news she gave him. "Connie, I didn't know! How did Leslie find out?"

"The day we had the reception, when you were campaigning. She couldn't help but see the marked resemblance to you."

It was hard for Marshall to comprehend. For 23 years he'd had a son—his own flesh and blood, raised and claimed by another man.

"Oh my God! Leslie has borne this burden alone all these years. Bless her sweet heart. I must get back home to her." He moved as if to leave, then hesitated. "I wish I could see my son, though," he said wistfully. "What are we going to do, or rather, what *can* we do about it?"

"I don't know. Imagine trying to tell a 23-year-old man the father who just died, wasn't really his father after all."

"Connie, you know I'd never do anything to hurt or embarrass you."

"I know, Chad, but I do want you to know
205

it was because we made love that day and conceived this little baby that I was able to establish a loving relationship with Jason. After that, we had another child and 14 happy, satisfying years, and all thanks to your insistence that I talk frankly about my needs and assume some responsibility in our relationship." Big tears welled up in her eyes and he felt that her marriage had been a good one.

"I'm happy to hear that. You're fortunate to have your children as a reminder of him and your happiness. And," he added, "because of you, I was able to wait for Leslie."

"Chad, I may have a solution for us." She was wiping the tears from her eyes. "John has just passed his bar exams and is looking for a job—"

"And I'll certainly offer him one in our firm. But do you think he'd ever want to leave Memphis?"

"That's no problem. He was planning to leave anyway—maybe New York or Cambridge where he finished school. He's never been interested in the conglomerate. The older boys, Jason's sons by his first wife, are running it. My children have trust funds and other responsibilities in the firm. John preferred to get out of the shadow of his father's influence and make it on his own. He's like that."

A knock sounded at the door and, as if on cue, John Thornton entered. Seeing his mother in tears, he naturally assumed she was crying over his father and being consoled by an old friend. He put his arm around her and shook hands with Marshall.

"John, do you remember Mr. Chadwick?"

"Yes, I remember you, Senator. " Marshall's skin fairly prickled as he looked into his own blue eyes and saw what Leslie had seen 14 years ago—his exact duplicate. He was almost inarticulate when Cornelia came to his rescue. "Chad and I are old friends and he just might have a proposition that would interest you."

"Now, Mother, I hope you haven't been pressuring the Senator to take in an unknown, untried lawyer—"

206

"No, nothing like that!" Marshall had recovered his equanimity. "In fact, I'm the one who mentioned we were looking for some young blood in our aging firm."

After that it was easy. Marshall was so fascinated and impressed with his son.

Before leaving Memphis, he telephoned Leslie. He felt such tenderness and love for her, he could hardly wait to get her back in his arms.

He by-passed the Jackson office and stopped at Denmark. When she heard his car in the drive, Leslie rushed out to greet him. With their arms around each other, they entered the house.

"I love you so much, Leslie Jane. You must know that no matter what happened in the past, you—"

"Don't apologize, Marshall," she interrupted him. "We were not married when that happened and I was the one responsible for delaying our marriage so long! You can't imagine how many times I've regretted not sleeping with you that night. I've grieved so long, thinking the Chadwick line would end with you because I couldn't give you a son—"

"You did give me a son, Leslie Jane," he interrupted, cupping her chin in his hand and kissing her tenderly. "If you hadn't asked her, it's unlikely Connie would have ever told me for fear of jeopardizing our marriage. It was so sweet and unselfish of you to want me to know about my son." He became so emotional, Leslie put her arms around him and soothed him.

Afterwards, he told her John had accepted his offer of a position in their law firm. "This way, at least we'll get to know each other. Then if the time is ever right, we'll tell him."

"We'll make him love us." Leslie was so enthusiastic. "Let's invite him to live in the guest house until he finds an apartment." She was looking so forward to this new adventure for them. Ever since she'd held that little 9-year-old boy in her arms, she'd longed for more knowledge of him.

Leslie often wondered, if she could have

foreseen the future and the impact John would have on their lives, would she have ever persuaded Cornelia to acknowledge John's parentage.

When he moved into the guest house at Inglenook, Marshall and Leslie couldn't have been happier. It was so easy and natural for him to become a part of the family. He seemed to just blend in like he'd grown up with them. Leslie tried hard not to smother him with attention. Living in the guest house assured his privacy and he had a standing invitation for dinner. It was such an effort for them to treat him as a junior partner and protege when both of them longed to put their arms around him and call him "son." The guest house and his association with the Chadwicks was so pleasant that John abandoned his search for an apartment, but insisted on paying rent which Leslie reluctantly accepted.

In the weeks and months that followed, Timmy introduced him around and he soon became a welcome addition to the young crowd which included Lee, Janie, Meg, and Mack. It was exciting to have an eligible man in their midst. He was equally popular with the men as he was an excellent golfer and tennis player. He also liked hunting and fishing.

Margaret hadn't paid much attention to John until he and Meg started dating, then she started asking questions. Any potential suitor of her precious Meg was always scrutinized unmercifully. It just seemed too contrived to her for Jason Thornton's son to settle down in Jackson, Tennessee as a junior law partner when he could be a part of a large conglomerate.

Leslie tried to evade her questions, but Margaret was persistent. One afternoon, following their DAR meeting, Margaret questioned Leslie again.

"I really can't say why he'd prefer to come here. Why don't you ask him? In the meantime, I have to fix dinner. Why don't you call Tommy to come over?"

"No, thank you. I must get home, but I do want some answers. Why? Why him? Now, don't

208

lie to me, Les." Then almost like she'd been struck by a bolt of lightning, Margaret screamed, "I knew he looked familiar the first time I saw him! Now I know!" She pointed an accusing finger at Leslie. "He looks like Marshall. Admit it, Les. John Thornton is Marshall's bastard son."

"Oh, Maggie, please," Leslie cried in anguish as she looked up and saw John standing in the doorway. He had come over to put his name in the pot for dinner. Leslie was devastated. It was so unlike Margaret to talk that crudely.

"John, wait!" she cried as he whirled around and rushed from the room. She tried to catch up with him, but he jumped in his car and skidded off down the driveway at breakneck speed.

Margaret was stunned as she realized what she'd done. "Oh, Les, you should have told me! I'd never have said that if I'd known. Please forgive me!"

"I must call Marshall." Leslie brushed Margaret aside and rushed for the phone. She caught him just as he was leaving the office. She was crying too hard to explain anything except that John knew. "I'll be right home."

Margaret was hysterical, "Oh, Les, I'm so sorry. What can I do?"

Leslie was calming down. "You can leave, Maggie. I don't want you here when Marshall comes." She and Margaret had always been like sisters, but Leslie could cheerfully break her neck now. Maybe she should have told her and Betsy, but it was just too private. She and Marshall had discussed it, but decided not to share it with anyone.

The days that followed were almost unbearable. Marshall had called Cornelia immediately to warn her, as he felt that John was probably heading for Memphis.

"We should have known this might happen," Leslie wailed. "He favors you too much for someone not to notice. I'm so sorry. Maybe I shouldn't have interfered in someone else's life after all."

"I don't know what's right or wrong

209

anymore," he said wearily. "I do know if you hadn't 'interfered' as you say, I would never have known I had a son and no matter what happens, I'll never forget the happiness and satisfaction I've felt these past few months getting to know him."

Even Marshall's warning left Cornelia totally unprepared for John's bitter, vitriolic denunciation of her. She cringed as he continued to berate her in the most abusive language. Ben heard the commotion and came in. The sight of his brother seemed to infuriate John even more. "Well, look who's here! How do you know you're not a bastard, too. Our mother's a bitch." Ben didn't understand what was happening but he involuntarily doubled his fist and slammed it in John's face, knocking him down. As John staggered to his feet, he hit him again.

Cornelia was weeping bitterly as she rushed to John who was lying on the floor in a dazed state. "Ben, darling, please leave. I'll explain it to you later. Ask Susie to bring me an ice pack." She was cradling John's head in her lap. He looked so helpless and vulnerable. She had to admit he'd always been her favorite child and now she had hurt him beyond redemption.

"I can't leave you alone with him, Mother," Ben protested.

"He'll be all right now. John didn't mean those awful things he said. He's had a dreadful shock and is hurting so badly. I'm afraid he'll never forgive me."

Leslie was at home the next morning when she saw John drive towards the guest house. Her car was being serviced so he probably thought no one was home. She debated whether she should go down to see him or not, but decided she must.

John was surprised when he opened the door to her knock. "Oh, Mrs. Chadwick, I'm sorry. I just came to get my things." The sight of his black eye and bruised chin completely dissolved her. She threw her arms around him, no longer trying to pretend he was just an associate. His

210

cold reserve seemed to melt as he put his arms around her also. The past night alone in a motel room trying to sort out his feelings had gotten to him. He was still confused and angry but this show of affection was what he needed.

"John, I hope you can find it in your heart to forgive me," she begged. "This has all been my fault."

"How can you possibly say that? You've been betrayed, too."

"John, dear, Marshall and I were not married when that happened. It was because I thought I was in love with someone else that drove him to Cornelia. They're such old and dear friends, he just needed to talk. Neither of them meant for it to happen—it just did. Please try and realize that once *we* were young, too, just like you are now—with the same desires and passions."

"You don't have to explain it, Mrs. Chadwick."

"John, I'm the one who asked your mother to tell Marshall about you. He had no idea he had a son. Because he's always loved children so much, I felt he had a right to know he had fathered a wonderful son! All we ever wanted was to get to know you and love you. It was never our intention to come between you and your real family. Jason Thornton is your father in every sense of the word. He and your mother are the ones who helped you grow up, nursed you through the measles and mumps, sent you to school, shaped your life so that you could become the fine young man you are."

She was crying uncontrollably. "If you only knew how proud and happy you've made Marshall."

"Aw, please, Aunt Les—" he unconsciously dropped the formality and called her what Meg and the other children did.

"I know you're hurt and angry and I can't say I blame you. We've handled it very poorly. But please understand this—we love you so much."

"Thank you. I'm sorry if I've been rude. It's just that I'm so mixed up. I don't know what to do."

"John, I hated my old dean at Vale University, but she did give me some good advice once. 'Never do anything or make decisions when you're angry. Give yourself some cooling off time first and then decide.' That's what I advise you to do."

Leslie held out a key to him. "This is the key to our cottage in Monteagle where we spent our summer vacations when I was growing up. I can phone the caretaker you're coming if you like. It's so beautiful and private. The tourist season is about over and the cottage is isolated. Go there, rest and relax and take your time deciding what you should do. Take your clothes and personal things with you. Leave the other things and I'll ship them to you if you choose not to return here."

He hesitantly took the key and Leslie left him alone.

"Aunt Les, tell me where did John go?" Meg demanded, rushing into the room. "I saw him leave but I couldn't get to my car soon enough to catch him."

Leslie knew it was useless to argue with Meg. "I can't tell you, Meggie. He needs to be alone and sort some things out for himself."

"Please, Aunt Les. I know what my mother did to him. I hate her!" she sobbed. "And I know she's not all that perfect or pure, either," she said maliciously. "Why don't you tell me about that Englishman?"

"Oh, Meggie, honey, don't be so bitter." Leslie put her arms around Meg, knowing she was hurting too. So many lives had been shattered by her bungling. Please Lord, don't let me make any more mistakes. "Yes, Meg, your mother once thought she was in love with my cousin Archie. Just like at one time I *thought* I was in love with Stephen, but both of us married the man we really loved. And let me remind you," Leslie just thought of a trump card to play, "wasn't it only last year you were supposed to be in love with Raymond?" Meg was somewhat taken aback.

"Oh, Aunt Les, please forgive me and don't tell Mother what I said but please let me see him."

Leslie found it hard to resist Meg's pleading and then she thought of a solution. On Monday the young adult class from the church was going to Monteagle for a Retreat. John would have two days alone before Meg could get there.

"Are you going on the Retreat with the church group?"

"Of course not. You know I never go on those things."

"You might enjoy this one."

"Oh!" The light suddenly dawned. "Thanks, Aunt Les. I'll go sign up right now." She threw her arms around Leslie and kissed her. "I love you."

John's voluntary exile hadn't been easy but the tranquillity and beauty of the mountains was ideal for the soul-searching he required.

He cringed when he thought of his bitter attack against his mother, especially when he recalled some of his own escapades. Leslie's remark, "Remember, we were young once just like you are now—with the same passions and desires," had really struck a sensitive chord. His father had bailed him out twice. Millie was paid off and the other one gave up. They later learned neither girl was pregnant. "But they could have been," shouted his father. He'd never forget the tongue-lashing Jason had given him but it had remained their secret. His mother never knew.

By the time Meg dropped by, he'd had enough solitude and was glad to see her, but didn't want to show it.

"What do you want?"

"I wanted to see you."

"Mrs. Chadwick shouldn't have told you."

"She didn't," Meg said quickly. "I'm up here with the church group. I recognized your car and decided to stop by."

John turned away, resisting the desire to take her in his arms. He couldn't look at Meg without thinking of her mother.

213

As if reading his thoughts, Meg said, "John, please don't judge me by my mother."

"She called me a bastard," he said bitterly. "And maybe you'd better leave before we create another one."

"I don't care. I love you, and I hate my mother. I'll never speak to her again," she said vehemently.

"Aw, Meg. Don't talk like that. You'll regret it." He relented then and put his arms around her. "I said the same things about my mother and that's why I'm up here now wrestling with my conscience trying to decide how I can make it up to her. I have some major decisions to make. First try and redeem myself with my mother and then where to practice law."

"Wherever you go, I want to be with you."

"Meg, my life has been catapulted into such a mixed-up muddle. I have to adjust to being a Chadwick and not a Thornton. I can't make amy commitment now. Maybe never."

"I can wait."

Leslie had some soul-searching of her own to do. Had she done the right thing sending Meg to John? Margaret would be furious with her if she found out. They were beginning to get back together. Margaret was so contrite and subdued, Leslie couldn't stay mad at her. Their ties were just too deep.

After a week at Monteagle, John called. Leslie choked up when she heard his voice. "Aunt Les, I want to come back—that is, if you and er—er, Dad, will have me."

"John, darling, of course we want you." Oh, thank you, God. If only Marshall could have heard him say "Dad." "But I think you should first fly to Memphis to see your mother. She must be hurting too. Just leave your car. We'll send for it."

John's reunion with his family was emotional but happy. When he tearfully embraced his mother and tried to talk, she put her fingers over his lips and said, "It's all over, darling.

Let's just forget it. I know you love me and forgive me. Nothing has changed except now you have two families to love you."

The boys accepted the news of John's parentage without shock. He was still their brother, so what? He and Ben were especially close. "You should have blacked both my eyes," was his reply with Ben tried to apologize.

When John returned to the guest house, Marshall and Leslie felt a completeness to their lives they didn't know was possible. Just having each other had always seemed enough to them but now they felt they had everything.

A few eyebrows were lifted when Marshall, with Cornelia's blessing, adopted John and he officially became John Thornton Chadwick. The lawyer explained that by just adding Chadwick to his name, it would be less complicated to change his records. Not to confuse future genealogists, his new birth certificate would show Cornelia as his natural mother and Marshall as his father.

John and Meg were married in Memphis. Cornelia arranged their marriage in her home with only immediate family members present. It broke Margaret's heart not to have Meg married at Forest Home but she dared not cross her because they were gradually beginning to bridge the gap between them. She even bit her lips and said nothing when John insisted on spending Christmas and Thanksgiving in Memphis with his family. Leslie gently tried to help by having dinner parties for all the family. John was always polite and considerate of Margaret but still refused to accompany Meg on her visits home.

"Just let it go, Maggie. It will work out eventually. He loves Meg too much to keep her from her family. He's been hurt and shocked but he's adjusting so well. Just give him time and be your sweet self. He can't resist you much longer."

Her own life was so complete and she couldn't have been happier when she learned of Mack's engagement. He was interning at Vale when he sent word to his parents that he was engaged and would be bringing his fiance home to meet the family. Of course they were all in a dither getting ready. This was the first time a prospective bride had visited White Haven since Leslie's brother Mack had brought Virginia Neal. The only information they had was that she was also a doctor, a graduate of Boston University, and interning at Vale.

The day finally arrived and everyone was waiting. Leslie's role with Betsy seemed to revert back and forth. Sometimes it was like mother and daughter, then "Big Sis" or just good friends, but always with love. Betsy was looking out the window when they drove up the drive."

"Here they come!"

"Calm down, Betsy." Timothy was trying to act unconcerned. "He's not the first one we've given away."

"I know. But he's the baby." Betsy rushed out the door. Leslie and Marshall waited in the background until Betsy and Tim greeted them. Having John now hadn't changed hers and Marshall's feelings for their godchildren, whom they'd helped raise.

Mack walked over and put his arms around Leslie. "Now here's my uncle and aunt. Aunt Leslie, Uncle Marshall, this is *Dr*. Florence Southall." He proudly emphasized the Dr.

Leslie felt a shiver go down her spine and caught her breath as she looked into a pair of snapping black eyes and saw a beautiful girl with long black hair. Surely not, she thought, her heart racing. Could it possibly be? Florence was Stephen's special name for her—maybe it was just a coincidence.

"So, you got yourself a doctor." Marshall stepped forward and stretched out his hand, giving Leslie time to recover. He still had an uncanny prescience where she was concerned. "What about that?"

"Welcome to the family," Leslie said, regaining her composure, as she put her arms around the girl. Janie, Lee, Timmy and their spouses along with Meg and John were all crowding around and Leslie turned gratefully to

Marshall. "Thank you, darling, but I do wish you would stop reading my mind."

"Then stop being so transparent. Does it bother you?"

"I'll have to admit, it gave me an eerie feeling, but that part of my life is over. Besides," she squeezed his arm playfully, "do you think I could even think of another man after these past twenty-two years with you?"

"I should hope not."

"Anyway, I may be jumping to conclusions. There's bound to be other Southalls in Boston besides Stephen."

"Why don't we go over and find out." Marshall kissed her on the cheek as they went over to join the family who had literally surrounded Mack and Florence. They were teasing their little brother and he was joking back at them. Florence was obviously enjoying herself but was overwhelmed with so much family. As they joined the group, she turned to Leslie and answered their question without being asked. "Mrs. Chadwick, Mack tells me you are also a graduate of Vale. Did you, by chance, know my father, Dr. Stephen Southall?"

"You might as well get used to calling her 'Aunt Leslie,'" Mack interrupted.

"Well, all right then, Aunt Leslie?"

"Why, yes," Leslie smiled. "As a matter of fact, we are old friends. I was about to ask if Stephen was your father. How are your parents?"

"Dad is fine. I never really knew my mother. She died when I was two years old. Dad has recently married one of the doctors on his research staff. I think he wanted to get me educated and settled before he married again."

Leslie again experienced a disquieting feeling as she realized that Ann must have died about the time she and Marshall married.

"I'm sorry. I didn't know. It's been such a long time. I've lost touch. Stephen's a brilliant doctor. I know you must be very proud of him and he of you."

"Oh, yes, I am. We have what you might call a mutual admiration society." Her eyes glowed as she spoke of her father. "And to think you two

217

knew each other. Well, you can get together again at the wedding."

Leslie and Betsy went to Boston a day early to make arrangements for the rehearsal dinner which she and Tim would host on Friday before the wedding on Saturday. This was Leslie's first visit to Boston. She couldn't help but recall how she and Stephen had planned for her to visit in February 1919. Well, she was just forty-five years late, she thought wryly.

Betsy was able to engage the Country Club, through Stephen's membership, for this all-important affair and Leslie tried to put aside her ambivalent feelings as she helped. Stephen had sent an invitation for them to stay at his home, but Betsy declined, explaining that with so many friends and family members planning to attend that it would be better to engage a block of rooms at the hotel. She could sense Leslie's feelings, even after so many years.

On the night of the dinner, Leslie went directly to the club to make last minute inspections and preparations while the rest of the family and wedding party went to the church for the rehearsal. She was glad to postpone her meeting with Stephen. She was hoping Marshall would soon arrive. He was tied up on an important case, but had promised that he, Timmy, and John would arrive in time for dinner.

Betsy and Tim were the first ones in and then it seemed the whole wedding party trooped in at once. Leslie spotted Stephen before he saw her. His hair was snow white and he wore black-rimmed glasses which emphasized his black eyes. He was still a handsome, distinguished looking man at age 69. His new wife must have been about his age, not very attractive, but apparently a brilliant person. She would have preferred to have Marshall at her side, but another part of her was glad he wouldn't come until later. It wasn't so bad after all. She really was glad to see him. He spotted her as she walked towards him with outstretched hands. "Hello, Stephen."

He ignored her hand and put his arms

around her and kissed her soundly. "Now, where's your husband?" He looked around. "I guess I'll have to account to him for this."

"You're in luck, Daddy," Florence laughed. "Uncle Marshall won't be here till later. Now, Aunt Leslie, I want you to meet my stepmother, Doris."

Leslie barely had time to acknowledge the introduction when Stephen put his arm around her and said, "Now if everyone will excuse us, Florence and I have a lot of—er, er, I mean Leslie and I have a lot of catching up to do." He led her towards the dance floor.

"Now I can hold you in my arms and no one can wonder about it." He held her closely and some of his old magnetism came through to her.

Leslie pushed back so she could face him. "Stephen, your wife? Will she mind?"

"Nope, not to worry. She knows about us. We laid all our cards on the table before we got married. Our marriage is not a very romantic one—I gave all that up when I lost you—but rather one of mutual respect and need. We even have a pre-marital contract. Florence is my sole heir and her niece is her heir. Walter, her husband, a dear friend and associate of mine, died about the time Florence left to make her own life and we sort of turned to each other. She understands and sympathizes."

Leslie felt a rush of tenderness and sadness for Stephen as she remembered his lonely childhood and now two marriages without real love. She was thankful he had found fulfillment in his work and in the rearing of a beautiful and talented daughter.

"Stephen, it's been so long. I hardly know what to ask you. My father and Aunt Margaret have died and so many of my family. What about yours?"

"My parents are gone, too. I finally made peace with my mother before she died. I guess she did what she did to us because she thought it was for the best, and actually I was as much to blame as she, although I wouldn't admit it for years. I rushed in headstrong and had a wreck. If only I had calmly talked things over with Ann, I

219

would have learned that she and Ben Roberts were getting serious about each other. However, after the accident, he visited her only one time in the hospital and never returned. Anyway, I made sure my mother never interfered in Florence's life, nor did I."

"Stephen, I have to believe things have a way of working out for the best. If you hadn't married Ann, you wouldn't have Florence, and I can't begin to tell you how happy Marshall and I are, after we finally got together."

"It took us both a long time to appreciate what we had all along," he said wistfully. "You were lucky to have a second chance."

"I know," she agreed. "And isn't it ironic that our children should bring us together again."

"Yes," he smiled. "And I'm glad. Otherwise, you might never have known that you have a namesake. What do you think about her?"

"She's adorable and I'm flattered that you named her for me although no one will ever know. You're the only one ever to call me 'Florence.'"

"That's why it's so very special." He held her closer. "It belongs just to us. She once asked me about her name and I told her she was named for the two women I loved. After that blunder I just made, she's probably figured it all out by now." The music stopped and Stephen led her out on the terrace.

"She favors Ann, doesn't she? Yet her eyes and mannerisms remind me of you, too."

"She has her mother's beautiful features. Ann died in 1942. She never got to know her baby."

"I'm so sorry. I didn't know until Florence told me."

"I called Sharon at the time and, ironically, she was just about to board a plane for New York to attend your wedding. We both agreed that you should be spared any more painful memories."

"Dear Sharon—always looking out for me." Big tears welled up in her eyes as she thought of their protective attitude towards her.

"After you moved to Washington, I became a regular reader of 'The Washington Beat' and I have followed the brilliant career of the famous senator from Tennessee *and* the frequent references made to his beautiful wife. I've never been far from you. I still love you."

"Stephen, it was just never meant for us to be together. We can live vicariously through the lives of Florence and Mack."

"Maybe they will find the happiness and fulfillment that was denied us." He put his arms around her and held her for a brief moment. She could look at him now with love—love without passion, even rest in his arms as a dear friend.

At that moment, Mack interrupted them. "Aunt Lessie, Uncle Marshall, John, and Timmy are here." He walked over and put his arm around her and looked at his soon-to-be father-in-law in an almost resentful manner. The vague references he'd heard in the past about his Aunt Leslie's lost love seemed to come back to him now and he wasn't sure he liked the way things were falling in place.

"Oh, good! Thank you, Mack." Then, noting his attitude, she patted his shoulder reassuringly. "Everything's all right, darling. Stephen and I haven't seen each other since before Florence was born. We just had a lot of reminiscing to do, that's all." She linked her arms between the two and they walked back into the club just as dinner was being announced.

Leslie found Marshall almost immediately. "There you are." He kissed her. She wondered now if maybe he had purposely delayed his arrival. "Are you all right?" He asked, observing her wet eyelashes.

"I'm fine. Never better, in fact. I've been talking to Stephen. I'll tell you about it later, but it made me realize for at least the thousandth time just how *very* lucky we are." She rested her hands on his shoulder and caressed his cheek, oblivious of the rest of the party. "I just hope you know how much I love you," she said earnestly. He looked deep into her eyes and seemed satisfied with what he saw and then with his mischievous grin, he said with mock
221

seriousness: "A bushel and a peck?"

She laughed as she flung her arms around him and finished the little childhood rhyme.

"And a hug around the neck."

Endnotes

1. *Historical Madison County*

2. *Martin Chuzzlewit* by Charles Dickens

3. "The Attempt to Capture the Kaiser," *The Tennessee Historical Society Quarterly Report*, Sept. 1961

References

Brigadier General S.L.A. Marshall. *The American Heritage History of World War I.*

Dickens, Charles. *Martin Chusslewit.*

Donaldson, M.L. *A History of Vanderbilt University School of Nursing 1901-1984.* 1985.

Ellis, Janice and Hartley, Cecil. *Nursing in Today's World.* Philadelphia: J.P. Lippincott Co.

Goldmark. *Nursing and Nursing Education in the United States.* New York: McMillan.

Historical Madison County

Lea, Colonel Luke. "The Attempt to Capture the Kaiser." The Tennessee Historical Society Quarterly Report. Sept. 1961.

Capping Ceremony
Vanderbilt University School of Nursing

Courtesy of Dean Colleen Conway-Welch
Vanderbilt University School of Nursing

About the Author

Elizabeth R. Lovell is a graduate of Jackson High School, Jackson Tennessee and Vanderbilt University School of Nursing, Nashville, Tennessee. She received the degree of Bachelor of Science from Columbia University, New York, NY.

She has worked 10 years as a public health nurse in Sumner County, Tennessee, 27 years as Director of Nursing, Williamson County, Tennessee and 3 years as Assistant Director of Nursing, Supervisory Training, Tennessee State Health Department. She has been retired from nursing since 1979.

Her memoirs *Home Visiting in Tennessee by Public Health Nurses*, were published in 1983.

She has also been a past president, Tennessee Public Health Association, and is now working regularly at family owned business, Franklin Flower Shop, Franklin Tennessee.

She is a widow and has two sons and four grandchildren.